Dedication

To my family who supported me when I needed them.

To Liliana Boulakieva and Nikolovi's family. They saved me by allowing me to live in one of their properties when I had nowhere to go. Without them, I may not have been able to publish this book.

1

It was Saturday, July 4th, 2022, and darkness had already fallen over the city of Chicago. It was hot as hell. The humidity pressed upon people as if they were in a sauna. Chicagoans were celebrating Independence Day. People were toasting one another by glugging tons of beers and any various types of hard liquor. Fireworks were blasting from everywhere; it looked like the sparkles would not stop anytime soon. It was as if America had been invaded by aliens who wanted to take over the entire planet. On that day, people were celebrating, partying, and having fun, but there was a girl who wasn't into celebration. She was running and screaming in panic, but no one could hear her. She was somewhere in Park Forest Preserve—an outback area filled with trees and large meadows. The girl had no idea in which direction to go. She was confused and terrified.

"HELP! PLEASE HELP!" she kept screaming. The girl had no idea what time it was either, because her smartphone was missing. The running girl looked to be in her mid-twenties and was dressed in a white A-shirt and blue jeans. Her blondish hair was tousled. Her breasts were bouncing playfully as she was running.

"HELP! PLEASE! HELP ME! I NEED HELP! OH MY GOD!" the girl kept screaming. She was sobbing and crying because she was scared to death. The girl wasn't alone—someone was chasing her. She kept screaming in terror and continued looking behind her to make sure her pursuer was far away. As she was speeding, she stepped improperly and collapsed on the ground. Her knees were injured, but she couldn't waste time checking for more wounds. She had to run for her life. In a few seconds, she was back on her feet and started rushing through the trees. These trees seemed to be watching her as she was running between them. Her youth and her years of school athletics gave her a slight speed advantage over her pursuer.

"HELP! OH MY GOD," the girl yelled pleadingly. She hoped to find the road where she might wave down a random car, some driver could stop, and she would be saved. The problem was that she couldn't hear any vehicles because of the noisy fireworks. The girl was getting out of breath. Even though she had an athletic body, her stamina waned. She wasn't prepared for such a chase. Her legs became weaker and more painful. The girl turned around to survey what was happening behind her. It was so dark that she could barely see the white color of her shirt. She was thinking, *Maybe I should grab something like a stone or tree branch and use it as a weapon!* Her thought blurred her concentration, and she stumbled on the ground for the second time. This time one knee got injured badly. The pain wouldn't let her rise to her feet. Then, out of nowhere, footsteps crunched nearby—someone was approaching. The girl was horrified. She thought this would be the end of her life.

"NO! PLEASE, NO! DON'T TOUCH ME! PLEASE! I'M BEGGING YOU!" These were her last words. A rod-shaped object swung and hit the girl. She was knocked out cold.

2

"Honey! Have you spoken with Ashley?" Tom Packer called to his wife. His daughter hadn't responded to his text, and he was worried.

"Jennifer, did you hear what I'm asking you?" he said. Tom was in his mid-fifties. Back in college, he used to play hockey, and he had been a good player. Now, the only thing he played with was the remote for the TV. He was 6'4", but he looked taller. His nose was misshapen as a green pepper, but his eyes were insightful, resembling those of Vladimir Putin. Tom worked in the construction industry as an electrician. He owned a small company and had a few employees. In 2006, he had acquired an Electrician's license that gave him permission to work in Chicago and the suburbs.

4

"Honey!" Tom repeatedly screamed as if there was an emergency.

"I'm coming. I'm in the kitchen!" Jenifer, his wife, yelled back. She was fifty-four years old, but people would complement her by saying she looked around the age of thirty-nine. She was a lovely Italian-American woman with a beautiful face. Her sensuously beckoning lips could melt people's hearts. Mrs. Packer had small breasts and a big ass, but she was still a sexy woman. She was short, 5'2", but that didn't bother her, except on rare occasions when Tom would make foolish jokes about her height. Tom was tall and Jennifer short, although the height difference wasn't a problem for their loving relationship. They had been married for twenty-six years. Tom, the electrician, used to date Jennifer's best friend, but the courtship didn't last long. In their college years, Jennifer pursued Tom wherever he went. They had gotten married in Las Vegas after a wild party, and now lived in a big house in Norridge, Illinois. Mr. and Mrs. Packer had a wonderful life together. They seldom fought, except when the electrician lost money at the casinos, which could result in Jennifer throwing silverware and other objects at him. However, most of the time they were a loving couple.

"Tom, what do you want? Don't you see that I'm busy with dinner?" Mrs. Packer protested.

"I know, honey. Have you talked to Ashley? She was supposed to be here already. I'm getting worried," the electrician said out loud. Mrs. Packer rolled her eyes as if she was listening to her obnoxious mother-in-law.

"Tom, I haven't talked to her. I told you I'm busy in the

kitchen. Don't stay like that! Call her," Jennifer became a little upset because her husband wasn't helping her. Without saying another word, he grabbed his smartphone and phoned his daughter.

"She isn't answering! That's weird. She has always answers her phone," he protested.

"Tom, don't you remember Christmas two years ago? Ashley wasn't answering, and then she showed up with her boyfriend. Relax, she is fine. She is a smart girl, just like me," Jennifer explained. Tom nodded, but he didn't agree with his wife. He sensed that something bad had happened to his daughter.

"Let me ask Brendan. Hey Brendan!" the electrician hollered.

"Tom, he can't hear you. He's upstairs. Go up there and talk to him," his wife suggested. Her voice was raspy. She sounded a little more upset. Tom did as his wife said and climbed the staircase to the second floor. Brendan was their son. He was in his early twenties and had recently graduated college with a computer science major. His specialty was cyber security. Brendan had started a job with a company based in Chicago. He had a six-figure salary, but still lived with his parents. Brendan, the computer genius, had never been with a girl. Usually, he jerked off watching downloaded porn on his laptop. Once, Jennifer had almost caught him as he forgot to lock the door of his room. He was as tall as his father, with a blondish pompadour and a sweet face, just like his mother. He was a handsome man, but his body was a little overweight. Brendan worked from home. He never went to an office. Sometimes, he hung out with friends, but mostly he was a homebody. His favorite trip was going to the bathroom or to the kitchen.

"Brendan, have you spoken to your sister today?" Tom asked, standing at the threshold of Brendan's room.

"Nope. The last time I spoke to her was last night," Branden responded. His eyes were wide open and he looked surprised.

"Call her, please. She was supposed to be here half an hour ago." Tom's words came quickly as if he was talking to a 911 operator. Brendan did as his father asked and dialed his sister's phone number.

"That's weird," Brendan said.

"What?" Tom asked.

"There is no signal. Her phone has no service," Brendan proclaimed, and his father looked at him as if he was saying, *"What the fuck are you talking about?"*

"The recorded voice said that her phone is disconnected!" Brendan declared.

They were staring at each other quietly, with questioning eyes. Then Tom and Brendan went to the living room. They saw Jennifer lying on the couch with her eyes closed. Her hands were shaking because she was terrified. The three of them brainstormed where Ashley could possibly go. Jennifer called her parents, and Tom called his parents. No one had heard anything from Ashley for the past five hours.

"Call Kimberly, her roommate," Jennifer said to her husband. She didn't just say it; that was an order.

"Honey, it's going to be okay. I'm sure Ashley is fine," Tom tried to calm his wife, but his effort was useless.

7

"Don't say another word! Call Kimberly. Oh, gosh! What happened to my kid?" Jennifer was furious. The worst nightmare for a parent was to lose their child or not have any idea where they could be. The same nightmare was chasing Mrs. Packer.

Tom spoke with Kimberly Shimmers. He left her on speaker so Jennifer and Brendan could hear.

"I have no idea where she is. The last time I spoke with her was four hours ago," Kimberly confessed.

"What did she say to you when you spoke with her?" Jennifer chimed in. Her child was missing; she couldn't be silent. Kimberly couldn't answer immediately. She was holding her breath in a state of utter confusion.

"I think she said that she would stop by Mariano's to grab something. Then she mentioned that she would head out to your house. That's what I recall," Kimberly uttered. She sounded assured in her words, but she was dubious. She was at a party at her cousin's house in Schaumburg. The music was loud; the booze was pouring freely. The alcohol was making Kimberly less dependable.

"If you hear anything from her, let us know, okay?" Jennifer asked. Kimberly confirmed she would. After that, Tom hung up the phone, and the three of them remained silent. Then Jennifer broke the silence.

"What about her boyfriend?" Mrs. Packer questioned. It seemed she was asking herself the question.

"What was his name, Jake?" Tom asked.

"Really? You don't remember his name? Your daughter has been dating her boyfriend for two years, and you don't recall his name? Josh! His name is Josh," Jennifer declared. She was furious. Her husband was making her angry.

"I was close!" Mr. Packer pointed out. He tried to sound funny, but it wasn't a moment for jokes. Jennifer ignored her husband's remark and looked at her son.

"Brendan, do you know anything about Jake?"

"I thought his name was Josh!" Tom interrupted his wife with a playful voice.

"I know! Tom, you're not helping me. Come on! I need you. This moment is very traumatic for me," Jennifer said, and Ton nodded.

"I think he is cool… like you know… I mean, I don't really talk to the guy, but my sister has never said a bad word about him," Brendan said quietly.

"Okay, I'll call him. What is his number?" Jennifer asked.

"Do you want to call him from my phone?" Brendan offered. His eyes were flashing with fear.

"Just give me the number." Jennifer's voice sounded calm, but it looked like she could explode at any second. The fear of losing her daughter was making her unruly.

"Oh, crap! He's not answering. I'll try again," Jennifer blurted out. She talked to herself as if the other two weren't in the house. Her eyes were stuck on the screen of her smartphone. Jennifer called twice, but there was no answer. Mrs. Packer left a voicemail and sent a text. Her hands were shaking; she had never felt so frustrated.

"I can't comprehend it. Where could she be?" said Tom.

"Tom, don't you get it? Our child is missing! Oh my God! This is not happening. This is…oh, what a nightmare. My stomach hurts, and I feel nauseous. I need to sit for a second. Hey, Tom, don't sit like that! Do something," Mrs. Packer ranted. Her emotions permeated the entire house.

"Honey, what am I supposed to do? Call the cops?" Tom Packer asked calmly. He couldn't just raise his voice at Jennifer; he respected his wife. That was what his parents taught him. He scratched his bald head. *Damn, I'm sleeping on the couch tonight*, he thought.

"No, silly. Call Spider-Man and tell him to fly over. Oh, gosh! Yes! Call 911," Jennifer commanded. Tom did what his wife told him to. While he was speaking to a 911 operator, his wife asked Brendan, "What do you think, sweetie? I mean, do you have any idea where your sister could be?" Ashley's brother rolled his eyeballs; he tried to come up with an appropriate answer, but he failed. His sleepy face showed how tired he was.

"I guess I can trace her using the "Find My iPhone" option. I tried to call her using NO CALLER ID, but she didn't pick up the phone." Brendan gave Jennifer hope. She stepped closer and hugged him tightly.

"Sweetie. Let's wait for the cops, and you'll tell them about this Find My iPhone option, okay?" Mrs. Packer declared, and Brendan nodded. He thought of asking his mom about what she had for dinner, but that wasn't the right moment. In the following minutes, the Packers family waited impatiently for the police.

**

Travis Delacruz was drinking coffee from Dunkin'. He was a police officer, a heavyset man of over 250 pounds. He was a white American who had lived most of his life in Illinois. Back in college, Travis used to play football as defense. He was a gifted player, but any hopes of a professional career disappeared when he knocked up his girlfriend. He had decided to become a cop to support his new family.

Travis was staring at his partner, Ray Wagger. They had been working together for the last three years. Ray was much smaller but taller than Travis. He was 6'5" with a scrawny body. He looked like a junkie who loved to poke himself with needles. Ray's face was rough and wrinkled. He seemed to be forever frowning, but actually he was a nice guy. Both cops were sitting at their police patrol. They hoped that the night on the 4th of July would go smoothly. Usually, on days like this, anything could happen. Travis finished his coffee and opened a can of Red Bull. Ray was watching him thoughtfully.

"Travis, you are a weirdo!" Ray said. Travis gave his partner the stinky eye as if to say, "*What the fuck are you talking about?*"

"What do you mean?"

"How can you drink a coffee and Red bull at the same time?" Ray asked.

"What are you sayin', though? I'm done with the coffee," Travis replied with a smirk.

"Come on, Travis! You know what I'm talking about."

"Listen, I have no idea what the heck you are talking about," Travis said dryly, and both burst into a laughter.

"Listen, Travis. I'm serious, man. This is not good for your heart. You gotta think about having a healthy life," Ray made his point. He wasn't wrong, but Travis wasn't buying any of his words.

"You sound just like my mother!" Travis said playfully, and Ray laughed his ass off. Their dispatch interrupted both officers by reporting that there was an emergency call for a missing person. Travis confirmed the location and drove off from Dunkin's parking. Five minutes later, the police vehicle with stickers saying "To Protect and Serve" pulled into the driveway of the Packer's house. Tom welcomed the officers and offered something to drink. Travis and Ray politely refused and started interviewing the Packer family. Jennifer was sobbing; she could barely pull herself together. It was not easy for her to remain strong at that particular moment.

"Okay, so, who is missing?" Travis asked. Tom, Jennifer, and Brendan looked at each other as if trying to determine which of them should answer the question.

"Our lovely daughter, Ashely, has been out of contact since noon. She is 98 pounds, soaking wet with blonde hair; she has green eyes, like emeralds. She's gorgeous, looks like the actress Beth Behrs. Here, this is a photo of her." Jennifer said. She took her smartphone and showed it to Travis.

"Oh, my. She's pretty!" Ray exclaimed, and Travis nodded agreeably.

"Does Ashley live with you?" Travis asked.

"Nah, she lives in Avondale Area. She attended De Paul University in the Lincoln Park area. And that was one of the reasons why she moved to Chicago. She graduated with an English major. Currently, she teaches at Christopher Columbus School. Ashley adores kids. She loves working with teens, which is why my baby decided to become a teacher. Ashley is a loving and outgoing person; she enjoys life, literally. She also loves to travel, play sports, or do outdoor activities, and so on. As a kid, she used to study a lot. We have never had any issues with her. Ashley is a scholar. When she was fourteen, I would make fun of her because she fell asleep with a book in her hand. Ashley is an outgoing person who helps others. If you ask her for directions, she will politely guide you. She is a corker. I just don't understand who would want to take my child from me…" Jennifer said and started sobbing. Tom was scratching his bald head repeatedly. He tried to hide his anxiety, but his effort didn't work out.

Ray said, "When was the last time you spoke with her?"

"I believe I texted her at noon," Jennifer said. She looked at Tom and Brendan as if she was asking them the same question. Tom and Brendan shook their heads synchronically like two pigeons who were walking on a sidewalk.

"Okay, so… Does Ashley live alone in Chicago?" Travis asked.

"No. Kimberly is her roommate; she's one of her friends from college. We had called her earlier. She said that she spoke with Ashley earlier this afternoon, but that's about it. Nothing unusual. Ashley was supposed to spend the holiday here with us, but…" Jennifer couldn't finish her sentence. She was about to shed more tears. She kept retelling herself that she needed to remain resilient, but the thought of losing her child terrified her. Travis and Ray exchanged a glance. They both were dead serious.

"So, the last time anyone spoke with her was this afternoon, right?" Travis asked. Ashley's family nodded.

"Does she have a car?" Ray chimed in.

"No. Usually, my baby uses rideshare platforms or rides a bike when she can." Thus far, Jennifer was doing all the talking. Tom and Brendon were quiet.

Ray Wagger asked, "Does she have a boyfriend?" That was an essential question. Travis, his partner, was thinking of asking that as well.

"Well, yes!" Jennifer continued, "We tried to call Josh, her boyfriend, but he didn't respond."

"So, Ashley has a boyfriend who didn't pick up the phone. That's important!" Travis remarked. He looked at his colleague as if he was talking to him.

"Yes. I think they have been dating for about two years. Ashley met him at college," Mrs. Packer replied.

"He seems to be a nice kid. We spent last Christmas together," Tom pointed out. Those were his first words since the police officers started the interview.

"He drinks!" Brendan added. Everyone in the room looked at him, wondering at what he had just said.

Officer Travis jotted in his little notebook the information about Josh.

"Did your daughter ever express anything negative about her boyfriend? Did they ever fight?" Ray questioned.

"Not really. I mean, she is in love with him. That's how my baby is; when she loves someone, no one cannot stop her, including me. She is just a loving person. I heard they were talking about marriage. I guess I should say that Josh is her fiancé," Jennifer proclaimed.

"A fiancé!" Travis repeated. His eyes widened. It was a wake-up call telling him that something wasn't okay.

"Ya, they went to Italy on vacation, and Josh proposed at the Colosseum in Rome," Jennifer continued.

"I heard him raising his voice at Ashley!" Brendan said sulkily. He was frowning. He wasn't a huge fan of Josh.

"How old is she?" Travis asked. He was mad at himself for not asking this question earlier.

"She is twenty-five," Tom answered automatically.

"Jeez! She's just a kid," Ray proclaimed, reminding himself how old he was.

"Okay! So, no one has seen or heard anything from Ashely for the past six hours?" Travis asked, chewing his lip.

"No one has any idea where she is. Brendan has posted an article about our missing Ashley on social media. Our friends are concerned, but no one has any information about her," Mrs. Packer explained.

"What's the next step, officers," Tom asked judiciously. Jennifer looked at her husband as if she was saying, "*Thank you for asking this question!*"

"Since she lives in Avondale, we will report to the City of Chicago. The City will look at the files and assign detectives who should take it from there. If Ashley doesn't show up for the next 24 hours, the police will announce her missing across the entire state. After 48 hours of her disappearance, the FBI will spread the news across the country," Travis finished his statement. Both police officers took the contact information of each of the family members. Then the cops strode to the main door.

"Don't worry, ma'am! We'll find your daughter. We'll touch base with you tomorrow," Ray said, and Travis shook his head agreeably. Then the police officers left the house as if they had entered the wrong address. Jennifer stared at Tom. She was thinking, *Hug me, idiot.* Tom was scratching his bald head and contemplating, *What did I do wrong?* In the next second, Mrs. Packer hugged Tom. He gave her courage and kept telling her that everything would be fine. Brendan went to his room. No one could tell what his thoughts were.

3

An unpleasant hangover woke Robert McCarthur. His name was Robert, but everyone called him Bob. *Gosh! How much did I drink last night?* he thought and checked the clock on his smartphone. It was 8:00 a.m., Monday, July 6th. Bob stirred around in his apartment in Roscoe Village. His one-bedroom place looked as if a severe earthquake had shaken it badly. In other words, it was a complete mess. Bob didn't give a damn what his apartment looked like. He was a fifty-one-year-old divorced hillbilly, still paying child support for his son who had just turned eighteen. McCarthur's parents were arguing about how he could pay for alimony, but some lawyers had proved them wrong.

Bob was born and raised in Dallas, Texas. After filing for divorce, he moved to Chicago. The Texan had been living in

Windy City for many years. Since 2010, Chicago had been his home.

McCarthur was a homicide detective who had a prominent name in the City of Chicago. Many police officers respected him because he was a good detective who had built a tremendous career in Chi-town. He was a big man, 6'4" tall, weighing over 230 pounds. McCarthur used to box in high school. He fought in heavy-weight divisions. After he won the Golden Gloves, Bob stopped competing and went to college. During his freshman year, he played football as defense. But he mostly bet on his education. His specialty was crime investigations. Bob had glistening long blonde hair, just like Patrick Swayze in the movie *Point Break*.

That Monday morning, his hair looked unkempt, just like his apartment. An hour later, his smartphone rang. He picked up the phone, and his blue eyes widened.

"Yeah! Gotha! I'll be right there!" he said and ended the call.

At 10:00 a.m., the same day, a black Chevy Tahoe was parked on North Lincoln Avenue— somewhere in the Lakeview area. McCarthur opened his apartment door and looked at the black SUV that was parked on the street. The Tahoe had tinted windows, and it looked inconspicuous, but not to him. He saw the vehicle and cracked his crooked smile. Bob was decked out in a pricy corporate suit; he looked more like a lawyer than a detective. He went down the stairs and opened the passenger's door of the Tahoe.

"What's up, chief?" a female voice echoed from inside.

"Fernandez! Where's my coffee?" McCarthur said. His face was frowning, but he was joking.

"I thought you quit the coffee!" the female said, and Bob chuckled. This was Lisa Fernandez. She had been his partner for more than five years. She used to call him *chief* because that was what most of the police officers called him. Lisa had a Mexican lineage, but she was a straight-up Chicagoan. Fernandez looked luscious as if she was a top model. Her hair had the color of coffee. Her beautiful face resembled the gorgeous actress Nina Dobrev. Even though she was pretty and sexy, Fernandez wasn't a chick that people could mess around with. In 2017, she became a flyweight UFC champion. As a UFC fighter, Lisa had a professional record of 14-0-1. Her body was muscular. Her sculpted abs looked as if she had been born that way. Fernandez was 5'8", but she seemed taller. McCarthur was fascinated by how she could stay fit at the age of thirty-five and simultaneously take care of her three kids. Fernandez was all woman and, at the same time, a tomboy.

"Where are we going? At the police precinct?" Fernandez asked. Bob raised his eyebrows and replied,

"Yes, but first, we need to stop at a strip club."

"Huh? A strip club? Are you for real? What are we gonna do there?" Fernandez asked. Her voice sounded friendly, but she was confused.

"To pick up my girlfriend," he replied, laughing.

"Give me a break!" Fernandez said and started throwing harmless punches at him. Lisa knew her partner was joking because he didn't date any girls, especially in strip clubs. Bob cracked his crooked smile. He found that scene extremely funny.

"Watch it! Take it easy. I'll end up in the hospital!" Bob, the Texan, teased Fernandez.

"You're an asshole! We're going to the police department, right?" She asked, and McCarthur nodded. Detective Fernandez was dressed in luxurious khakis and a corporate shirt that accentuated her astonishing figure. Her breasts were small, but they looked big under a push-up bra. Bob avoided looking at his partner's chest. He couldn't allow himself to be that disrespectful.

Ten minutes later, Fernandez drove the black Tahoe toward the southwest side of the city. At the intersection of Belmont and Lincoln/Ashland, Fernandez saw a guy wearing a hat beating the shit out of a homeless man.

"Hurry up! Something is going on up there," the female detective exclaimed and jumped out of the car. Fernandez could be described by two words: go-go. She loved her job and was devoted to her career. That was something that McCarthur admired. He also jumped out of the car and called the dispatch. They needed backup.

"Stop it! What's the matter with you," Fernandez hollered at the guy in the hat. She stood between the two men who were exchanging profanities.

"He started first!" the man wearing the hat said, "He came to my car and hit my side mirror." He continued cursing the homeless man. His hat fell to the ground, but that didn't stop his rage. He was a white man in his mid-thirties. His southern accent was easy to catch; his French Crop hair looked stylish, but his head looked like a pumpkin. The man wasn't big but surely bigger than Fernandez. A person's size didn't bother her. She was a warrior, willing to fight for justice and pride.

"Hey! Knock it off! I'm warning you!" Fernandez said to the man with the southern accent. She sounded polite, but her tolerance was about to disappear.

"I'll fuck you up," the vagrant yelled. "Come on, tough guy! What's the matter with you? Are you hiding behind the chick? You ain't shit! Show me what you've got!" He was behind Fernandez; the female detective turned around and looked at him. The homeless man had red eyes and no teeth; he was in his fifties with long silver hair and an emaciated body. His clothes were dirty; the man reeked of dried urine. The homeless guy hadn't eaten anything for the past 36 hours. The hunger destroyed his inhibitions, and he had become violent.

"Come on! You motherfucker!" the homeless person antagonized the other man. The guy with the southern accent went out of hand, and tried to swing a punch, but Fernandez blocked his blow. She stepped laterally, grabbed his hand, and did a hammerlock. Then she forced the man onto the ground and twisted his arm in a way that prevented him from moving. The pumpkin-headed guy moaned and screamed like a toddler. The pain was unbearable.

"Come on, motherfucker! I thought you were a tough guy," the vagrant yelled.

"You shut up!" Fernandez yelled back to the homeless man. In a second, Bob came over and helped Fernandez. They handcuffed the pumpkin-headed man, and Fernandez declared "You're under arrest. You'll be charged with assaulting a police officer. You have the right to remain silent. Everything you say can and will be used against you. You understand?" Fernandez asked.

"I didn't know you were a cop," the guy mumbled.

"What difference does it make? You cannot throttle people just like that!" Bob said. The Texan was out of breath, having run to the scene of the fight. *I'm getting old!* he thought.

The backup police patrol came over. There were three police patrol vehicles that blocked the intersection. Two of the officers were needed to regulate the traffic jam. There were so many stalled cars as if the Chicago Auto Show had just opened.

"Good job, Fernandez," McCarthur said and gave her a fist bump. She flashed a smile; her charming dimples made her look younger. Lisa handed the brawler off to the other officers. In the meantime, Bob was still trying to catch his breath.

"Are you okay?" Fernandez asked her partner.

"Ugh, yeah! What a morning, right," the Texan asked, and Lisa nodded. Both detectives returned to the Tahoe. Lisa drove to the Police department. At noon, they went to speak with the Police Commissioner. His office was in Downtown Chicago.

Lavance Makuba was the Police Commissioner of the City of Chicago. He was an African-American man, born and raised in the south side of the city. His family was Nigerian, and they were proud of him. Makuba loved his parents; they were very close. He had been in the police force for over thirty years. He had short curly hair and a ducktail type of beard. His body was overweight, but his hands were as strong as hammers. Lavance was an astute and erudite man.

In his early twenties he had been a motivational speaker, visiting churches and schools. Besides being a motivator, Makuba loved comedy. Once in a while, he performed at a few stand-up comedy events.

McCarthur and Fernandez stepped into the office of the Police Commissioner.

"It's good to see ya, Lavance," Bob greeted the Commissioner with his crooked smile.

"Good old McCarthur," Makuba said, "Hey, Pard, have you read the report from Norridge?" Lavance asked. He teased McCarthur by calling him "Pard". He called him that because Bob used to wear a Leopard pattern jacket, which looked funny on him. Makuba used the word "Pard" because it was the short version of Leopard. Hearing the joke, the Texan cracked his crooked smile.

"Yes, I did. I thought you were playing golf today!" McCarthur responded. He made a joke because Makuba sucked at golf. He laughed his ass off. Bob and the commissioner had known each other for eleven years. They were good buddies and often made fun of each other.

"What report? I haven't read any report!" Fernandez protested. Lavance and McCathur looked at each other as if they were saying, "*You tell her.*"

"Lisa!" Lavance said. He sat on his office chair with arms folded as if he had some stomach problems and continued, "A girl has been missing since the night of the 4th of July. Her name is Ashley Packer. Age twenty-five, a school teacher in Chicago. She lives in Avondale."

"Do you have a picture of her?" Fernandez asked.

"Yes. Actually, we have her Instagram profile," Lavance answered.

"Holy shit! She's beautiful. She looks like the famous actress… ugh… what was her name," Fernandez asked.

"Beth Behrs!" the Texan replied.

"That's right! It was on the tip of my tongue, though. Who was the last person she spoke with?" Fernandez questioned. Her mind was concentrated on the missing girl.

"Here's the scenario. Her family lives in Norridge. Ashley was supposed to spend the night on the 4th of July with them. After her family realized that Ashley's phone was dead, they called 911, and a police patrol stopped by. The Norridge police patrol gave us the report because Ashley has been living in Chicago for five years. What we know is that Ashley allegedly spoke with a Kimberly Shimmers before she disappeared."

"Who is Kimberly Shimmers?" Fernandez asked. Lavance and Bob exchanged a glance.

"Her roommate. Kimberly and Ashley know each other from college. They have been living together since February 2020," McCarthur proclaimed.

"Okay. So what are we waiting for? Let's go to her apartment and speak with this girl, Kimberly," Fernandez suggested. The female detective was impatient because when it came to a missing person, she took it personally.

"Hold your horses, my dear," the Texan said. He called his partner *my dear* because he had a fatherly affection for her.

"What is it?" Fernandez asked.

"Her boyfriend, Josh, didn't pick up his phone on the night of her disappearance. The day after Ashley was reported missing he told the cops that he'd been partying at his cousin's house. He made the excuse that the music was loud and he couldn't hear his phone.

"That's BS! Why were they not together?" Fernandez questioned.

"Huh?" Bob grunted.

"Why didn't Josh and Ashley spend the holiday together?" Fernandez asked.

"That's a good question. Josh told the cops that they had decided to be apart for the evening," McCarthur proclaimed.

"I believe we need to speak with him in person," Fernandez stated.

"Hell yeah! I was just thinking the same thing," Bob declared. He stared out the window of Makuba's office intensely as if he was watching a hovering UFO.

"What is it? Are you okay?" Fernandez asked. She stared at McCarthur. He had been looking weird all morning.

"I'm fine. Don't worry about me. I'm like Bruce Willis in the movie *Die Hard*; strong like a rock," Bob lied. The truth was that he was in pain, but he was hiding it, even from himself. Fernandez continued to gawk at her partner. The female detective nodded as if she understood what the Texan was saying, but actually she was confused.

"Let's go, Fernandez!" McCarthur said, and both detectives made for the door.

"Talk to you later, boss," Bob said and waved at Lavance.

"Pard, let me know if you find something interesting," Lavance said and waved back. Lisa Fernandez and Bob strolled to the black Tahoe.

"What do you think, chief?" the female detective asked.

"Agh! Nothing! Let's talk to this Josh Rodriguez, Ashley's boyfriend. I'm interested to hear his side of the story."

"Where does he live?" the UFC fighter asked.

"Not far away, like Lawrence and Pulaski. I think that's Mayfair."

"Great! Let's go!"

"Hold your horses, my dear. I have an idea," Bob said with a smirk on his face. Fernandez was flustered. She couldn't comprehend what her partner had on his mind.

**

An hour later, the black Tahoe parked on Montrose Avenue. There was a gym across the street. The sign on top of the gym read: GLADIATOR. The detectives burst into the door and walked to the front desk, where a sturdy young man was chilling at the desk.

"Hello! I'm looking for Josh! I'm detective McCarthur, and this is my colleague, Lisa Fernandez," Bob stated.

"Hi, Guys! It's nice to meet you. I'm Josh! Before we continue, can you sign this waiver? This is a policy that every visitor needs to sign," Josh pointed out. He had a fauxhawk haircut and the handsome face of a model. His skin was baby-smooth and his body was jacked. He looked like he lived in that gym. The detectives exchanged a questioning glance and took the clipboard.

"Excuse me, guys, I need to use the restroom. I'll be right back with you," Josh said and walked out to the south side of the gym. Fernandez started scrawling her name. The Texan looked thoughtfully at her. Suddenly the detectives stared at each other as if they had had a telepathic connection. They exclaimed together, "HE FOOLED US!"

Fernandez ran through the gym. The Texan started after her, but he was too slow. Lisa saw Josh standing fifteen feet away and said, "Don't move, young man! We just need to ask a couple of…" she couldn't finish because Josh started running away.

"HEY!" Fernandez shouted, chasing after the young man. Josh slid out of the back door and rushed through the alley. Fernandez wasn't far behind. Her training kicked in, and she switched on her full speed. Josh, the bodybuilder, looked behind to have an idea of how close she was. Suddenly, a car loomed from the alley and almost hit him. The driver honked and screamed, "Hey! Watch where you are going, Punk!" The bodybuilder thought of giving him the finger, but he didn't have time for that. Fernandez was right on his tail.

"Stop, or I'll shoot you!" the UFC fighter yelled. Josh ignored her threads. The handsome guy knew that Lisa wouldn't shoot at him; he was right; the female detective was bluffing. Josh was running as fast as he could. Then the black Tahoe blocked his way. McCarthur nimbly jumped out of the vehicle and aimed his service weapon at him.

"Don't move, or I'll blow off your head," Bob yelled. Josh wanted to look defiant, but he was so spooked that he almost peed in his pants.

"Lift your hands up so I can see them!" Fernandez hollered and searched the handsome guy. She then handcuffed him.

"Why did you run from us? We just wanted to ask a few questions!" Detective McCarthur asked.

"Shit! I thought you were going to arrest me!" the young man with the muscular body mumbled.

"For what? Have you done something illegal?" Fernandez questioned. Her brown eyes were stuck on Josh.

"No. But it looked like you were going to arrest me," the handsome bodybuilder protested. He accidently prophesized what was about to happen.

"We just need to ask you some questions," McCarthur declared.

"Why? I didn't do anything!" the bodybuilder asked. He was breathless from the running.

"That's what we are going to find out. Come on!" Fernandez yelled.

Josh was taken to the police department in Avondale and escorted to an interrogation room. The bodybuilder hated being in police departments because he had been harassed by the police several times before. He was scared; his hands were shaking. At 3:00 p.m., McCarthur and Fernandez barged into the room where Josh was kept. Fernandez walked hurriedly with a coffee in her hand, and Bob closed the door.

"Why am I here? I told you already. I didn't do anything," the handsome guy spoke with frustration. Fernandez took off the handcuffs from the bodybuilder. He held his wrists and feigned pain.

"Where were you on the night of the 4th of July?" Bob grilled.

"I've already told that to the cops. I was at my cousin's house."

"Can you prove it? Do you have any evidence that shows where you've been?" Lisa asked.

"Absolutely! I shot a video that night. Give me my phone back, and I'll show you." Fernandez handed him his phone, and Josh started scrolling through the screen. The video displayed how fireworks had been blasting in the yard of a neighboring house. There were no humans in that video footage.

"This video is unclear! Anyone could have taken it," Fernandez scolded the young man.

"When was the last time you saw Ashley?" Bob asked. He didn't take his eyes off the bodybuilder.

"We went to a lunch at Wildberry Pancake by the Water Tower on the 4th."

"And… What had happened there?" the female detective asked. She hated when people were cutting the details.

"Nothing unusual. We ordered some food, chit-chatted about the holiday. After we finished the food, Ashley had to go to a beauty salon, and that's how we split," Josh replied. Sweat formed on his forehead.

"Do you remember the name of that beauty salon?" Bob asked.

"A… Not really!" Josh seemed baffled. He struggled to give a good answer. Then McCarthur looked at him with furious eyes. The bodybuilder disliked how Bob was eyeballing him.

"Let me get this straight. You have been dating Ashely for two years, and you still don't know the name of her favorite beauty salon. Come on, man! Cut the crap." McCarthur was pressing Josh.

"I don't know, sir. Honestly, she switches beauty salons

as often as I change my T-shirts," Josh protested. Fernandez looked at the young man from the corner of her eyes. She wasn't buying any of his words. The female detective could swear that he was not telling the truth.

"I don't understand. Why would you spend the holiday separately? We know that your relationship with Ashley was getting serious. I mean, she is your fiancé. Am I correct?" Lisa asked.

"Ugh...uh... yeah. We were having conversations about getting married," Josh spoke slowly. He stuttered as a result of his confusion.

"Then why would you spend the holiday separated? Don't you care about your fiancé, what she wants and where she goes? Don't you think that is your responsibility to be with your future wife?" the female detective longed to make Josh uncomfortable.

"Ma'am! We decided to spend the weekend in different places. I promised my cousin to visit him on the 4th of July. I then asked Ashley to come with me. She refused because she wanted to be with her parents. There is nothing wrong with that. I mean, that's not a crime!" Josh raised his voice a bit, and that drove Fernandez nuts.

"You're a liar!" Lisa exclaimed and hit on the empty table.

"Lisa, come on, dear. Mellow out. Cool your jets," McCarthur urged. He laid a gentle hand on her shoulder.

"But he's..."

"Relax. Go outside, get yourself another coffee, and take a deep breath. I'll finish the interrogation," Bob said. Fernandez didn't like his idea, but she listened to him. In a second, the female detective left the room. Then Josh made a useless comment.

"What's up with this chick?" Bob ignored that question.

"Your last name is Rodriguez, right," the detective asked.

"Yeah!"

"Mr. Rodriguez, you'll have to pay a fine of $250 for obstructing a police officer's order."

"Put it on my tab," Josh said indignantly.

"I beg your pardon!"

"Yes, sir!" Josh responded as if McCarthur was his commander in the Navy.

"I'll let you go, but that doesn't mean we won't talk with you again. And… Oh, yes. Don't leave the state or the country. Do you understand what I'm saying?" the Texan questioned.

"Yes, sir!" Josh exclaimed. This time he sounded more respectful. The detective didn't like how Josh was responding, but he couldn't do anything— not at that moment. An hour later, the bodybuilder was released from police custody. The detectives didn't have any evidence to press any charges. McCarthur watched how Ashley's fiancé walked out of the police precinct. *No law could prevent or forbid saying respectful words in a disrespectful way, but people could easily get fed up by listening to similar expressions,* Bob thought. He disapproved of young adults' sarcastic behavior, especially as he helped them, and the kids acted with no ethics or moral virtues. A few minutes later, the Texan was in the passenger's seat in the black Tahoe. He was quiet, but his brain spoke loudly. *Nowadays, people don't use the phrase "respect your elders" anymore. Many might have no idea what that means.*

A lot of parents misinterpret what it is to be a good parent. Being a good parent doesn't mean allowing their kids to have anything they want. Nothing wrong with that, but there has to be a balance. A parent's job is to teach their kids about ethics or how to behave among society and how to respond to the community. Ah! Who am I kidding? I'm not a good parent either, Bob's inner voice whispered. At around 4:00 p.m., Fernandez dropped McCarthur at his apartment.

"I'll talk to you later. And don't worry about today. You did a good job, my dear," the Texan said, laying his hands on the Tahoe's door. Fernandez thanked him and said, "I just empathize with Ashley's parents. I can only imagine what it would be like if one of my kids disappeared."

"I know your frustration. I am a parent like you. Trust me, we will find her. Go and rest. It was a hectic day." The big detective stared at Lisa thoughtfully. Fernandez nodded and drove off. The female detective was driving fast because she had to pick up her daughter from school. The Texan spent the night reading a Stephen King novel. He loved to read. Books kept him away from doing unwise things, like swigging alcohol till the early hours of the morning.

***

On the following day, the black Tahoe parked on a side street called Irene Avenue. Both detectives jumped out of the car. The heat outside made them frown, especially Bob; he was sweating too much. On Irene Avenue, a few townhouses were lined up like soldiers. The townhouse where Ashley lived looked renovated. Fernandez was impressed by the modernized building. She even envisioned how she could live there. The Texan wasn't impressed with the building; his mind was concentrated on the missing girl.

A Columbian man was waiting for them at Ashley's building. His name was Mario. He was the owner of the property. Mario came illegally to the United States in the early 2000s. Eleven years later he got his green card and started working as a real estate agent. He was a slender man in his early forties. The Columbian had always lied about his height. He claimed that he was over 6 feet, but actually, he was 5'11". He had two little girls from two different women. He was a good guy who took care of his family. The Columbian landlord loved to dress in expensive attire. No one could explain how he had money to wear such bling-bling clothes while simultaneously paying for private schools for his kids. He looked more like a pimp or a drug dealer than a property owner.

"Hello, guys!" Mario exclaimed. His smile widened as if he had just won the lottery. He stretched out his arms as if the detectives were his siblings. Then Robert and Lisa introduced themselves to the landlord.

"How are you doing, sir?" Fernandez asked.

"Agh! You know, living in paradise! HA-HA-HA," Mario laughed. The Columbian landlord appeared to be comfortable speaking with the detectives, but actually, he was a little nervous.

"Let me ask you this: where were you on the night of the 4th of July?" Robert was curious to scope out more information.

"I was in Wisconsin," Mario proclaimed. Fernandez got a little upset because He was skipping the details.

"What did you do up there?" the female detective asked.

"My parents lived there for over twenty years, so I decided to take the wife and the kids and drove there, HA-HA-HA," Mario kept laughing as if he were watching Pete Davidson on SNL.

"Okay. Can you show us the apartment where Ashley lives?" Fernandez questioned. Mario agreed without hesitation and walked the detectives to the third floor. As he and both detectives stepped up the staircase, the stairs creaked as if screaming from pain.

"Do you know if Kimberly is here?" Fernandez asked.

"I have no idea. HA-HA-HA," the Columbian landlord laughed repeatedly. He became a little annoying with his fake giggle. Then Mario knocked on the door, and Kimberly opened it. She was a sweet white girl, the same age as Ashely. Her body was curvaceous, but that didn't bother her. Boys were all over her like a bunch of seagulls attacking a half-eaten burger left on a beach. The detectives and Kimberly exchanged a few pleasantries, and Mario took his leave. Kimberly had blue hair. She wore glasses that made her look luscious. She was cordial and kind. She offered them coffee, tea, and cookies. The detectives kindly refused and casually nosed about the apartment as if they were looking for something.

"Miss Shimmers, can you show us Ashley's room," Fernandez politely asked, and Kimberly walked the detectives to her roommate's room. Her bedroom was neatly organized. The nightstand uncluttered, as was her wardrobe. The entire room looked as if no one had been in it for a while. Bob was surveying Ashley's belongings when Fernandez asked, "When was the last time you spoke with her?"

"I believe it was around 1:00 in the afternoon on the 4th of July," Kimberly answered quietly. Detective Fernandez glimpsed at her partner as if she needed permission to proceed.

"What did she say?" Fernandez asked.

"Ashley talked about spending the weekend at her family's house. She said that she would stop at Mariano's before heading to her family's house."

"Did she use an Uber as a transportation option?" Bob queried. He was eager to learn more from Kimberly Shimmers.

"I would guess so. Ashley often commutes with Uber." Kimberly shrugged off. There was a pause. Bob stared at the ceiling as if he was a child looking at the stars.

"Do you know her boyfriend, Josh Rodriguez," Fernandez asked, and in the meantime, McCarthur was snooping around like a police dog searching for evidence.

"Oh, yeah! That douchebag is annoying," Kimberly cried out. Her tone suddenly changed.

"Why is that?" the Texan interfered.

"He's like an Instagram and TikTok model. He posts pictures and videos every hour or so. It's a bummer to watch him. He always talks about his body and lectures about how to have a body like his and blah-blah-blah. I mean, give me a break; who the heck does he think he is— Dwayne Johnson? His ego is bigger than New York City," Kimberly explained. Fernandez and McCarthur looked at each other questioningly.

"A-aa… How would you describe Ashley's relationship with Josh?" Fernandez asked.

"To be honest, I would not say that Ashley was happy with him. She trusts Josh but also she is scared of him."

"What do you mean *scared*?" Bob questioned.

"I heard that he would punch walls and other objects while they were having heated conversations." Once again, both detectives shot a glimpse at each other.

"Have you ever seen any bruises or injures on Ashley?" Fernandez asked.

"No, I have not. Ashley was constantly let down by Josh. Two weeks before she disappeared, she found text messages on Josh's phone from another woman," Kimberly explained.

"So you are saying that Josh cheated on Ashley?" Fernandez chimed in.

"Yes, I would say so. They had a bunch of quarrels because of that," Kimberly agreed.

"And that was why Ashley wanted to spend the weekend with her family rather than being with Josh?" McCarthur asked.

"Yes, I would guess so. But I can't be 100 percent sure. Ashley was a bit secretive. Especially for the past several weeks," Kimberly said in a low voice.

"Wait! What do you mean she was *secretive*? Don't you guys confide in one another?" Fernandez asked. She felt that she was on to something important.

"Not like we used to. For the past few months, Ashley has become alienated, and I can't really tell why. Every time I tried to speak with her, she said that she was okay, but she wasn't. She refused to talk. She always came up with some excuse, or she just left the apartment. I feel like I lost my friend." Kimberly started sobbing, and Fernandez hugged her. The Texan was motionless, but his mind was active. He was contemplating his next question. He also thought about how much he loved his son, Jeremy. Bob's son lived in Dallas with his mom. McCarthur retold himself that he needed to call Jeremy and tell him how much he loved him. He then focused his thoughts on work and asked, "Miss Shimmers, this guy, Josh, how often has he visited this apartment?"

"I can't really tell. Maybe, a few times in a week. He was in and out, then Ashley spent some weekends at his place," Kimberly replied. Fernandez stared at her partner as if she was saying, "*Let's get outta here.*"

"Okay, Miss Shimmers, thank you for your time. If you think of anything useful, please, call us. We may contact you again. Here's my card. Have a nice day!" Bob said, and the detectives left the apartment. On the way out, McCarthur exchanged a few words with Mario. He advised the building owner to cooperate if they needed him. Then they walked to the black Tahoe. The Texan was quiet. He sank into deep thoughts about what Kimberly had just told him.

"What do you think, chief?" Fernandez asked while getting into the vehicle. It took a few seconds before he could answer.

"Chief, are you okay? I'm worried about you, man," Fernandez went on. The Texan took a deep breath. He was having some respiratory problems, which he kept to himself.

"Obviously, Josh lied to us. They were arguing, and Ashley

wanted to spend the weekend with her parents because she was afraid of him," he declared.

"Or, she was let down by his infidelity," Fernandez continued.

"Exactly! Here's the thing, I doubt if we ever find Ashley's phone, but if we can, that would sort out the puzzle," McCarthur pointed out, and Fernandez agreed. She stared at the dashboard, but she wasn't looking at it. She was confused and simultaneously convinced that the bodybuilder had something to do with Ashley's disappearances.

"Do you think that Kimberly is telling the truth?" Fernandez asked. She kept staring at her partner.

"Lisa, my dear, I'm hungry. I can't think with an empty stomach. Let's go and eat something. I'm buying it today."

"But you took care of the check the last time," Fernandez objected.

"Did I? Who cares! Drive to Topo Gigio. They have the best Italian food in the city. Let's go, Raggaza! Yee-haw!" McCarthur cried out, and Fernandez burst into laughter.

4

It was Friday, July 12th. The weather was gorgeous. Usually, at this time of the year, the humidity could feel like man being clenched in an octopus' tentacles. Sunlight shone over the Chi-town, reminding the Chicagoans how beautiful that city was. Many locals and tourists enjoyed the end of the summer, but not Tom Packer. He was working on a new commercial project somewhere in the southwest burbs. The construction perimeter was laid out for a new pizza place. Tom had been working on this project for over six months. He was a busy man, working on multiple projects. He needed money because the mortgage couldn't wait. On that day, Mr. Packer worked on the electric panel of the unit. He was installing all the circuit breakers that powered the entire retail space. Mr. Packer needed to pay close attention to what he was doing because the main power, supplied by the electric meter from outside, was turned on. In a little later, Tom looked at his Apple watch. It was 3:00 o'clock. The heat inside was tolerable, but the high temperature was dangerous. The electrician was covered with stinky sweat. That didn't bother him because he was used to that smell. Instead, something else disturbed the electrician— the thoughts of his beloved Ashley. It had been a week since his daughter was reported missing, and he missed her a lot. His mind evoked memories of quality time with Ashley. He remembered how he and Jennifer organized Ashley's birthday parties when she was a little girl. He also recalled how goofy he was, trying to impress his daughter. While the electrician was sailing in the river of precious memories, his work in the electric panel became careless. He grabbed a white wire (the neutral) which was supposed to be attached to a bar that had all the white wires from each circuit. The white wire slipped out from his fingers and touched the coppered bar to which each breaker had been connected. Then BOOM! An explosion blasted and tossed Tom away from the electric panel; his eyes were closed as if he was sleeping. His body didn't move.

***

Two hours later, Tom opened his eyes. He looked around to survey where he was. At first, he was confused. He couldn't understand what had happened to him.

"Where the heck am I?" Tom asked out loud, but he already knew the answer. He was in an ICU unit. The electrician was alone in the room. Just a second before Mr. Packer was about to shout his question again, the door opened. Jennifer burst over the threshold like a bulldozer scurrying through a cabin. Brendan was a few feet behind his mom. It was difficult for him to keep up with his mother's pace.

"Come on, Brendan! Hurry up!" Jennifer exclaimed without looking behind her.

"Tom, what the hell happened?" She went on, "Why are you in the Hospital?" Mrs. Packer stared solemnly at her husband as if he had told her bad news, such as The City was about to conduct a foreclosure on their house.

"I was asking myself the same question," Tom confessed. He looked like a student who failed to understand a simple math equation.

"Tell me, how are you feeling?" Jennifer asked. She turned around and exclaimed, "Brendan!"

"I'm coming, MA!" Brendan yelled. His angry voice sounded as if he was saying "*Stop bothering me!*" Jennifer ignored Brendan's answer and turned her attention to her injured husband. Tom had this ignorant stare which many considered annoying, but somehow it looked attractive to Jennifer. That was one of the reasons why she found herself fond of his charismatic yet foolish behavior.

"I… I guess I'm fine. I have a headache as if Iron Mike had knocked me out cold, but other than that, I feel fine," the electrician said, "Have you spoken to Nick, my employee?" Jennifer gave him the stinky eye as if he had just insulted her.

"Yes! So here's what I've heard. The explosion threw you away. While falling on the ground, you hit your head on an

EMT pipe. Your employee, Nick, saw you lying there as if you were being killed. He called the ambulance, and they brought you here. The doctors said you hit the back of your skull. Fortunately, you don't have a concussion or any serious injuries. Also, you don't have any burns. Tom, you are a lucky man. Gosh, I'm so glad that you are fine. What's the matter with you? You could have been killed!" Jennifer said sulkily. Her big black eyes stared at her husband as if she was trying to hypnotize him. The electrician couldn't tell if his wife was scolding him or just projecting her Italian temper. He scratched his bald head as if he was a scientist that couldn't understand how his innovation project had failed.

"Yeah… I guess I screwed something up and that caused an immediate explosion. I don't know, honey. I have been thinking about our girl lately. It's not easy to focus on work while my daughter is missing. That's the only rational explanation I can come up with," Tom muttered. He didn't sound honest, but he was telling the truth. He loved Ashley so much that he could do anything to find her.

"You'll be okay, dad," Brendan managed to comfort his father. He sounded somehow wiser than Tom.

"Thanks, bud," Tom said and ruffled Brendan's hair. He then looked at his wife and asked,

"How long do you think I'll be kept here?" Hearing this question, Jennifer frowned. Her face looked as if she was saying, "*How am I supposed to know that!*"

"I don't know. Listen. I gotta go. Call me if you have any updates, okay? Come on, Brendan. Let's go. Your father needs to rest," Jennifer said and hugged her husband. He waved at his family as if they were going on vacation somewhere overseas and would not come back anytime soon. Tom scratched his bald head as he usually did. He was confused; he couldn't understand why he had been so careless. The electrician made an immature mistake as if he was a greenhorn who had never worked on an electrical panel before. Mr. Packer quit those murky thoughts and contemplated his missing daughter. Tom was scared. He tried to hide it, but his fear was transparent. His eyes oozed. The nostalgia made him sad, but he looked like a man coping with the situation successfully.

"Hey, Tom! How are you feeling?" a man's voice echoed in the ICU unit.

"I'm fine," Tom mumbled tiredly. The man approached the bed, where Tom lay, and gave him a fist bump. His name was Nick; he had a Greek lineage of which he was proud. Nick was an easygoing man. Normally a smile was carved on his face as if he had been born like that, but at this moment, he was serious.

Not long after Nick's father succumbed to cancer, his mother moved to Greece. His father was an affluent man. Nick inherited most of his dad's wealth. He was in his early forties, a single man; no wife, no kids. He had been Tom's employee for the past two years. Unlike most people, Nick didn't work for money. He got his paychecks, but he didn't work for the payroll. He worked because he needed to stay away from gambling. Betting was his greatest vice. He was putting money on everything; horses, boxing, football, anything he could think of. He even bet on who would be the first person landing on Mars. He loved the feeling when he had money on something and how the anticipation of winning kept him hooked. Gambling was the passion that stuck with him for years. Tom met Nick at a sports bar in Norridge a few years ago. They had had a long chit-chat about gambling and had become good friends since. That was the reason why Nick worked for Tom. Actually, he did him a favor because Tom struggled to find a devoted employee.

For a moment, Mr. Packer surveyed his friend. Nick was grossly overweight. He was short, around 5'8". His nose was so big that he could hang his car keys on it. His face looked to be that of someone who had struggled a lot over the years, but actually, he was a carefree man.

"What happened?" Nick asked his employer. He stood by the medical bed as if he was a horrendous ghost who spied on Tom.

"I don't know, man. I was connecting the circuit breakers, and I guess the neutral wire slipped from my hands and touched the power bar in the electric panel. I haven't done anything like that in 20 years of working in the industry. I really fucked up," Tom said. He then started laughing. Mr. Packer couldn't tell why he laughed. He tried to compose himself in that embarrassing situation.

"Yeah. The panel looked like a fried chicken. It actually resembled a bunch of burned steaks left on the grill. HA-HA-HA," Nick laughed his ass off. Tom smiled, but he did not think it was funny. Mr. Packer and Nick chit-chatted for about five minutes more. Then Nick left the room. He was making an excuse that he had to do something important, for instance, betting on college football. Ashley's father spent the night in the hospital. The doctors monitored his vitals, describing him as stable in his medical report. On the next day, Jennifer came and picked him up. The electrician was happy to leave the infirmary. He hated hospitals. It made him feel distant from his family, and that depressed him.

***

On Monday, the 18th of July, the black Tahoe turned into the driveway of Ashley's parents' house in Norridge. Fernandez got out of the vehicle. She was dressed business casual; her blue shirt was tucked into the black slacks she wore. Her figure looked phenomenal, as usual. Her abs could be seen even through the shirt. Her muscular body looked sexy as if she had been drawn in a comic book filled with superheroes. Lisa Fernandez tied her charming coffee-colored hair into a ponytail. The female detective looked hot as if she had won Miss America; she was so attractive that she didn't need makeup or eyeliner. Her beauty was natural. Bob McCarthur also hopped out of the car. His breathing was heavy. He moved so slowly that Fernandez had to wait for him at the door.

"Hey, chief! Are you okay?" Fernandez asked; she peered at her partner with great commiseration. Bob took a deep breath. He didn't want to answer, but he couldn't be quiet either because Fernandez wouldn't stop until she had answers.

"I'm fine. Strong like a bull," Bob said confidently. But he wasn't honest. He disregarded the question about his health and focused on work. Fernandez nodded and punched the doorbell. She thought of asking, *Are you sure?* But then she rejected this instant whim. Jennifer opened the door, projecting her genteel hospitality. She invited the detectives to sit on the sofa in the living room, offering drinks as if she was getting paid to do it. Fernandez refused, but McCarthur asked for a bottle of water. After serving the water, Jennifer yelled,

"Tom, Brendan! Come over. The detectives are here!" Two minutes later, Tom artistically ambled over the living room as if he was walking on a stage of a renowned theater. Jennifer eyeballed her husband and beckoned him to come closer. She whispered to make sure that the detectives would not overhear the conversation.

"Where is Brendan?" she asked. The electrician gave her the confused stare of a person who didn't understand the question.

"I don't know. Isn't he in his room?" Tom asked, scratching his bald head.

"No! That's why I'm asking you! He was supposed to be here. Don't look at me like that. Man up and call your son!" Listening to his wife, Tom lumbered to the kitchen and dialed Brendan. Then a few seconds later, he returned to the living room, where Jennifer had already talked with the detectives. Mr. Packer gave his wife a nod that could be interpreted as, *"He'll be here soon."* He then sat next to her and listened to the conversation. Bob stated that he and Detective Fernandez were assigned to resolve the case and that they were going to collaborate with the police in Norridge city. It was paramount for the parents to share any information regarding their missing child, and Detective McCarthur longed to follow the rule of thumb.

"At this point, we found out that Ashley's fiancé, Josh, had allegedly been having an affair with another woman. Do you know anything about it? Has Ashley mentioned anything?" Fernandez asked. Jennifer and Tom looked at each other with foolish stares as though they'd heard a ridiculous statement.

"Gosh! I have no idea. Ashley didn't mention anything about Josh being unfaithful," Jennifer replied. She was a bit confused and surprised. Tom was scratching his bald head repeatedly. He then grabbed his wife's hand and gripped it tightly.

"She was happy with him. Ashley told me that she wanted to get married to Josh because she was deeply in love with him. She said that he was taking care of her and making her feel loved," Jennifer went on.

"What is your relationship with Josh? What do you think of him as a person?" McCarthur asked.

"He seems to be a nice kid. He spent a few holidays with us, including Christmas and Thanksgiving. He is an affable person, respectful," Mrs. Packer responded. Up until this moment, she did most of the talking. Tom was quiet. He wasn't the type of guy who would talk much.

"Do you think that Josh is an honest person?" Fernandez asked. At that moment, the door swung open, and Brendan came in.

"Where have you been? I told you that the inspectors would stop by to talk with us," Jennifer scolded her son in a low voice. She wasn't happy. Brendan mumbled something unclear and greeted the homicide detectives. He took off his backpack, sat on a chair, and joined the conversation.

"I'll repeat the question. Does anyone consider Josh a dishonest person?" the female detective asked.

"Yeah. Josh is a hinky guy. I don't trust him!" Brendan exclaimed, and everyone in the living room stared at him.

"What makes you think like that? Has he ever lied to you?" the Texan asked. His deadpan face projected that he was studying Brendan.

"I'm not sure. Josh hasn't been as trustworthy as he may seem. He is a layabout. He thinks himself the sexiest man on earth," Ashley's brother spoke with his typical girly voice. He was an effeminate guy who got sketchy from time to time.

"We've checked his files and found that Josh had been arrested for shoplifting in a 7-Eleven store. He did four months of community service and had to pay a fine. Do any of you know about that?" Fernandez asked. Tom, Jennifer, and Brendan were dumbstruck. None of them expected that the bodybuilder could be involved in such foolish delinquency.

"When was he arrested?" Mrs. Packer asked. She was still shocked by the detective's revelation.

"He was busted in December 2019. At that time, he hadn't known Ashely, I suppose," Lisa Fernandez responded. She shot a questionable glance at her partner and continued,

"When was the last time you spoke with your daughter?"

"I spoke with her at noon on the 4th of July. We had a short chit-chat about when she would come over. That was it," Mrs. Packer answered.

"Did you notice anything unusual in her voice or something out of the ordinary?" McCarthur asked. Jennifer shook her head no. Detective Fernandez and Bob exchanged another questionable glance.

"Brendan, how is your relationship with your sister? Are you close?" the Texan asked. The young man rolled his eyes as if he was saying, "*WTF? What does this have to do with her disappearance?*"

"Growing up, we were good friends. She is my big sister, and I love her. Often, we would hang out together. We used to play games and watch movies. However, after she left home for school, she became less available. She was studying a lot, and I was busy with college. As grownups, we barely see each other," Brendan responded calmly. Bob nodded and glanced at his partner.

"Do you mind if we take a look at her room?" Fernandez asked politely.

"Not at all. Please go ahead," Tom declared. Bob and Fernandez got up go to Ashley's room. They were skeptical about finding anything essential, but they had to check it out. *There was an old saying: You never know which top hat a rabbit could be hiding in*, Bob thought as he was walking up the stairs. In the following seconds, the detectives went into Ashley's room. They moved around like two hungry squirrels looking for food.

"Mrs. Packer, do you know where Ashley keeps her journal?" Detective Fernandez asked. Jennifer stood on the threshold, staring at Fernandez with hope.

"Oh, my goodness, I don't know if she has one," Jennifer answered. Hearing that, Lisa's face changed. She was surprised. *How come she doesn't know that?* the female detective thought.

"When was the last time Ashley visited you?" Bob asked.

"Ashley and Josh stopped by for lunch on Easter. After we finished our meal, they left to watch some basketball game." Jennifer was responding to each question asked by the detectives. Tom sat next to her, scratching his bald head and keeping his mouth shut. The detectives exchanged quizzical glimpses.

"Okay, Ma'am. We need to go. We'll be in touch. Hopefully, we'll find your daughter soon. Thank you for your cooperation and for the water," McCarthur said, flashing his crooked smile. Hearing that, Jennifer burst into tears. Detective Fernandez stepped closer and proclaimed, "I'm speaking as one mother to another mother; we'll do everything possible to find your child." She then hugged Jennifer.

"Thank you!" Mrs. Packer said, sobbing.

It was already dark outside when the detectives left the house and walked toward the black Tahoe. Detective Fernandez stared at her partner and asked, "Do you think we will ever find Ashley's smartphone?" Bob shook his head no.

"I doubt it," McCarthur replied. He thought, *Nowadays if you don't have a phone, it's like you don't have a name.* Both detectives jumped in the black Tahoe. Bob's cell phone rang. He picked up and said, "Hello! No! You've gotta be kiddin' me. Are you serious? Okay, we are coming!"

***

A few minutes later, Fernandez was speeding through the streets of Chicago. She was driving so fast that Bob thought he might throw up. He looked at his smartphone to check the time. It was 9:30 p.m. The ride took about twenty minutes, but Bob felt like it was no more than five. The black Tahoe drove in at a huge condominium building in Lincoln Square. There were at least a dozen police vehicles parked in front of the building. Sirens of a fire truck blared from a block away. The fire truck approached the condominium in seconds. EMT providers scurried quickly and entered the building. The residents in the building gathered and stared at the police officers like a bunch of pigeons on a telephone wire. McCarthur and Fernandez snaked through the crowd and boarded the elevator. The elevator stopped on the 11th floor. There were around ten cops who kept the premises clear for the forensic experts and the detectives. Most of them nodded at Bob and Fernandez as if they were neighbors who had known each other for 20 years. The detectives went through an apartment filled with more police officers, EMT technicians, and others. Fernandez was walking upfront; Bob was trying to catch up to her pace. In a minute, both detectives eased into a bedroom. They saw a recumbent corpse on the bed.

"What is the victim's name?" the Texan asked one of the officers.

"We found his wallet in the kitchen. His ID was in there. His name is Jack Hammer. A twenty-five-year-old man."

"Gosh! He was just a kid!" Detective Fernandez exclaimed.

"Who called 911?" McCarthur asked the police officer.

"The landlord, sir. Jack Hammer didn't pay the rent for the previous month. The landlord said that he was trying to reach out to Jack, but he didn't respond. The landlord got pissed and decided to check the apartment in person. He found Jack lying here, on this bed," a burly officer explained.

"M-mm. Where is the landlord?" McCarthur questioned. His face looked like he had shit in his pants.

"He is in the foyer, sir. Do you want to speak with him?" the burly man asked.

"Later. First, I need to examine the body," the Texan said, sighing. He then looked at the body. Jack Hammer had a stylish man bun. His weight was about 180-190 pounds, and his height was about 5'11". Jack was a white man, but his baby face looked brown. His body reeked unpleasantly, like a carcass that was smashed on a highway. The officers were frowning because of the unpleasant reek. The forensic experts came in and started snapping photos of the entire apartment. Bob and Detective Fernandez looked around the body. Then they surveyed the apartment. The EMT providers came over and took the body for an autopsy. McCarthur closed his eyes for a moment. He covered his face as if he was ashamed of something he had done. For a moment, the Texan pictured his son lying dead on the same bed where Jack was. Bumping into dead bodies was something that he hated.

"Are you okay, chief?" Detective Fernandez asked.

"Yeah. Let's talk to the landlord," the Texan said, and Fernandez nodded. They took the elevator and eased to the parlor of the building. The landlord was explaining something to a police officer. He was a Polish man in his early forties. His curly hair looked phenomenal. His big nose looked more like a beak of an eagle. His face resembled a penguin. His name was Julian Lukasz. He was dressed in some eccentric clothes that portrayed many different colors. It was no secret that Lukasz was the type of guy who preferred to sleep with another man. Lukasz waved his hands left and right in frustration. Finding a dead body on his property was something new to him. McCarthur and Fernandez approached Lukasz. The Polish landlord joyfully introduced himself and gave a dead fish-type handshake to the detectives. Robert sized him up. He then cut to the chase and asked, "Mr. Lukasz, when did you find the body?"

"Here is what happened. Jack hasn't been returning any of my calls for the past nine days, and I had to come over and check him out. As I opened the door, the apartment looked spooky, as if no one had lived there for years. Anyway, I sneaked in and checked the bedroom. Jack's body was lying on the bed. I'm horrified. I can't imagine how his parents would feel over the loss of their son." The Polish landlord was blabbering. He hadn't actually answered the question in his long monologue. Fernandez decided to make it easier. She asked, "Do you remember what time it was when you found the body?"

"Immediately, after I saw the body, I called the police. A-aa… About forty-five minutes ago," the Polish landlord replied.

"Was the door locked when you got here?" Robert asked.

"No, I suppose he forgot to lock it."

"Can you describe Jack as a tenant? When did he move in here?" Detective Fernandez questioned. Lukasz looked at both detectives and smiled, especially at Bob.

"Jack Hammer has been here for about two years. I posted this apartment for rent on Zillow, and he reached out to me. I checked him out, you know," Lukasz winked at Bob and continued, "He was a very disciplined and respectful young man. His credit score was above 750, and he had a well-paying job."

"What was his job?" Fernandez asked automatically.

"I don't know exactly. Something related to computers. I don't really care what job he had. He was paying every month without delays. He was a good tenant. I mean, a really good and handsome tenant," Lukasz answered. He was animated and exhilarated.

"Where were you before you came to check the apartment?" Bob asked gravely. Lukasz touched his lips with his fingers as if he had just tasted an expensive meal.

"At my house in Evanston."

"Can someone confirm that?" Fernandez asked.

"Yes!" Lukasz cried out.

"Who?" the Texan asked curtly.

"My cats! HA-HA-HA!" Lukasz giggled. Fernandez didn't find anything funny at this tragic moment. She looked at her partner as if she was saying, "*Let's go. I can't stand this person.*" Bob understood her glance and proclaimed, "Mr. Lukasz, we'll touch base with you in the next couple of days. Don't leave the state without checking with us, okay?" McCarthur waved an admonitory finger at the Polish landlord and walked to the car. Lisa followed him like a dog following its master. They both jumped in the black Tahoe. Fernandez was exasperated. It was around 10:30 p.m., and she hadn't seen her family since she left her apartment in the morning.

"What do you think, chief?" the female detective asked.

"Can't really tell. We need to wait for the autopsy. The coroner will have the answers," the detective with curly hair replied.

"Do you think it was a murder?" Fernandez asked. She drove the vehicle impatiently. She wanted to drop Bob off as soon as possible, but that didn't stop her from asking questions.

"It's possible. We need to check the kid's background. We need to know where he worked, where he peed, and where he took a dump. Everything," McCarthur replied.

A few minutes later, detective Fernandez dropped Bob at his apartment. He got out off the Tahoe and said "Don't stress too much. You need to rest. You look tired."

"No. I'm not," Fernandez said while she was yawning.

"Yeah, I can see that," the Texan countered. Fernandez smiled, showing her charming dimples. Then she drove off almost immediately. McCarthur went straight to his bedroom. His apartment was a mess, but he didn't care. Nobody would be visiting him, and he was too tired to care about anything but sleep. He dragged his feet slowly to the bedroom. The breathing problem was making him lethargic. Around midnight, he dozed off at once.

5

It was Wednesday, the 20th of July. McCarthur and Fernandez went to have lunch at a place called Tasty Greens. It was a vegetarian food chain that had an eye-catching design. Tasty Greens looked so refined and modern that Bob thought he lived in the future when he was there.

Tasty Greens had an inventoried list of offerings called the Meta-menu. This menu provided a convenient option for ordering without interaction between employees and customers. Meta-menu projected a 4D software object with the shape and type of a particular dish, spinning in front of the customers; the 4D objects came from infrared light produced by an electric sensor installed inside the countertop. The flying objects hovered in the air like tiny UFOs. These software objects were so lifelike that they looked like floating dishes. Both detectives had a new type of peach salad. This type of salad had been invented a few years ago, and every young adult loved it. The detectives sat in a booth with a table shaped like a salad.

"What is this place?" McCarthur asked.

"This is a new era of vegetarian food. Everyone talks about this place. What do you think?" Fernandez asked. The Texan looked around like a confused tourist lost in New York. His eyes lit up with admiration. He was impressed.

"Yea, the place is dynamite. How do you know about it?"

"My kids. They know all the modern places in the city," Lisa Fernandez responded. She sighed and went on, "I've read Jack Hammer's files. He is clean. Never been arrested. He had e few parking volitions, but that's all."

"Have you talked with his parents?" the Texan asked.

"Yeah, with his father. His mother was very upset; she refused to talk. His father didn't reveal any useful information. He was shocked. Jack Hammer didn't have any enemies, but he had a lot of friends, one of whom could have turned against him …" Fernandez couldn't finish the sentence because her mind was filled with ambivalent thoughts.

"Right! That makes sense, though," the Texan agreed with his partner.

"Yeah. I asked his father to give me the names of his best friends. One of them is named Isaac. Jack and Isaac used to be very close. We need to scope out some information from this guy. He may give us…"

"Wait a second," Bob interrupted Fernandez because his phone was ringing.

"Hello! Yeah. Okay, I'm on my way," Bob said and hung up.
"Who was it?"
"The coroner!"

***

Bob and Detective Fernandez rushed to the Chicago Morgue. The coroner was expecting them. He was a bespectacled African-American man in his mid-thirties. He wasn't tall, but he wasn't short either. His name was Marcus Johnson; he was one of the best forensic doctors in the city. Johnson had graduated from UIC with remarkable grades. He was a quiet guy who lived in Hyde Park. Johnson loved to splurge on his hairstyle. He had expensive hair dreads. His hair looked just like J. Cole's had back in 2014. Marcus was still single, but that didn't bother him. He was taking his time, looking for the right one.

"Hey, Marcus! How you doing," Bob greeted the coroner. Marcus politely responded and asked the same question. They exchanged a few pleasantries then Bob asked, "What is your opinion, Marcus?"

"Jack had been dead at least a week before the police found his body."

"What was the reason for his demise?" Detective Fernandez asked the question that Bob couldn't wait to hear the answer to.

"I found a large amount of Potassium cyanide in the victim's body," Marcus replied.

"What does it mean in plain English," Fernandez asked.

"Potassium cyanide is a highly toxic chemical asphyxiant that interferes with the body's ability to use oxygen. The toxic substance can be used in the air or can be ingested in food or drinks. The victim had died from asphyxiation. In other words, he was poisoned," Marcus had finished his profound conclusion. Detective Fernandez was shocked; Bob didn't look surprised.

"What a mess!" Detective Fernandez commented. It seemed that she spoke more to herself than to the others.

"If it was a murder, there must be a motive. Dr. Johnson, did you find any bruises or traces of physical attack?" Bob asked.

"Not really. The victim drank some type of liquor or could be water, then he rapidly fell on the floor and died while he was suffocating," Marcus responded.

"Wait a minute! We found the body on the bed. Marcus, do you think Jack Hammer could drag himself and lay on the bed without any help?" Detective Fernandez inquired.

"It's possible! If he was in the bedroom at the moment of drinking the cyanide."

"Do you think it was a suicide?" Fernandez asked. McCarthur lifted an eyebrow in surprise. *Right on, my dear!* he thought. Lisa had just asked a vital question, but Marcus couldn't answer. He lifted his arms and shrugged.

"It's possible! I mean, I didn't know the person," Marcus said. Bob nodded and announced,

"We'll talk with his family to figure out if he was a suicidal person. Nowadays, everything is possible. Thank you for your time, Marcus. I'll talk with ya later." The coroner nodded, and both detectives hastily left the morgue. As they were walking to the black Tahoe, Lisa Fernandez glanced at her partner. The Texan was silent. He ruminated over the circumstances.

"What is it, chief."

"They couldn't find Jack's smartphone," he replied. Fernandez cringed and made the face of a person listening to someone speaking in a foreign language.

"Yeah, we talked about it. But I'm not buying it. What are you trying to say?"

"We couldn't find Ashely's phone either!" Bob speculated. Fernandez's eyes widened. She fathomed Bob's statement.

"You think that's a coincidence?"

"I highly doubt it," McCarthur replied. The detectives discussed the possibilities of the murder. Then Bob's phone chimed. He answered,

"Hello! Yeah. What! You've gotta be kidding me! Okay." He hung up and said, "Ah, dammit!"

"What?" Lisa asked.

"Let's go for a ride," Bob replied. His short answer confused Fernandez.

***

At 3:00 p.m., the same day, the black Tahoe rolled through the streets of Chicago. The vehicle wasn't speeding, but it wasn't driving slowly either. Half an hour later, the Tahoe pulled up into the parking space at a gym that had a big neon sign saying: GLADIATOR. In a minute, the detectives jumped out of the vehicle and hurried to the door. The gym was packed; every single fitness machine was occupied. Some people were waiting to use particular machines. It was as if the gym were offering a free day. Josh was at the front desk assisting a customer. When he saw the approaching detectives, his face looked like he was about to throw up. McCarthur stepped closer and interrupted the conversation that Josh was having with his customer.

"Hey, Josh! How you doing, buddy? We need to talk," the Texan said in a cheerful way, but he wasn't happy. His crooked smile looked slightly threatening.

"Hello, officers. Can you give me five minutes? I'm in the middle of something…"

"NO!" Both detectives exclaimed simultaneously. Josh nodded. He called out his mate to cover him at the desk and took the detectives to the office. His office wasn't big, but it was sumptuous. There was an expensive black leather couch across from the door. On the north side of the room was a computer desk with a brand new Mac. Behind the desk was a shelf filled with of trophies. Josh sat at his desk and politely offered non-alcoholic drinks. The detectives politely refused. Bob couldn't wait any longer and asked, "Josh, are you the owner of this gym?"

"Nah, it's my uncle's. I just run the business. I don't have that much money. HA-HA-HA," the bodybuilder laughed embarrassedly. Both detectives were dead serious as if Josh had just insulted them.

"Josh, do you know a guy named Jack Hammer?" McCarthur asked.

"Nope. Never heard of him," Josh confidently replied.

"Don't lie to me, Josh. Spill the beans," the Texan urged the bodybuilder to talk. Josh looked at both detectives and sighed.

"Okay, here is the thing. One day, Jack came to the gym. He asked about personal training. He wanted to know about the breakdown and the prices. I printed out all the options for him. He took the copy and left the gym. Never seen him since then," Josh confessed. He looked calm and confident. Bob and Detective Fernandez didn't believe his statement. They thought he was bullshitting them on purpose.

"When did he visit the gym?" Fernandez asked. Josh's answer was important to her. The purpose of her tricky question was to confuse the bodybuilder.

"I don't know, guys. Thousands of people are coming in and out of that gym on a daily basis. If I have to guess, probably a month ago!" Josh answered. His confidence irritated Detective Fernandez; she wasn't buying any of his words. McCarthur stepped close to the bodybuilder. He was staring at him with his dagger eyes and stated, "We found traces of Ashley's hair in his apartment," McCarthur continued. "Jack Hammer is dead. His landlord had called the police a few days ago because Jack wasn't responding." The Texan flashed his crooked smile. Josh's confidence evaporated like the smoke of a cigarette in the wind. His face looked puzzled and even terrified. Bob's plan worked well. He wanted to make Josh uncomfortable. *When people were being pushed, their concrete mindset cracked,* the Texan thought.

Lisa glanced at her partner and said, "We've checked Jack's social media. He was friends with Ashley. They had posted some pictures together. Do you know anything about that?"

"No, ma'am!" Josh said automatically. McCarthur showed his crooked smile for the second time and laid out, "Let me get this straight. You're telling me that your fiancé had pictures with Jack on social media, and you've never seen them."

"A-aa, yes! That's correct, sir," Josh replied. He tried to sound polite because the conversation wasn't going well.

"Bullshit!" Lisa Fernandez exclaimed. Her patience broke into pieces because she couldn't stand Josh's disdainful behavior. The bodybuilder acted as if he was a celebrity who had some kind of immunity that could be used against the authorities. That was why she accosted him so aggressively.

"Lisa," the Texan said in a low voice. By saying *Lisa*, he meant, "*Cool your jets. I got this.*" McCarthur and Fernandez had been working together for many years. A single word uttered between them was easily construed.

"Josh, listen bud. I have to be blunt with ya. You're the main suspect in first degree murder," the Texan declared.

"Huh? What are you talking about?" Josh pretended that he was confused. Faking his puzzlement was a good idea; his acting skills were impressive.

"Let's face the facts. You saw the pictures that Ashley and Jack had taken. You became mad and jealous. Then you visited Jack at his apartment and poisoned him. You planned to make it look like a suicide. You were mad at Ashley. You had a falling out with her. She said to you, "it's over." And you flipped out, got panicked, and kidnapped her. Josh, where is she?" Bob asked.

"Huh? Officers, I swear to God! I have no idea what you are talking about. I didn't kill Jack. I didn't know that he was dead until you told me. I'm telling you the truth. I'm innocent," Josh said quietly, but he was about to explode with anger. The muscular guy disliked the Texan; he thought of him as a crooked detective. Bob shook his head disagreeably; he had tried to gaslight Josh and test his resolve, but the kid was resilient, not a dummy. McCarthur and Fernandez looked at each other. They had their usual telepathic conversation. Then Bob blurted out.

"Okay, Josh. At this point, we don't have any more questions. Although, you can be sure that we'll want to speak with you again soon," the Texan said, and both detectives left the office. Josh remained motionless. His eyes were cast down to the floor as if he had been somehow disgraced. His deep thoughts made him uncomfortable.

***

It was Sunday afternoon in Chicago. The fresh breeze of August induced Chicagoans to hang out with friends. Downtown was blooming. The city was filled with young people, just like bees in a beehive. People were enjoying the weather and having fun, but Robert McCarthur wasn't into any of these activities. Detective McCarthur walked into his crib. His apartment was on the third floor of a well-restored townhouse. He had bought the apartment a year ago; it seemed to be a good deal. The neighborhood was fine and not far from the downtown area. The Texan bellied up to the fridge and opened a bottle of vodka. Too often he drank alcohol, though he knew he shouldn't. That was his way to escape from the problems he had.

The Texan sipped a glass of vodka, went to the balcony and sat on his rocking chair. He was mesmerized by the Chicago dusk. He watched how the sun was gradually hiding beyond the horizon. The police detective thought about his vivid memories of how he met his wife twenty-eight years ago. His crooked smile flashed for a moment, then it disappeared, and his serious face switched on. The Texan reminisced about how happy his family had been. He then remembered the countless arguments that he and his wife had. Thinking about his past, Bob knew how foolish he was. But it was too late for apologies. He had messed up his family. The remorse for his deeds made him sad. He comprehended how wrong he was, and the outcome of his efforts was taking him in the wrong direction. The alcohol helped him to swallow the pain. He drained the glass and refilled it. The drinking problem was making him depressed. For the past few years, this problem has grown bigger. His doctor had advised him to stop drinking. However, Bob neglected his doctor's suggestions and drank to get hammered. He had to work the next day, but that didn't stop him from drinking. Morgan Wallen was singing "Talkin' Tennessee" on the JBL speaker left on the table next to him. The music wasn't loud, but he could clearly hear it. Bob's eyes were filled with tears. He missed his wife and his son. He hadn't seen them for six months. His wife Teresa refused to speak with him. She was mad at him because he was mean to her, calling her horrible names and telling her what a bad person she was. More tears were falling from Bob's eyes. At work, he showed his strong, straightforward character that could break any criminal. But at his place, he was weak, lamenting about his life. Bob drained another glass. He then got on his feet and walked to the fridge. Another bottle was waiting in the freezer. He took the bottle and wobbled back to the balcony. McCarthur sat on the rocking chair and took another sip. The detective was checking his social media. He wasn't interested in anything in particular. He was killing time while the alcohol was making him dizzy. The Texan had more than a thousand contacts in his phone, but none of his friends would call him and say, "Hey, Bob? How are you doing? Is everything okay?" None of his friends seemed to care about him. He was alone. Only Siri was keeping him company. Regularly, he asked Siri about things that could pop up in his mind. It was funny to him that he lived in a digital age where people turned into half-cyborgs, having conversations with their smartphones. Back in the 1970s, Bob was a loving kid, playing basketball with his friends from school. He never imagined a time when people would only communicate with their phones. There were no smartphones back then, and Bob had to be at home at a specific time. After the school bus dropped him at his parent's house, he always went home. If he got there late, repercussions waited for him. In the 70s, kids played together and had fun on the streets, but they also had to follow a strict curfew. If someone came home late, they would be in trouble. Bob remembered that one day, his sister didn't return from school. At that time, she was fourteen. The entire city was looking for her. Two weeks later, the police found his sister's body somewhere in the gorge. She had been raped and murdered. Not long after that, the police found the murderer at his house. He was a Caucasian man in his thirties, a mentally unhinged college professor. After years of a dysfunctional marriage, he metamorphosed into a pedophile and murdered Bob's sister. Since then, McCarthur had vowed to become a detective who would catch killers.

The Texan drained another glass. The vodka made him dizzy, but that didn't stop him from refilling. The detective thought about Ashley, the missing girl. It was his duty to find her. Ashley reminded him of his sister. Deep inside in his soul, he prayed that she was still alive. He was focused on how he could find something that would resolve the case. Her boyfriend, Josh, was a liar. Bob was convinced that the bodybuilder had the motive for kidnapping his fiancé. He then poisoned Jack Hammer because he was jealous. *Someone is hiding something!* he thought. The Texan knew that Josh wasn't telling the truth about Ashley. The wind was blowing and playing with his curly hair. Robert stared at the empty glass as if he was looking for something specific. All of a sudden, he started to cough badly. His throat hurt and made him nauseous. McCarthur kept coughing as if he had just toked a strong blunt.

"What the…" he managed to say, then coughed more. *I'm getting old,* he thought, then got on his feet and went inside. The alcohol shook his vision; he could barely walk. He went to the kitchen and fell on the floor.

***

Lisa Fernandez looked at her Apple watch. The clock was displaying 10:05 a.m. It was Monday, and she was supposed to pick up Bob as she usually did. This morning, the Texan wasn't showing any sign of coming down to the car. That made Lisa anxious and edgy.

"Come on, chief. What the heck are you doing?" She asked herself. Lisa Fernandez waited in the black Tahoe for a few minutes more. She looked through the window and gawked at Bob's apartment. She couldn't tell if he was in there.

"Come on, chief! Let's go!" Lisa whispered under her breath. Fernandez became nervous; patience wasn't her strongest quality. In the next few minutes, she called Robert. His phone was working, but no one was answering. She snuggled her firearm in its holster and jumped out of the Tahoe. Fernandez wore a blue Polo shirt and black Ariat breeches. Her ponytail looked outstanding. Fernandez walked quickly, but she was extremely cautious. She headed to the intercom and punched a four-digit pin code. An annoying buzzing sound blasted, and she yanked the door. Stepping nimbly up the stairs, she approached Bob's apartment and knocked on the door.

"Come on, Chief! Are you okay? Hey, Bob!" Lisa raised her voice. She kept pounding on the door.

"Bob!" she repeated. Lisa leaned forward and pressed her ear against the door. There were no sounds—nothing. It seemed like no one was in there. But that didn't deter Fernandez. She grabbed the doorknob and turned it clockwise; the door was unlocked, which was unusual. Lisa tiptoed into the apartment.

"Chief! Are you in the shower? What's going on?" Fernandez

exclaimed. She looked around the condo. Bob's apartment was a disaster; clothes were thrown everywhere. A bookshelf filled with junk stood on the east side of the living room. The white leather couch across the room was covered with jeans and socks. A box with Chinese leftovers was on the coffee table; flies hovered around the food like little helicopters. Fernandez tiptoed to the kitchen. The sink overflowed with filthy dishes

"Bob! Are you okay? Is anybody here?" She repeated. Her fingers were touching the holster. Fernandez figured that something had happened. She checked the bathroom. It was clean; there was no sign of her partner.

"Chief! If you are here, answer me! Hey, Bob!" Fernandez was cautious and prudent. The veins in her neck were pulsating with dread. She sweated as if she was in a sauna. The adrenaline made her heart pound. The only room that remained unchecked was the bedroom. The door was closed, which wasn't a good sign. Fernandez didn't see any blood in the apartment, which was good, but that didn't help her either.

"Chief! I'm opening the bedroom door. Do you hear me?" There were no answers. Fernandez grabbed the doorknob and turned it. She slowly opened the door, and her face froze. She was dumbstruck. She looked down and covered her mouth in disbelief. Then she laughed out loud. McCarthur was sleeping in his bedroom like a baby. His mouth was wide open as if he was singing. Fernandez assumed that Robert had gotten drunk and passed out the night before. He was wearing the same clothes he had on for the past two days. The entire bedroom reeked like a distillery.

"Come on, Chief! Let's get to work!" Fernandez spoke loudly. She tried to wake him up. In a few seconds, Bob stirred a bit. He opened his eyes and saw Detective Fernandez giggling.

"I slept in. Dammit!" he burst out sleepily. In spite of his slowly moving body, Bob took a shower and got dressed in about 30 minutes. Even Fernandez was impressed. She was waiting at the threshold by the main entry. Bob trudged down the stairs at a slow pace, continuously rubbing his face. His eyelids were blinking like a broken-down traffic light. He was feeling dizzy, but he successfully managed to disguise it.

"Come on, chief. Do you want a beer?" Fernandez voiced playfully. Bob's hangover entertained her. The Texan cracked up. Then his face cringed. He said, "It's not funny!" And both laughed loudly as if they were smoking blunt. They jumped in the Tahoe, and Fernandez fired up the engine. She asked, Police station?"

"Yea, but first, stop at a 7-Eleven store. I need to snack up and maybe get a coffee." Fernandez nodded and sped the Tahoe. The vehicle stopped in a parking space at 7-Eleven at the corner of Western and Grace Street.

"Do you want something?" McCarthur asked softly. Fernandez shook her head no. Bob nodded and got out of the vehicle. He walked to the store. Just before he opened the door, a voice disturbed him.

"Hey, excuse me! Do you have a cell phone?" a panicked man asked. He stood a few feet from the Texan. His voice sounded urgent.

"Yea, what's goin' on?" McCarthur asked.

"They just stole my car! I went inside to grab a 12-pack, and when I came out, the car was gone!" The man's voice sounded unfriendly. He wore a cheap cap and disheveled clothes. He looked to be in his fifties, but he acted like an angry adolescent. The brown color of his skin alluded that he had a South American lineage. His slender body made him look like a wino who drank more than he ate. His white beard aged him, but his face looked somehow youthful.

"Hold on! Get it together. Did you see who took your car?" the Texan asked while he was dialing the operator.

"Nah, man. I didn't see anyone! Here are my keys, man!" The guy pulled out two car keys and a bunch of other residential keys.

"Okay, I got you. I'm a detective. The patrols are on their way," Bob declared. He looked at the 12-pack beer that the man held and asked himself, *It's 10:30 Monday morning, and this man already thinks about drinking.* The detective contemplated the odd situation. Then he looked at the man and asked.

"What's your name?"

"Victor Ortiz," The man responded automatically. His eyes looked angry as if he was about to start a fight.

"Okay, Victor. The police patrol is coming. They'll take care of you, okay?" Robert said. Victor nodded, but he looked like he didn't understand what Bob had told him. McCarthur went into 7-Eleven and grabbed some croissants. He left the store and wished Victor good luck. Then he hopped in the Tahoe. Fernandez looked at him and asked,

"What's up with this guy?"

"Ugh! I don't know. He claimed that someone had stolen

his vehicle while he was in the store. I called the 20th district. They will take care of him. Honestly, I think this man is nuts," the Texan replied.

"Why?" Fernandez quizzed and drove off from the parking space. McCarthur looked through the side mirror. He observed how Victor was complaining to other people. Then he looked at Fernandez and said,

"Because I don't trust him. I'm incredulous. You know that. Besides, how could a thief start an engine without the key in less than a minute? This is not a James Bond movie." Bob concluded. Fernandez agreed without saying a word.

The black Tahoe sped to the police headquarters in Chicago, near the West Side area. Later on the same day, Bob and Fernandez spoke with a few cyber security experts to trace the social media of Josh, Jack Hammer, and Ashley. The Texan contacted a few of the biggest social media platforms. He wanted to catch Josh because he was 100% convinced that he was responsible for Jack's murder. Robert believed that Josh was surreptitious, making up stories to blur the truth. He also knew that if he found potassium cyanide in Josh's apartment— the pretty Latin boy would be incarcerated. Later on, the detectives checked Josh's parents. Mia, his mother, emigrated from Mexico back in the 90s. Her files indicated that she was clean. Mia had worked many jobs over the years. In 2012, she graduated from DePaul University and became a psychiatrist. Mia had been working in the same private clinic since 2013. Josh's father was a different story; he was born in the Logan Square area in the early 70s. His name was Raul. At age of eighteen, Raul started working as a busser in a prominent restaurant in the downtown area. Ten years later, Raul opened his own restaurant. At first, his restaurant wasn't going well, but then it turned out to be a gold mine, and Raul made a decent living. Years later, he became a high roller. He was splurging money on casinos, cars, and clothes. In 2014, Raul got a DUI. In 2015, he was arrested for possession of a half-pound of marijuana. In 2018 Raul's restaurant burned down while it was closed. The police report stated that someone who worked in the kitchen had left the stove on, causing the fire. Later the same year, Raul filed for bankruptcy. Four months later, he opened a big deli market in Franklin Park. Allegedly, Raul received a payout from his insurance for the burned-down restaurant, but it was unclear how he pulled out two million dollars in cash with which to start the deli market. In 2019, Raul opened a car dealership. This business started making him more than just decent money. Josh's uncle, the owner of Gladiator, lived in Mexico. His name was Juan. He was an American citizen and hadn't been back to the U.S. since 2016. His life in Mexico remained mysterious to Chicago's detectives. According to the IRS, Juan was paying his taxes on time. The reports on Josh's family were long and engaging. Bob had the feeling that he was reading a John Grisham novel.

Around noon, both detectives headed for lunch at the Fulton Market area. The restaurant where they decided to eat was called Shumsters. It was one of the newly opened places in the area. Also, the restaurant had a Michelin Star, which helped to attract more people. Shumsters was an Italian restaurant embellished with a comprehensive design with many oval columns built to entice customers. The vestibule, where patrons waited had a huge electronic fireplace. McCarthur and Fernandez sat in a round booth that massaged them while they ate. Bob liked the idea of having his ass shiatsued while he waited for the food. Both detectives ordered Fettuccine Alla Bolognese.

As they were eating, Bob stated,

"I'm waiting for the judge. He was supposed to give us a search warrant last Friday. I think we'll have it by tomorrow. We need to check Josh's apartment."

"Do you think we can find something useful?" Fernandez asked.

"I'll say that I'm optimistic about finding something crucial. I mean, Josh is the main suspect, and he seemed to be uncertain in his statements," Bob responded.

"What about Jack's best friend, Isaac?"

"Yeah. I spoke with him two days ago," McCarthur replied quietly.

"And what he said," Fernandez impatiently asked.

"He moved to London four months ago. Isaac declares that he hasn't seen Jack for five months," the Texan paused, then he went on, "After lunch, we'll go back to Ashley's apartment. I need to speak with Kimberly, Ashley's roommate."

"Why?"

"I need to ask what she knows about Jack Hammer. Her information can be helpful. Trust me on this," Bob replied, and Fernandez nodded. The lunch was over.

***

An hour later, the black Tahoe was stuck in heavy traffic, and that made Fernandez pissed. She hated Chicago's gridlock. At 5:05 p.m., the Tahoe parked on North Irene Avenue. Fernandez briskly hopped out of the vehicle; Bob needed a little more time. He moved slowly.

"Are you okay, Chief?" Lisa asked. The Texan showed his crooked smile. His stomach looked like that of a pregnant woman who was in pain.

"Yeah, I think it's from the Bolognese. Don't worry. I'll be all right. Come on. Let's talk with Kimberly," the Texan suggested. Both detectives climbed the stairs to the third floor and knocked on the door. No one responded. McCarthur was confused because Kimberly had promised to talk with him. The detectives looked at each other with surprise. Bob and Fernandez had another telepathic connection. Often, they communicated with just a few glances. McCarthur looked at his partner. Fernandez nodded as if she was saying, "*Gotcha!*" The door was open. Both detectives tiptoed inside as if they were thugs trying to rob the apartment.

"Kimberly! Are you here? This is Detective McCarthur. I'm with my partner, Detective Fernandez. We spoke two days ago about coming over and asking you some questions. Are you here?" Bob raised his voice. The apartment looked spooky. No one was answering, which made Bob nervous. Both detectives split in different directions; Bob checked the kitchen, and Fernandez the bedroom. The Texan looked around. There was no sign of Kimberly.

"Kimberly!" he shouted while he was walking into the bathroom.

"Bob! Here! Come here!" Fernandez exclaimed, and McCarthur quickly went to the bedroom.

"What! Ah, dammit!" the Texan cried out. He saw Kimberly lying dead on her bed. The picture was terrifying.

***

Twenty minutes later, North Irene Avenue was filled with police vehicles, a firetruck, and an ambulance. The police troopers and EMT technicians were scurrying around like ants in an anthill. The apartment where Ashley and Kimberly had lived looked like a police station. Forensic experts were taking pictures as quickly as paparazzi taking photos of celebrities. Kimberly's body was lying on the bed as if she was taking a nap. She was covered in blood. Her eyes and mouth were wide open as if she had watched a horror movie just before she passed away. There was a note left on the bed by Kimberly's head. The letter read:

To Mom and Dad,

I'm sorry for what I'm about to say. You have given me a life and everything I could possibly ask for. I will always love you, don't ever forget that. I know you guys wanted me to grow up happy, and I was. But I'm not happy anymore. I hate that the entire world is flooded with a bunch of monsters. I also want to confess that lately my life has been a nightmare. I've lost my job. I spent all my savings on payments and bills. I lost my best friend, Ashley. I feel like I don't want to live in this cruel world. I just can't take it anymore. People around me were treating me like a low-life piece of shit. It had been like that for years. My life isn't worth it. I need to release my soul and let the spirit hover around like an angel. I feel like no one could understand me, so I made my choice. I will always love you.

Goodbye.

Love, Kimberly

"So, it was a suicide! But why would she kill herself?" Fernandez asked. She was flustered. The Texan looked at her as if he didn't understand the question. He took a deep breath and said,

"It looks like...Agh. Wait a minute! Was she the type of girl who would commit suicide? We have to speak with the coroner." Bob's thoughts confused even himself. He went to the kitchen and leaned forward to the sink. He felt nauseous. It looked like he was about to regurgitate, but he did not. The detectives and deputies had a tough job to do. There were many questions of which the answers remained elusive. The chaos in Chicago increased.

6

A day after Kimberly was found dead, Bob and Fernandez drove to the Chicago Morgue. They were both anxious to speak with the coroner, especially Bob. His gut feeling whispered ominous possibilities to him. The coroner, Marcus Johnson, waited for them in the autopsy room. He was dressed in a white lab robe, although his pants looked flashy. Marcus looked debonair as usually he was.

His fluffy dreadlocks made him look like a model for a men's hair magazine.

"Marcus! How you doing, buddy?" Bob exclaimed while flashing his crooked smile.

"I'm cool. What about yourself?" the coroner replied and gave him a fist bump.

"Can't complain. You know me. I'm not bored. However,

I'd decided to stop by and see what you're doing," Bob stated. Marcus nodded and kindly greeted Detective Fernandez. The three state officials were chit-chatting casually for a minute. Then McCarthur changed the subject.

"Marcus, what have you found so far? Was it a suicide? Did Kimberly kill herself?"

"No. It was a murder! Someone stabbed the victim twice. Kimberly was already dead when the murderer stabbed her the second time," the African-American coroner stated. Fernandez was shocked, but Bob didn't look surprised.

"Did you find any fingerprints or any traces of DNA?" Fernandez asked. Marcus shook his head no.

"Whoever killed Kimberly, he must have been a very smart guy. He knows how to cover his tracks," Marcus went on.

"Marcus, did you see any bruises or injures on Kimberly's body?" Bob asked and sighed in frustration. Marcus looked at him for a second. Then he said, "Follow me." Both detectives walked behind the coroner. They strolled to a different chamber where the corpses were kept. The room looked spacious and spooky. Scary like the set of a horror movie. Also, it resembled an ominous food court with no chairs. The ceiling was festooned with a bunch of 2 x 4 light fixtures. The lights were so bright that a person could get a headache looking at them.

The coroner pulled out Kimberly's covered body. He then uncovered the corpse's head. He leaned forward and showed a bruise on the back of the skull.

"What is that?" Fernandez asked. The bruise resembled a big black blotch hidden under Kimberly's hair. Bob looked thoughtfully at the corpse. He then stared at Marcus and asked, "Do you think she could have been hit with some sort of object?"

"Yeah, absolutely! In my professional opinion, I would guess that the murderer had used a pan or skillet. As you can see, the bruise is on the back of her head, which implies that she was attacked from behind," Marcus shared his opinion. Both detectives nodded simultaneously.

"Maybe she turned around... then Bam! The murderer hit her!" Fernandez said.

"Exactly! I think after the hit, she immediately fell on the floor, unconscious," Marcus asserted.

"With that being said, it is clear that Kimberly knew her murderer!" Bob questioned. He was filled with excitement. His big blue eyes lit up; his heartbeat raced, like a man skydiving for the first time in his life.

"So that's why the door was unlocked. Kimberly had voluntarily opened the door. Most likely, she chatted with her murderer before he killed her," Detective Fernandez finished her rational statement.

"Bingo!" Marcus exclaimed.

"Same thing happened at Jack Hammer's apartment. His door was also unlocked. That's what the landlord told us, remember?" Bob told Fernandez. At this moment, her eyes lit up as if she found out that she had the chance to fight for the unified world UFC title. Detective McCarthur stared at Lisa. He saw how her brown baby skin shone under the light, and her seductive lips portrayed her gorgeous face. Detective Fernandez was probably the hottest chick on the police force. Yet she could have been a model or an actress. She could have had a remarkable career in Hollywood, but she had chosen to be a detective because she wanted to help people, and this was one of those moments.

"Maybe there's some connection between Jack's death and Kimberly's murder," Fernandez concluded.

"Marcus, what type of person would be able to knock Kimberly out?" Bob asked. Marcus looked at him, puzzled.

"You say what?" the coroner questioned. He didn't understand the question.

"Was the murderer a male or female?" McCarthur rephrased.

"Ah, yeah. I would say a male. Female couldn't perform such a powerful strike unless she is a UFC champion," Marcus stated and looked at Fernandez. The female detective frowned. She gave him the stinky eye as if she was saying, "*C'mon, man! Give me a break!*" Marcus realized that Fernandez didn't buy the joke and ad-libbed,

"I'm joking! HA-HA-HA." The coroner cracked up. He had such a contagious laugh that it made Fernandez snicker. Bob joined the laughter, but he wasn't amused. His mind was focused on the mystery of Kimberly's demise. His gut feeling was making him restless. In a minute, the autopsy's room became awkwardly quiet.

"We need to find the weapon that the murderer used to kill Kimberly," Bob spoke out loud.

"There is something that you should know," Marcus stated. McCarthur gave him a look as if to say, "*Go ahead.*"

"The victim was pregnant," Marcus pointed out. His lucid eyes surveyed the detectives.

"Huh!" Fernandez exclaimed. Her mind was immersed in a lake of confusion.

"She carried a month along. I know it's very unusual and sad," the coroner responded.

"You ain't joking with us, right?" the Texan asked, even though he knew the answer. Marcus was dead serious. He took his job seriously, and McCarthur knew that.

"There is more!" Marcus announced, and both detectives froze. They looked like wax figures.

"I took a swab test and found something shocking. Guess who the father is!" Marcus announced, and both detectives exclaimed in disapproval.

"Who! Agh, dammit!" the Texan exclaimed. He had already figured out the answer.

"No way! You've gotta be kidding me!" Fernandez burst out. She couldn't believe Marcus' words. Yet, he seemed to be quite serious. As a matter of fact, Marcus Johnson seemed to be offended.

"I'm not finished! Marcus has more surprises," The coroner pointed out kindly. He went on, "I found a strand of hair from another female and took a DNA test. Apparently, Kimberly had a sexual relationship with that person. Her name is Monica Shingles. Sound familiar?" Both detectives shook their heads no.

"Who is Monica Shingles?" Detective Fernandez asked. Her glowing brown eyes widened. She looked frightened, but actually, she was disgusted. Bob glanced at her, saying,

"I guess our buddy might have known the answer." His words came with confidence. In the next minute, both detectives briskly left the room. The chaos in Chicago grew greater.

***

It was 10:30 a.m., Wednesday, July 26th. The sky was overcast. Clouds were dull as if it was a sign of the apocalypse; the wind was blowing and shaking the street signs and the trees. The temperature was around the mid-sixties, which was unusual for the season. The weather forecast had predicted scattered storms throughout the day. A torrential downpour was expected by mid-afternoon. None of this bothered the black Tahoe that rolled on the I-90 expressway. Detective Fernandez was behind the wheel; she was focused on the road. Her gorgeous brunette hair was tied in a ponytail, as usual. She wore an expensive blue raincoat and black trousers. Under her coat, she had a black V-neck shirt. As she paid attention to the road, Fernandez looked at a humongous billboard that projected Ashley's colorful image. The sign displayed the word: MISSING. Bob sat on the passenger's seat. His eyes were stuck on the paperwork that he was reading. The tips of his curly hair were dangling playfully. He wore a brown fedora, a black North Face coat, and black jeans. Ironically, both detectives loved to dress in black. Silence filled the black Tahoe, but not for long because Fernandez wanted to talk.

"Chief, do you think we will ever find Kimberly's smartphone?" She asked. Her partner took off his reading glasses and said,

"Nah. I don't think so. Allegedly, the killer collects victims' phones to cover his tracks. Although, if we find the knife which the murderer used to kill Kimberly, then we can track him down. The problem is: he is too smart. To catch a guy as smart as this is equivalent to finding a needle in a haystack. I feel like we are heading toward a dead end," he paused for a second and continued, "Kimberly's parents confirmed that she didn't write that suicide letter. At this point, we are certain that she was murdered. With that being said, many more questions arise. Why would someone kill her? What is his motive?" Detective McCarthur questioned loudly—yet in a mellow tone.

"If Kimberly didn't write that note, then who did it? The murderer?"

"I would say so."

"Do you think that Josh killed all of them, including Ashley?" Fernandez asked. Bob glanced at her. His confused mind struggled to come up with a straight answer.

"Either he is the killer, or he must have been his accomplice. I believe he has teamed up with the murderer, and right now, he acts like he's a fall guy who has nothing to do with killing people. But that won't last long. Mark my words; we'll catch this slimeball," Bob said confidently, but he wasn't completely sure. *Resolving a murder case is like playing a puzzle; all the missing pieces must be fit together to have the final result,* the Texan thought. Detective Fernandez agreed with her partner. She gripped the steering wheel tightly as if she was trying to break it. The female detective was nervous. The problems in her household were multiplying, and on top of that, she

84

was determined to unravel this complicated investigation. Fernandez had been so busy that she didn't have time for training in the gym. She needed to kick someone's ass. She had to release the emotional pressure because her anger elevated to a much higher degree.

In 2001, three boys accosted her in the girls' restroom at the public school she attended. At that time, Fernandez was in the 8th grade. She was frightened and scared. The boys were bigger and older than her. The three brats took her belongings and beat the shit out of her. Fernandez was embarrassed and brutally abused by those three boys. The assault terrified her, and she bottled up that unpleasant encounter deep down in her mind. She had never told this story to the school principal. Her parents saw the bruises and asked her what had happened. Fernandez made up a story, saying that she had fallen on the stairs. The gorgeous Latina lied because she was embarrassed and humiliated. At that time, she thought that if she revealed the truth, the three brats would attack her again. At the age of seventeen, Fernandez started training in martial arts and took a vow that she would never let anyone abuse her again.

Back in the Tahoe, Fernandez was restless, but she looked calm. She restrained her emotions and acted professionally. That was one of her best traits. Her character could be described as a formidable flaming boulder that could crush everything in its way, but her blissful soul resembled that of a nun.

Thirty minutes later, the black Tahoe parked on Foster

and Kimball Street. Fernandez killed the engine and looked at Bob as if she was asking for approval to proceed.

"Are you ready, chief?" She asked quietly. McCarthur flashed his crooked smile and showed thumbs up. Then both detectives jumped out of the vehicle and walked across the street where there was a big neon sign that read: GLADIATOR.

***

Bob and Detective Fernandez went through the door. The gym was crowded as usual. Both detectives exchanged a questioning glance as they walked around. There were so many people in Gladiator that the Texan was forced to ask one of the employees to find Josh. A guy named Hugo spoke with Detective McCarthur. Hugo had started work at Gladiator four months ago. He was a diminutive guy of Mexican descent. He pointed to where Josh trained. Bob and Fernandez approached a machine called a "Seated Press." Josh was instructing a beautiful red-headed girl on how properly to use that machine. Both detectives stepped to the young bodybuilder, and McCarthur cried out, "Josh, buddy! How you doing? Do you mind asking you a couple of questions?" Bob's voice was friendly as if he had known Josh for many years. He stared at Josh's developed muscles thinking, *How the heck had he gotten so cut?* Josh glanced at Bob, and his happy face immediately changed to that of a frowning man suffering from sudden diarrhea.

"Hey, guys! What a surprise. Can you wait a second? I'm in the middle of something…"

"I'm afraid that we need to talk. Right now," Bob said. His friendly voice changed to the hoarse tone of an angry customer. Josh rolled his eyeballs reluctantly, excusing himself to the beautiful girl. He walked the detectives to the office. Josh wore a thin, white tank top. His ripped body could be seen easily through the fabric. The veins on his biceps popped up. It looked like his body could explode at any second. Josh had a well-trimmed beard. His Faux Hawk haircut was stylish and looked fine on him. Also, he wore mini playboy earrings that glowed a little too much. Josh sat on his chair and kindly said, "So, how can I help you today?" The bodybuilder smiled. It seemed that he was having fun. Fernandez took a deep breath and asked "Josh, where were you between the hours of 6:00 p.m. and 10:30 p.m. last Monday?" Her voice was thin and imperative. Josh raised his perfect-looking eyebrows in frustration. This question surprised him; he was caught off guard.

"Uh... I watched the Cubs game with my friends. We were in a sports bar close to Wrigley."

"Can anyone confirm that?" Bob quizzed.

"Hell yeah! I mean. Yes, sir. My buddies were there," Josh spilled out these words automatically. He looked calm and a bit cocky. Lisa Fernandez squinted at Josh. She then glanced at her partner as if she was asking for approval, then proceeded,

"Mr. Rodriguez, did you hear about Kimberly's death?"

"Yeah, yeah. Are you kiddin' me? I mean, it was all over the news. That's horrible," Josh paused. He then looked at both detectives and continued.

"You don't think that I did it, right? I mean, c'mon. I do

have an alibi." His elated voice disappeared. He was no longer cheerful.

"What was your relationship with Kimberly?" the Texan asked.

"Uh… friends. I mean, she's a close friend to my fiancé, though," Josh shrugged. Fernandez shook her head in frustration.

"Mr. Rodriguez, did you know that Kimberly was pregnant?" Fernandez interrogated. The bodybuilder seemed baffled.

"Pregnant! Nah… I mean, I think she was… you know. Let's put it this way: she liked to sleep with other girls," Josh carefully picked his words. He tried to sound more respectful while speaking with homicide detectives. But that was BS. The detectives didn't believe him.

"Well, apparently, she was bisexual. Josh, cut the crap. What happened? Help us out. We need to catch the perpetrator," the Texan said calmly. Fernandez admired how McCarthur maintained his professional attitude in such a critical moment. Josh took a deep breath. He then said, "Okay. Two weeks before Ashley disappeared, I went to her apartment. I needed to grab a few gym items. At that time, Ashley wasn't there. She went to a book signing in Milwaukee. Some prominent author that she liked was attending an event out there. Ashley was very excited to see him. She asked me to come with her, but I'm not a big reader. I've read two books in my entire life. Anyway. So, as I walked to my fiancé's apartment, I accidently bumped into Kimberly. Her friend was there too. What was her name…uh?"

"Monica Shingles?" Fernandez butted in.

"Yeah! That's right. So we talked about, you know, school, friends…you know, like casual stuff. Kimberly offered me a drink. To be honest with you, I think she had already been hammered because she was talking too much. They both drank some sort of whiskey. And as you may know, alcohol makes people socialize. Next thing I knew, I woke up in bed with Kimberly and her friend. My *buddy* was sore. As I went to the restroom, I peed all over the toilet. So I figured I might have had sex with Kimberly and her friend. But that was a mistake, though. We took a vow to keep it secret, especially from Ashley. Kimberly and Monica agreed. That was all," Josh finished his confession.

"Let me get this straight: you had a threesome with your fiancé's roommate and her friend, yet you didn't know that Kimberly was pregnant?" McCarthur asked.

"Yes, sir! I didn't have a clue that she was pregnant. She didn't tell me. It's all messed up. Yeah, I mean, I cheated on my fiancé, but that doesn't make me a killer."

"That doesn't exonerate you either," Fernandez pointed out. She tried to maintain her professional behavior. It was not easy for her because she thought Josh was a piece of shit.

"Ma'am! I love Ashley. She is the person I want to spend my life with. You have to believe me," the bodybuilder said. He was persuasive. That made Bob sail into a river of thoughts building up to his next question.

"Did Ashley know about your hanky-panky business?" Fernandez said quickly. She couldn't hold back. The whole story irritated her.

"I don't think so. But I thought Ashley cheated on me

with Jack Hammer. That was why we had some fights before she disappeared. Just because I had a falling out with Ashley doesn't make me a killer. I have never hit a girl in my life. Why would I? I don't want to go to jail. That's the truth," Josh declared. He looked at the detectives with his innocent eyes. His words made a lot of sense, yet at the same time, he confused both detectives. Bob and Detective Fernandez looked at each other quizzically. An awkward pause occurred for about a minute. Bob looked down at his shoes as if he had dropped something. He then raised his head and said,

"What is your relationship with Monica Shingles?"

"What do you mean? I don't understand the question," Josh replied and frowned. The Texan stared at him as if he was saying, "*Really?*"

"I think my question was crystal clear and straightforward. In other words, I was asking: do you talk to her on social media? Do you hang out with her?" Bob grilled. He took off his fedora and ran his hand through his curly blond hair.

"No! I mean, we are friends on Instagram, but that's all. I haven't seen her since, you know…" Josh couldn't finish the sentence. The bodybuilder was embarrassed to talk about his lewd encounter. Another pause occurred. McCarthur studied Josh closely. He looked at Detective Fernandez as if he wanted to ask, "*What do you think?*"

"Do you have any more questions? Because I need to get back to work," Josh asked politely. It was not a secret that he didn't care to talk to the detectives. Bob looked thoughtfully at Lisa Fernandez. He flashed his crooked smile and said, "Nah. At this point, we don't have any further questions. But you know the drill; don't leave the country or the state without contacting us. We'll touch base with you later. Okay?"

"Yes, sir!" Josh respectfully replied as if he was answering his father after messing something up. The bodybuilder escorted the detectives to the exit doors. He wanted to make sure they would leave the premises. Bob and Fernandez crossed the street. The rain was still pouring down fast. They jumped quickly into the vehicle to avoid getting wet. Fernandez woke up the engine. She looked at her colleague and asked, "What do you think, chief?" The female detective was eager to hear his opinion. McCarthur stared at her questionably. His eyes looked tired as if he was falling asleep.

"He's disingenuous. His statements throw me for a loop. He wants us to accept his story. But I believe Josh Rodriguez killed Jack because he was jealous. He had the motive. I bet he knew that Ashley cheated on him, and that made him upset. When people get upset, they act without taking a second to consider the ramifications. After killing Jack, our buddy decided to wipe out Ashley's roommate to cover his tracks."

"But what about Monica Shingles?" Fernandez asked. She had the "aha moment."

"Yes! Here is the catch. We need to talk with her as soon as possible. Her life can be in great danger. Besides, I need to hear her side of the story. In the meantime, we'll have Josh staked out," Bob finished his thoughtful response and made a phone call. He requested information about Monica. The black Tahoe quickly drove off. Bob's conclusion took both detectives on an urgent trip.

***

At 1:30 p.m., the same day, they parked the black Tahoe in front of a condominium building in Downtown Chicago. This building was located on Illinois Street, a block away from the Ferris Wheel. The condominium was a tall building constructed from a curtain wall. Sumptuous. A masterpiece created by a prominent architect in the early 2010s. Bob and Fernandez walked through the foyer of the condominium. Inside, the interior looked luxurious. Various plantings were tastefully placed the entire length of the foyer. The floor consisted of over-sized tiles that glowed through the entire premises. The walls also were built from expensive tiles. They were 4x4 large, made from a polished black stone that sparkled through the vestibule. The ceiling was painted white and had two levels, each one with embedded lights. A large chandelier hung in the center of the ceiling. It looked so bright that a man could be dazzled if he stared at it. The detectives stepped closer to a big front desk covered with a black marble that shone through the vestibule. The marble on the desk perfectly matched the walls. A young African-American lady stood behind the desk. She was dressed in a tasteful white suit that looked glamorous on her. Her name was Precious; she had side braids leading into a ponytail, flowing onto her left shoulder. Precious had an enthralling smile and beautiful glowing eyes.

"Oh my God! I love your hair!" Fernandez complimented the lady at the desk. She outran Bob's eagerness to speak. Both females exchanged pleasantries while Bob surveyed

Precious, exposing his crooked smile. The detectives asked the lady if they could get a hold of Monica Shingles. The African-American lady called Monica and informed her about the situation. She then hung up the phone and gave the detectives a sign that they could proceed.

"On which floor does she live?" Bob asked thoughtfully.

"She's on 55th, sir," Precious replied. McCarthur swallowed hard. The trepidation made him restless. Nausea bothered his stomach. His heart raced. But he looked calm, almost tranquil.

"Oh, the view must be gorgeous!" Bob exclaimed. He tried to sound polite because he had acrophobia. In a second, the detectives stepped into the elevator, and Fernandez punched the button. The Texan closed his eyes for a second. He needed a break to deal with the sensation of an unnatural vertical ascent.

"Are you okay, chief?" Fernandez asked. McCarthur had never told her that he was scared of heights. He just never talked about it. He was ashamed of being a grown-up man in his early fifties, and at the same time having silly phobias.

"Yeah. I'm fine. Let's talk with Monica and get the hell outta here," the Texan said in a low but frustrated voice. Fernandez nodded agreeably. She knew that Bob's frustration didn't get along with long discussions. The elevator stopped on the 55th floor. Both detectives scuttled through the hallway. Barking dogs could be heard from each apartment. The dogs barked so loudly that Bob felt like they were in a dog shelter. Fernandez knocked on Monica's door and pressed her ear close to the frame.

"I'm coming! Just give me a second," a female voice echoed.

A dog barked aggressively from the other side of the door. McCarthur and Fernandez exchanged questioning looks.

"I'll be right there!" the same female voice blared. The door opened, and a small white Bichon Frisé immediately charged at the detectives. The puppy jumped happily at Fernandez's legs. The small dog looked friendly, but snarled aggressively. Bob thought that the dog might start biting him.

"I'm sorry. Usually, he is not like this. C'mon Pierre. Stop barking!" a cheerful female voice echoed from the door. Monica Shingles was stellar; she had the body of a model. Her brown hair glistened like honey. She was 5'8", but somehow she looked taller. Shingles had snow-white skin as if she had never exposed her body to the sun. Her blue eyes glittered like diamonds; she wore a black sleeveless, flared dress. Her legs were gorgeous. Fernandez adored Monica. Bob was shocked by her perfection; his heart pounded. The Texan thought that if he met any more beautiful woman like this, it might result in a heart attack. He could barely get it together.

The detectives introduced themselves, and Monica led them into her condo. The apartment was worth millions of dollars. The furniture was cutting edge. The colors on most of the furniture were white and gray, just like the walls. Monica's apartment had an exquisite view, facing Lake Michigan. From her apartment, the breathtaking scenery stretched the length of the North and South Lake Shore. Lisa Fernandez was awestruck. She loved Monica's apartment. The detective moved around the condo as if she might like to buy it. Bob kept a safe distance from the windows. He liked the view, but his fear of heights made him feel queasy. Detective Fernandez kept asking questions about the apartment. But she could quickly switch from a casual chat to more formal language. A few minutes later, she cut to the chase and changed the subject.

"Monica, what was your relationship with Kimberly?"

"Close friends from college. We weren't besties. Like… you know. Like… something like that. However, we kept in touch from time to time," Monica answered. She used the word "like" pretty much in all of her sentences.

"Miss Shingles, do you know why we are here?" McCarthur asked. He sat on the white sofa that was far away from the windows.

"I'm not really sure. Like… I was asking myself the same question. HA-HA-HA," she laughed.

"Miss Shingles, do you know that your friend, Kimberly, was found dead this past Monday?" Bob asked quietly.

"Oh my God! Are you serious?" Monica exclaimed. Her eyes filled with tears. She covered her face with her hands and started sobbing. Lisa stepped closer and hugged her.

"Woof! Woof!" Pierre barked.

"Shush, Pierre! Knock it off!" Monica commanded.

"Woof! Woof!" The dog repeated. The unexpected barking seemed like the dog was trying to add something to the conversation.

"Stop it! Knock it off. I said," Shingles snapped. She excused herself, took her Bichon Frisé into the bedroom, and closed the door. After a minute, she returned to her guests. Monica was devastated; her heart was broken. She hadn't known that her friend was murdered. Kimberly always supported her when she needed help. They'd been solid friends over the years. Kimberly was someone who could be trusted.

"I'm sorry. I just can't take it. I can't believe that my friend is gone. Who could do something so horrible to her? Like... what the hell. She was the most amazing person that I had ever met, though. She would give away her lunch to a homeless person... you know... just to make them happy. She would come to a stranger and say, 'Happy Friday! I hope you have a great day!' Or something like that! I just can't take it anymore!" Monica cried more. She had to cover herself because she felt heartbroken. Miss Shingles became very emotional, which was normal for her. Bob and Fernandez exchanged glances. Their telepathic communication had kicked in.

"Miss Shingles, what is your relationship with Josh Rodriguez?" McCarthur asked. He chose his words carefully.

"Josh?" Monica cried out. At first, it seemed as if she hadn't heard the name correctly. She then continued. "This cocky ass! Like...he acts like he is a superstar or like... someone who we need to pay reparation to for his existence. I don't talk with that guy. Besides, I have a boyfriend. Like...you know... Well, technically, we're not together, but we are working on it. Actually, we are taking baby steps in our relationship." Monica protested as if railing at customer support service for messing up her bank account.

"How did you meet Josh?" Fernandez asked. That question was paramount because it would clear some of the confusion in this investigation.

"Here's what happened. On a random night, Kimberly called me. She wanted to... like... hang out, and I said, 'Fine.

I'll come over.' Like… I agreed. She begged me to visit her because she wanted to talk with me. So I got to her apartment, and you know… we started drinking. As we chatted, suddenly, the door opened. We were both surprised because she wasn't expecting anyone. We planned it to be just the two of us. Like…you know. Anyway, so this guy, Josh, walked into the apartment. It became a bit awkward. Kimberly and I were staring at each other like… WTF… you know. So this so-called adonis, Josh, came over. He wanted to have a drink with us. Kimberly looked at me like… she was saying, "*What should we do.*" I wanted to be polite, and… you know… like… we both were…like… 'Fine, dude! Let's drink.' Then Josh sat between us and started chatting. I don't know why, but he acted a little…weird," Monica finished her monologue.

"What do you mean by *weird*?" McCarthur asked, raising his eyebrows.

"Like… he became flirty with us. He was inquisitive, asking us a bunch of questions. Like…what we wore, what we liked, and all these types of questions. Then the alcohol kept pouring. We started chugging shots, and you know…I woke up with a hangover, intertwined in the same bed sheets with Kimberly and … him. That was the last time I saw him," Monica said. She paused for a second. The tears in her eyes interrupted her speech. Her hands were shaking as if she was sick.

"Miss Shingles, do you know Ashley Packer?" McCarthur queried.

"Not really. Like… I've met Ashley before, but we've never done anything together. Like… we chatted about the usual stuff. You know…girl talk. But I wasn't close to her. Like…

I'm not friends with her on social media. However, I can tell she was a very nice person. Actually, she was a loving person. Like… her vibe was okay, and she had a friendly attitude in general. She was also a very educated woman. Like… she talked as if she was a scientist working for NASA or something like that, you know," Monica said. Both detectives nodded. They looked calm, but their minds were stressed.

"And just out of curiosity. What do you do for a living?" Bob asked. He wasn't interested in her portfolio. He was trying to collect more information that could help him find the murderer.

"I'm CEO of a marketing and social media publication. Like…I work for a fashion entity that establishes its own clothing. You know…like…we are targeting local and global business," Monica responded. Her eyes looked tired as if she hadn't slept for the past couple of days. The Texan nodded. He ran his hand through his curly hair as if he was checking for bruises on his head. A second before he managed to say something more, Monica interrupted him. She shot her question with the speed of a supersonic aircraft.

"Do you think? Like…Josh had killed Kimberly, and now he is targeting me? I'm so scared. What if he comes here—to my apartment? This is so embarrassing. Like…you know what I'm sayin'? How am I gonna sleep tonight? I don't know what to do?" Shingles started sobbing. She was terrified. Her eyes were filled with tears. Her voice became hoarse as if she had a sore throat.

"Miss Shingles, we'll send a police patrol to watch your building. Josh will not have any access. We'll make sure that you are protected. We suggest that you do not leave the State until this case is resolved. I need you to remain strong. We'll catch the guy who killed your friend. Everything it's going to be fine," Detective Fernandez said. Her words sounded confidently, but she wasn't sure of her statement. Monica showed that she comprehended what Fernandez said, but she doubted the detective's assurances. Her heart felt disintegrated. Shingles was scared to death; her stomach was in great pain. She felt nauseous and dizzy. She craved to kick out the police detectives because she wanted to be alone. Monica stared at both of them as if to say, "*I need to be alone now! You need to get the hell out of here!*" The Texan studied Monica. He interpreted her subtle message and proclaimed, "Okay, Miss Shingles. Thank you for your time. I appreciate it. We'll keep you posted. Here's my card. It's a direct line. Call me if you need anything, okay? Stay safe." Bob's words sounded trite, but he spoke from the bottom of his heart. Monica nodded. She went to her bedroom, opened the door, and Pierre scurried out on its little legs.

"Woof, woof!" The Bichon Frisé barked angrily. The dog barked as if it was saying, "*Fuck off! Annoying humans. Leave my Monica alone!*" Both detectives left the apartment, and Monica slammed the door. She leaned against the wall, striking the back of her head into the drywall.

***

After they finished the conversation with Monica, Bob McCarthur and Lisa Fernandez took the elevator down to the front desk. Precious, the gorgeous employee there, instructed them where the office of the building manager was. Bob looked at his smartphone. It was 4:30 p.m. The building manager was still in the building, and both detectives power walked to catch him up before he left the office. A minute later, they saw a door with a glowing sign that read: BUILDING MANAGER. The Texan knocked on the door, and a male voice shrieked,

"Yeah! Come on in!" Bob and Lisa stepped inside the office. They saw a guy in his late forties, dressed in corporate pants and wearing a blue shirt bought at Walmart. His name was Eric Morris. He was a douchebag who acted uppity, especially when he chatted with hot chicks. Eric had a flop-quaff on which he spent a lot of money. His eyes were sparkling blue, and his smile was charming. Eric Morris lived alone with two cats. He was a divorced weirdo. His nine-year-old daughter came to visit him from time to time, but other than that, he never had any guests. He was a good-looking guy— for his age.

"Hello, guys. Welcome to Royal Point. How can I help you," Eric said with the sketchy tone of a man who didn't want to be bothered. Bob explained the entire scenario of Kimberly's murder. He provided a photo of Josh Rodriguez and asked for Eric's cooperation. The building manager agreed not to allow Josh in the building until McCarthur said otherwise.

"Is he a criminal?" Eric Morris asked, surprised by the detectives' revelation.

"That's what we are trying to figure out. But he is the main suspect in two murders, and we think that Josh may try to come here to harass one of the residents in this building," the Texan responded. Suddenly, Eric became speechless; he couldn't believe what he had heard half an hour before he was about to leave his workplace.

"Okay! I will make sure this person won't get close to my building. That's important. Besides, I don't need criminals here," Eric said grumpily. He wasn't happy to hear that, especially after a long day in the office. McCarthur nodded and added, "I'll send a police patrol to watch the building. They'll be on the lookout for Josh. They will be across the street if you need them." The Texan calmly mumbled as if he was a man telling children stories. The two detectives left the building buried deep in thought. As they strolled to the Tahoe, Detective Fernandez broke the silence.

"That's weird. There is a discrepancy between Monica's story and what Josh told us."

"Someone is lying," McCarthur replied. Fernandez nodded and asked, "Chief, did you speak with the judge about the search warrant?"

"Yeah. It's not gonna happen," Bob said while hopping in the Tahoe.

"Wait a minute? Why? What did he say?" Lisa Fernandez looked shell-shocked. She climbed into the driver's seat and fired up the engine.

"We don't have enough evidence. Josh has a motive, but up until this moment, we can't do anything. We need to find more evidence that will put him behind the bars," McCarthur responded with frustration as if he was announcing the death of his friend.

"What! This is not right!" Fernandez exclaimed. She shook her head, frowning.

"Yes. I agree, but I can't change his mind. The judge is adamant. Anyway, I'll tell you what I'm gonna do. I'll put Josh on a stakeout. I'll send an undercover unit to watch him 24/7. Don't worry. We'll catch this slimeball. You have my word," the Texan declared. His face looked disgusted. Detective Fernandez agreed without saying a word and put the Tahoe in gear.

7

It was Friday, August 24th. The weather was in the high eighties, torrid and humid. The sun had already dropped behind the horizon, and darkness slumped over the city of Chicago. The hot weather didn't bother Brendan Packer. He was in his room watching some foolish videos on Tik Tok. He spent many hours at his laptop, but when he needed to go somewhere, he was out for hours. Tom and Jennifer didn't bother him because he bristled when he heard the question: "*Where are you going*?" For that reason, his parents let him do his own thing without much interference. Brendan loved his laptop; he had been working with his computer for five years and felt like it was part of his life. His beloved laptop was the most valuable thing he had.

Around 9:00 p.m., Brendan ordered a chicken sandwich

combo from McDonald's and had it delivered with Uber Eats. After he gobbled the food, he looked at his laptop and watched more funny videos, this time on YouTube. The next second, his face froze as if he had seen the ugliest creature alive. Brendan took off his computer glasses and rubbed them into his T-shirt. Then he put them back on. Ashley's brother couldn't believe his eyes. There were no words to describe the picture displayed on his laptop's screen.

"Mom! Dad! Come here! You have to check this out!" Brendan exclaimed in a state of terror. He heard no answer from his parents. The cybersecurity guy got a bit frustrated and repeated, "Mom! Dad! Come up here!" This time he raised his voice as if he was crying for help. Tom and Jennifer power walked to Brendan's room because he kept screaming. They whispered something while taking the stairs to Brendan's room.

"What is it, dear?" Mrs. Packer piped up at the threshold of her son's room. Tom walked slowly; he was a few feet behind his wife.

"Mom, come here! Look at the screen," Brendan pointed out at his laptop. Jennifer stepped closer and said, "Brendan, why did you scream and… oh my God! What the hell!" Jennifer's face froze. She couldn't believe what she saw. Tom stepped over and looked at Jennifer and his son who were mesmerized by the screen of Brendan's laptop. He became curious and looked at the screen as well. His face froze, just like the others.

"Play it over," Jennifer commanded, and Brendan did what his mother ordered. The three of them watched a YouTube video showing Ashley tied to a cheap chair in a room painted in red. She had a ball gag on her mouth to prevent speaking. Her body shivered from fear. Ashley looked exhausted as if she had been screaming for hours. Her eyes could barely stay open. Her beautiful blonde hair looked uncombed and unclean. The gorgeous girl moaned in an attempt to say something, but the ball gag in her mouth muffled any sounds. She sounded more like a dying animal that was groaning disturbingly. Tom, Jennifer, and Brendan looked at the screen, hypnotized. Jennifer was horrified. She covered her face and started weeping. Tom attacked his bald head like he wanted to rip the skin off of it. His fingers flexed the air and eyes burned red hot with a lust for retaliation. At 0:15 seconds into the video, someone stepped in front of the camera. Ashley was hidden behind the unknown person. The person was dressed in a black hooded robe and wore the famous "The Guy Fawkes Mask" that every computer hacker used to cover their face while streaming in videos on the internet. The mask had a creepy white face painted with big eyebrows and a black handlebar-type of mustache. The villain moved around prudently as if he was walking on a tightrope. The person spoke with confidence and contempt.

"You'll never find her. You hear me. You'll never know where she is. No one is smarter than me. You miserable people who live your mediocre lives with your boring jobs cannot understand what I am doing. You'll never know who I am," the villain grumbled. He was aggressively tapping at the camera lens. The voice of the unknown person was computer-distorted to hide his identity. It sounded as if the greatest wrestler of all time, André the Giant, was speaking. It was no secret that the villain wanted to remain anonymous. The Packers family couldn't specify the villain's gender, either. This unknown person kept repeating the same words over and over again until the camera fell to the ground, and that was how the video ended. The video went viral and reached over two million views in less than an hour.

Jennifer was on the edge of having a panic attack. She had a pounding headache. She had to sit down fast, otherwise she might tumble onto the floor. Tom helped her and put her on a chair by the east end of Brendan's room. He kneeled next to his wife and whispered, "Honey, how are you feeling? Do you need something?"

"I'm dizzy. Bring me a bottle of water, please," Mrs. Packer implored, and Tom scuttled down to the first floor. Brendan observed his mother's struggle without saying a word. The cyber security boy had no idea what he had to do. Jennifer had been more than stressed out since her daughter was reported missing. She had visited a few psychologists referred by her doctor. She spent countless hours talking and sharing her fears with Tom. Jennifer was terrified by the possibility of losing her child. She didn't know what to do. She worried that she might not see her daughter ever again. *Losing a child is the biggest fear that any parent can experience,* she thought.

An hour later, Tom put his wife to bed. He fretted about his wife's condition. He was an attentive husband who would die for his family. But Jennifer wanted to be alone. Mrs. Packer insisted on having silence around her because she was on the verge of a mental breakdown. Tom left his wife and eased into the living room. He then poured a red California wine into a fine wine glass and sat on the sofa. He turned on the TV and started scratching his bald head. The electrician switched the channels as if looking for something specific. He played *Goodfellas*, the movie from the 1990s. But he wasn't watching it, his head was preoccupied with thoughts about his baby girl. His love for Ashley couldn't be depicted with a few words. Tom covered his face using his hands and burst into tears.

***

Bob McCarthur watched the YouTube video showing Ashley bound, gagged, and helpless. He didn't understand the message that the person wearing the Hacker Mask repeatedly uttered. Watching the video several times, the Texan was confused but determined to find the person who kidnapped Ashley.

"What do you think, chief?" Detective Fernandez asked. The UFC fighter leaned against the wall in the detective's room in the police precinct. She was chewing gum nervously as if she had to make a decision on which her entire career depended.

McCarthur glanced at his partner and kept watching the video. He sat on a computer chair at his desk. He took a deep breath as if he was about to jump from a helicopter and uttered, "I don't know, Lisa. I've never seen anything like that in my entire life." His eyes were hypnotized by the YouTube video. Lisa Fernandez nervously walked around the room. She was making meaningless circles like a shark in the sea. She was frustrated because she couldn't stand violence against innocent people.

"C'mon, chief! Tell me your opinion. We have been working together for more than five years; I know that look. You know something. What is it? Tell me!" Lisa's voice sounded inductive. Bob sighed. His small blue eyes crossed hers. His expression was saying, "*I don't know what to think.*"

"Okay, I think this person is definitely a man, judging by the way he moved, but I cannot be completely sure. First thing in the morning, I'll speak with FBI and ask for a computer expert to trace the source of this video. Also, I'll talk with a criminal psychologist to analyze this person's behavior. At this point, that's all I can come up with," he declared. His words came out with confidence, but he wasn't sure of what to do.

"What about Josh? Do you think he is the guy in this video acting like a stupid geek looking for attention?" Fernandez said, and instantly Bob's eyes widened. He stared at her as if he was about to confess something that he had been hiding for years.

"Crap! Lisa, that's it!" the Texan exclaimed. Detective Fernandez looked at her colleague as if he had just taken off his pants and chanted, "I don't need clothes anymore!"

"Huh? Bob, you aren't making any sense, man. What are you tryin' to say?" Lisa questioned. She sank deeply into a state of confusion. Detective McCarthur answered without wasting a second.

"Our guy is seeking attention or some kind of validation! I mean, that's my raw opinion. We still need some analysis from an expert, but that's a good start. Good work, Lisa."

Bob looked like an excited boy who was just about to see the boobs of his first girlfriend. Detective Fernandez didn't completely sympathize with her colleague's exhilaration. She then confidently fired off her next question.

"Yeah, that's definitely a decent start, but that doesn't answer my question. Do you believe that Josh was behind that mask?"

"I see what you're sayin'. That's why I sent undercovers to be on the stakeout. There is something else. If Josh is our guy, then where could he have been hiding Ashley? Anyway, my gut feeling is telling me that we are close to unraveling this case," the Texan said. In the next second his iPhone rang. He picked up the phone and said, "Yeah! What! Fuck! We are on the way," and quickly hung up.

"Who was it?" Lisa asked. She was desperate to find out what this phone call was all about. Her eyes were glowing with interest. She was mesmerized by her partner.

"You won't believe it!" McCarthur cried out.

***

While Bob and Fernandez brainstormed the YouTube video in which Ashley was exposed as a hostage, Matt Marinos sat impatiently in his police vehicle. He was 6'2" tall with a semi-muscular body. Matt had been working in unmarked units for more than five years. His long, pushed-back hair looked outstanding, and his eyebrows were bushy, underlining his tired face. His black eyes were glowing. Matt Marinos had the carnivorous look of a wild hyena. Some people got scared by the way he stared at them. Even though he was undercover, Matt wore police gear and a vest. He was in his late thirties, born and raised in Chicago, though his family had emigrated from Greece a long time ago. Matt's parents made sure their son would be well-educated, and though Marinos didn't fulfill their dream of becoming a doctor, he felt proud to serve as a Chicago cop. To him, the Windy City was one of the most beautiful cities in the country. The Greek cop was watching the clock on his iPhone. It was 2:00 in the afternoon.

"Where the heck is he? He's supposed to be here already," Matt mumbled under his breath. The Greek cop had been at work for eight hours and he was starting to lose patience. Matt looked out of the unmarked vehicle, a dark blue Ford Edge. The unit had no police markings but had portable emergency lights in the back and the front windows. Matt was standing on North Tripp Avenue, a side street located a little west of Lawrence and Pulaski. The Greek cop had had a stressful day. His wife was in her ninth month of pregnancy and had been on his nerves throughout the entire day. She kept him posted with her anxieties by text every 20 minutes. Matt loved his wife, but, sometimes, he hated being around her because her moods were difficult to bear. As Matt was texting back to his wife, the door of his car opened, and another man hopped in.

"Damien, what took you so long? I've been waiting you for twenty minutes," Matt protested.

"Man, I had to talk with this Indian chick that works behind the counter; she is kinda cute," Damien replied. He was Matt's partner. He was 5'8", with hands powerful like a bench vise. He was a Cuban in his mid-twenties. His body type was average, nothing too special. The Cuban cop ended to gain weight easily because he loved junk food. Damien had a beautifully shaped nose and a square chin that looked like it was made from stainless steel. His green eyes seemed to be a little too close to each other. He had grown up in Milwaukee, Wisconsin. In 2019 he became a Chicago cop, and recently was assigned to work with Matt.

"Did you get her phone number?" Matt asked. He was smirking at his colleague.

"Whose phone number?" Damien asked, befuddled.

"The chick that you were just talking about. C'mon, dude!" the Greek cop blurted out.

"Here's the thing. I'm building strong communication with this chick. Eventually, she will voluntarily give me her digits," the Cuban cop said.

"Okay, so, did you get the number?" Matt asked.

"I got her Instagram," Damien murmured.

"Pussy!" The Greek cop cried out. His face looked deadpan, but he was messing around with his partner.

"Blah-blah-blah. Tomorrow, I'll get it. Mark my words!" Hearing this statement, Matt burst into laughter. His laugh annoyed Damien.

"Hey, Damien! Where's my doughnut?" Matt protested while scavenging through the empty Dunkin' bag.

"You didn't say anything about doughnuts?" the Cuban piped up. His facial expression depicted a pure state of confusion.

"I said: go to Dunkin', get me a large coffee and a doughnut.

What's the matter with you? Are you falling in love with this chick?" Matt pointed out furiously.

"Nah! You didn't say anything about doughnuts."

"Yes, I did," Matt said confidently.

"Okay, I'll get you a doughnut," Damien said in a low voice and reached to open the door.

"Don't go. It's fine. Forget about it!" the Greek mumbled under his breath. He looked disappointed, but he was just breaking his partner's balls. Matt loved teasing his colleagues. That was just the way he was.

"I thought you were on a diet!" Now Damien was the one who joked with his colleague. Matt looked at him as if he was questioning some stranger who'd just passed him walking on the sidewalk.

"That was yesterday," the Greek cop mumbled.

"Shut the fuck up!" Damien exclaimed, and both laughed out loud. Then Matt looked out through the windows of the unmarked vehicle.

"Shush!" There he is! Our *Cupcake* is heading somewhere," Matt exclaimed, and both cops were staring at Josh Rodriguez who was walking out of his apartment. Josh had been under police surveillance for a week. Matt and Damien had to follow wherever he went. It was an obnoxious assignment because the bodybuilder was tended to go all over the city of Chicago.

"What is he doing?" Damien asked. His question made Matt pissed.

"Shush! I said. He's going to his Mercedes!" Matt answered. Unaware of the unmarked police car, parked around fifty feet from his apartment, the bodybuilder strolled to his white

2015 Mercedes. Josh's car looked luxurious, painted white with glowing black rims. The VLT of tinted windows was under 5%, which made it difficult to see through them. The Mercedes looked like something a mob boss would drive. Josh opened each door of his vehicle. It looked like he was searching for something. The bodybuilder didn't seem to be finding it because he was moving jerkily as if he was pissed. The handsome Latin guy opened the Mercedes' trunk and rummaged inside. He then looked up as if someone was calling his name.

"What is he doing?" Damien whispered.

"Can't tell! He didn't take anything from his vehicle. Could be anything," the Greek cop replied.

"He's just fooling around. I'm telling you straight. This guy is clean. We've been watching him for a week, and what? Nothing," Damien complained. Matt didn't respond. He was silent as if he didn't hear his partner.

Josh closed the doors of his Mercedes and walked back to his apartment. It looked like he hadn't taken anything from his car. Ashley's fiancé returned to his apartment as fast as if he would miss The IFBB (World bodybuilding & Fitness Championships).

***

"Nothing!" Damien reiterated this word for the fourth time already. His grumpy behavior was annoying Matt. For the next ten minutes, the cops chilled in the Ford Edge. Damien was bored. He watched daffy videos on TikTok to kill some time. Suddenly, an old SUV, a Buick Enclave, pulled into a parking spot designated for disabled people who held permit number 182. A young white man in his mid-twenties hopped out of the Buick. He wore a black shirt and black pants of an unknown brand. His hair was long and greasy. It looked like he hadn't washed his hair for months. His slender body resembled that of a basketball player who played only for fun. The guy with the long hair looked like an adult trapped in a teenager's body. The man stepped quickly to his car trunk and took out a black plastic bag. He then slammed the trunk and walked down the sidewalk. He looked around to make sure that no one was watching. His plan failed because Matt and Damien had already spotted him.

"Man, I hate these assholes who parked illegally. He deserves a ticket," Damien protested, and Matt agreed.

"Where does he think he's goin'? Look at him. He's going into Josh's building," the Cuban cop said. A few minutes later they heard an unusual sound. Matt's eyes widened as if he saw an approaching ghost.

"DID YOU HEAR THAT?" Damien almost shouted, and Matt nodded.

"Should we call for backup?" the Cuban asked. He became nervous; his heart was racing.

"Hold on! Let me check his plates," Matt responded and accessed the small portable computer mounted in the car. In the meantime, the bony man with long hair was walking rapidly to the Buick.

"I've got an idea!" Damien announced and got out of the unmarked cop car.

"Where the heck you think you're goin', dammit," the Greek cop hissed, but it was too late for any debates because the Cuban cop was already halfway to the Buick.

"Excuse me, sir! I'm Officer Damien Velasquez. Do you… what the f…" The Cuban cop couldn't finish his sentence because the man with the long hair pulled a gun and took a shot at him. Damien crouched and kneeled next to the nearest car.

"Police! Drop your weapon. Put your hands in the air! Drop the gun and put your hands in the air! Drop your weapon, man," Damien shouted while pulling his sidearm from its holster. The bony man with the long hair paid no attention, but jumped into the Buick and drove off.

"FUCK!" Damien screamed. Matt pulled up and screamed, "JUMP IN!" Damien hopped into the car. The passenger's door wasn't closed yet, and Matt sped off immediately.

"OPERATOR! OPERATOR! GF1269. SHOTS FIRED! I REPEAT. SHOTS FIRED! We're in pursuit of a red BUICK SUV. The vehicle has an Illinois plate number: VB4-247976561. The suspect is armed. He even shot at me! I repeat. The suspect has a gun! He is taking Lawrence West. He'll probably jump on the highway!"

"ROGER THAT, UNIT 7. BACKUP IS ON THE WAY!" The voice came out the radio speaker mounted in the police car. The Buick was driving madly, ignoring signs or traffic lights. The car chase became insane because the SUV ran through a red light and almost hit another vehicle. Matt was driving behind with flashing lights and loud siren. Damien was right; the Buick sped on West Lawrence Street and took

115

the ramp, heading for I-94 northbound. The traffic was mild, giving the suspect a perfect opportunity to increase his speed. Matt was tailgating the Buick's bumper. The Greek cop kept close, trying to stop the speeding vehicle. The Buick was switching lanes each second, avoiding other cars on the road.

More city police vehicles and even state police joined the insane chase. The Buick was speeding faster, but his pursuers were closing the gap. The man with long hair drove in the emergency lane and the shoulder because they were empty. In a couple of minutes the Buick started to slow down because of heavy traffic ahead. Most of the other cars ahead of him barely moved. The suspect kept changing lanes until a state police's vehicle cut him off and blocked his way. In a split second, the Buick was surrounded by police cruisers.

"DROP THE WEAPON AND PUT YOUR HANDS IN THE AIR SO I CAN SEE THEM!" an officer's voice yelled madly. Around ten police officers were pointing their weapons at the suspect. The man with the long hair was still behind the wheel. He was out of options.

"DROP THE WEAPON!" another officer repeated. The man in the Buick held his gun under the steering wheel, while a swarm of cops stuck their weapons directly into the driver's side window.

"DROP THE WEAPON. PUT YOUR HANDS ON THE DASHBOARD!" another cop screamed while pointing his gun at the suspect. The man with long hair calmly obeyed the officer's order. Damien opened the door of the Buick and yanked the man out of the vehicle. The Cuban cop pressed the suspect to the fender of the Buick and handcuffed him as quickly as possible.

"What is your name? Why did you shoot at me? You crazy ass," Damien shouted. The man with the long hair didn't say a word; he was as silent as a corpse.

"What is your name?" Damien repeated. This time his voice sounded more aggressive. He was pissed because the suspect had shot at him and was simultaneously relieved that he hadn't been injured. The Cuban cop shoved the suspect into the rear seat of one of the police patrol cars. He closed the door and tapped on the roof, signaling the driver to take off.

Later on the same day, the police burst into Josh's apartment. The front door wasn't locked because the long-haired man had left it open. Josh's apartment was on the first floor. His pad looked extravagant and luxurious. There was a 65 inch TV hung on the south wall of the living room. An expensive gray-colored couch faced the TV. A pricy blue coffee table in the shape of a shell was before the couch. At the end of the living room was a small hallway leading to the kitchen. The officers barged into the kitchen and found Josh's body lying on the gray tiles. A large puddle of blood spread out under his head. His eyes remained open as if he was still alive. The forensic experts searched the entire apartment. They collected fingerprints and other pieces of evidence.

***

The suspect was taken to the 19th police district at 2452 West Belmont in Roscoe Village. Three police officers escorted him through a dark hallway and locked him in a free holding cell. The officers were shouting questions through the cell door, but the man with the long hair refused to speak. He looked calm and carefree as a man with no problems. But that was just how he looked. In his mind, he was furious. His heart was filled with growing hatred which many would have found hard to understand.

On Monday, the 27th of August, Bob and Fernandez entered the main entrance of the 19th police department. Both detectives seemed to walk faster than usual. McCarthur was holding a clipboard with the suspect's details. The name of the man with the long hair was David Sparrow. He was twenty-four years old, with no wife and no kids. Sparrow had grown up in a dysfunctional family. His mother lived in Florida with a guy named Shorty. His father was a nice guy who stayed out of trouble. But he had cheated on his wife multiple times. That was why David's parents were separated. His father was a truck driver, making decent money. With his father's help, David Sparrow had no commitments whatsoever. David lived in a small studio in Park Ridge, Illinois. He was a lounger. The boy didn't know what it was to work a real job. He was playing Texas hold 'em on a daily basis. His poker endeavors brought him an inconsistent income. Occasionally, David had to borrow money from his father because he was broke. David Sparrow was a quiet guy with few friends. In 2018, he dropped high school because he had never been encouraged to study.

Bob McCarthur was walking and, at the same time, reading David's files. Detective Fernandez walked next to him. She was quiet, but her mind was occupied. One of her daughters had problems in school, and that made her restless. Both detectives stepped into a room containing nothing but a one-way window. From that window, the detectives could see into another room in which interrogations were conducted. The suspect, David Sparrow, had been waiting in that room. His hands were cuffed because he was charged with murder, shooting at a police officer, and running away from a crime scene. Bob McCarthur surveyed the man with the long hair through the one-way glass.

"We've got him. There is no escape. What do you think, chief?" It seemed like Bob hadn't heard Lisa's question. He stepped close to the window and eyeballed the suspect. McCarthur had the eyes of a cheetah watching its prey.

"Chief, do you have a plan?" Lisa said, "Because I do."

"Huh?" Detective McCarthur hissed.

"We can play 'The good and the bad cop'. You remember the movie?"

"What, *Bad Boys*?" the Texan asked and showed his crooked smile.

"Yeah, it may work… you never know," Lisa pointed out. She was excited as if she was about to jump into a UFC cage and fight a tough opponent. She stared at her partner, craving to hear his opinion.

"Lisa, hon, we are not on a set of an action movie or CSI show. This is not a game. You know that better than anyone else. We can't just jump in and start playing movie characters. We have to force him and make him spill the beans. You follow?"

"Absolutely! That's why I suggested *the good and the bad cop*. I'm telling you, he will talk," Detective Fernandez protested. She was dressed in a gray T-shirt that demonstrated her astonishing figure. Her breasts, hidden behind her bra, bulged out of her shirt. Her chest held most of the police officers spellbound. Her black Relaxed Fit Straight pants were exposing her muscular legs. Lisa Fernandez had a body that most girls could only dream of, but the female detective wasn't someone who would brag about her clothes or how she looked. She was a fighter that was ready to die in the UFC cage. She was a tough, confident and successful woman whom Bob admired.

"Let's see how it starts, and we'll go from there. Sounds good?" Bob asked and gave Lisa a fist bump. He wore a black shirt that read *I am your Devil* on his chest. His belly bulked out a bit, but not too much. His hair appeared as though it was styled with a grapevine clip.

"After you," said Lisa, "We got him. He will talk." With that being said, both detectives exited the observation room and headed to the interrogation room where David Sparrow waited. The interrogation room reeked of mold and damp cement; it was an old building, constructed over forty years ago. The walls inside were painted dark green. Two cameras were attached to the ceiling at the corners, facing diagonal to each other. A darkened blue table, built from unknown metal, was at the center of the room. A light fixture hung down from the ceiling and shone on top of the Sparrow's long hair. The suspect sat on a double-hinged black vinyl metal folding chair. His eyes were barely open as if he was about to fall asleep. His white face looked calm, but he was restless. David had a small nose and big blue eyes. His face looked like a man who was always pissed at something. His emaciated body looked as if he was sick from a deadly infection or he didn't eat properly. His black shirt and pants looked like they were from the 1990s. The detectives stepped into the room, and Lisa closed the door. Bob aggressively dropped some files on the table. He grabbed the metal table and leaned forward, close to the suspect.

"David Sparrow, how you doing?" Detective McCarthur said, "I read your report. Gotta admit; it doesn't look good, buddy. The weapon you used to shoot at the officer matches up to the bullet in Josh's head. You are charged with shooting at a police officer and first-degree murder. That's a heavy indictment. I'm telling you straight; your case is not okay. The court will be in order after three days; the judge will give you at least thirty years. David, you've reserved your spot in prison. Do you understand what I'm saying?" the Texan bluffed. There was no response. Sparrow looked straight ahead at the door; he avoided any eye contact with either detective. McCarthur repeated his question, and again there was no answer. He then flashed his crooked smile and laughed out loud, though he was getting angrier. He walked around the suspect, hoping to make him nervous.

"Answer the question!" Detective Fernandez screamed and pounded on the table. She tried to put more pressure on the interrogation. It seemed that her plan didn't work because David didn't flinch.

"Lisa!" Bob snapped. He alerted his partner by gesturing

121

to take it easy. Lisa Fernandez nodded and shot daggers at the suspect as if she was about to beat the shit out of him. McCarthur took a deep breath. He looked up at the ceiling. Then his eyes met Lisa's.

"David, you think you are a tough guy, huh?" Bob asked. "In prison, you'll be everyone's best girl. The inmates will give you a lot of love, literally." McCarthur's voice rumbled the room as if he spoke with a bullhorn. Yet, David could have been a deaf-mute. If he was listening, he wasn't buying any of Bob's words. Lisa looked at her partner as if to say, "*What now!*" The Texan showed his crooked smile. His facial expression was saying, "*I've got an idea!*"

"HEY, CUPCAKE! I'm talking to you! Do you understand what I'm sayin'?" Robert questioned.

"Who you calling a cupcake?" David said his first words since he had been arrested. The words coming out of his mouth sounded eerie. The man with long hair looked at the Texan with creepy eyes. Robert flashed his crooked smile as if he was saying, "*It worked!*"

"Well, what do I know? It's a miracle! The mute man can actually talk," the Texan proclaimed, "Did you kill Kimberly and Jack Hammer?"

"Huh?" David grunted. He didn't like the question; his face cringed as if he had been insulted. Detective Fernandez repeated Bob's question.

The suspect looked at Fernandez and said "I need to speak with my lawyer." The Texan projected his crooked smile and shrugged.

"You'll get the chance to speak with your lawyer, but first,

I need to know something, and I think you already know what that is. Where is Ashley?" David didn't answer. The Texan repeated the question. And again there was no answer.

"David, I know that you keep her somewhere in the area. Would you mind telling us where Ashley is?" Detective Fernandez asked politely.

"You'll never know where her body is," the suspect said in a low tone. David's hatred was almost tangible. His bitterness could be sensed as if a ghost was hovering in the room. The detectives exchanged a questioning look. McCarthur tried to remain professional while Fernandez was about to go ballistic. She walked to the door, turned around, and closed her eyes. Her fists were clenching and shaking simultaneously. Then, Fernandez turned back with lightning speed and stepped close to the suspect.

"What is all this about, huh? What are you trying to prove by killing all of those innocent people? Where is this hatred coming from?" Lisa belted out. Her eyes were fuming. David was getting to her, and she could barely stay still.

"Lisa, calm down. Take it easy," Bob implored. "That's not necessary. You know that better than anyone else."

As the detectives talked to each other, David started laughing hellishly. Bob turned around and said,

"What are you laughing at, dipshit?"

"Now you're calling me a dipshit!" David spoke in a low but unpleasant voice. The suspect was teasing McCarthur. It was no secret that they didn't like each other. The Texan rolled his eyes and took a deep breath. His patience had been seriously tested.

"David, why don't you just tell us where you're hiding Ashley, huh?" Bob asked. He had vowed to find the culprit responsible for kidnapping the blond teacher. He couldn't imagine how he would feel if his son was reported missing. Both detectives took this case personally because of their parental instincts for their own children. The interrogation room became silent as if no one was there.

"May I have a cigarette? I'm trying to quit, but my vices are resilient," David said. His face looked flippant, resembling the TV version of Denice the Menace. The suspect was playing mind games with both detectives. Hearing his appeal, Bob laughed, flaunting his crooked smile.

"We're not filming a *Blue Bloods* episode. I'm afraid that you gonna have to get used to the idea of quitting smoking," Fernandez said. What she didn't grasp was the fact that David was playing with her by asking provocative questions. In one sense, his plan worked but not for long.

"Aren't you the one who wore this bizarre costume in the YouTube video?" the Texan asked politely.

"What video? What are you talking about?" David replied. His face looked confused. Robert wasn't buying any of the suspect's words. He knew that Sparrow was just playing dumb. Bob pulled out his iPhone and played the video that had gone viral a few days ago, where Ashley was bound to a chair, and someone wearing a costume and mask was speaking to the camera.

"You'll never find the truth," Sparrow said. "That's for sure!" The suspect made his statement clearly, but the detectives felt uncertain of his words. Lisa could barely stay still. McCarthur sighed. He had become as frustrated as Lisa.

"I see where you're heading with these answers. Are you sure you don't know where Ashley is?" the Texan asked. Detective McCarthur avoided eye contact with the suspect because he was about to freak out.

"I didn't say that!" David piped up. "All I'm saying is that …"

"Wait a minute," Bob interrupted the suspect, "So, you actually know where she is. Isn't that right, Mr. Sparrow?"

"No! I didn't say that either. Don't put words in my mouth," the suspect protested. The heat between the suspect and the detectives escalated.

"Quit playing your foolish games! Answer the question. Dammit!" Lisa cried out and hit the table aggressively. She couldn't restrain her anger. The UFC fighter in her was at the edge of crossing the line.

"LISA! Get it together! Dammit!" Bob snapped. He gestured to his partner, and both left the room. They had a private chat in what seemed to be a dark corridor.

"Stop it! Lisa, what's the matter with you, huh? If you hit the suspect while he is being interrogated in handcuffs, the prosecutor will cut you off from this case. Is that what you want? Get it together! We got him. We have enough evidence to lock him up for the next thirty years. He is fucked, and he knows it. Do yourself a favor; go outside and take a deep breath. I'll see you in a minute, okay?" McCarthur finished his speech, and Lisa nodded. She didn't agree with her partner, but she also knew that there was no use in arguing with him. Detective Fernandez did as she had been told and went outside. She lit up a cigarette. Usually, she didn't smoke, but when the shit hit the fan, she puffed ciggies. The Tabaco helped her to release the stress.

In 2002, Lisa's father died during military service in Afghanistan. Ever since her father passed away, her life had been dark and difficult. Her mom became an alcoholic after the loss of her husband. Lisa Fernandez had had a hard time growing up. Her brothers helped her when she needed them, which was often back in the early 2000s, but Lisa was mostly on her own. At age of twenty, Lisa started her bachelor's degree and worked part-time at Taco Bell. She was also taking care of her mom. Unfortunately, her mother's alcohol problem worsened. She became aggressive, throwing empty bottles of vodka at Lisa and her brothers. Lisa had no choice. She had to put her mother in a nursing home. A year after university graduation, Lisa fell in love with a man named Rick and they decided to get married. In the following years, they had three wonderful kids. Fernandez had a happy family, but Rick didn't help much with the kids, which was unfair to her. That was why she was on edge while interrogating David Sparrow. McCarthur finished the interrogation with David, but he wasn't completely done with him. The Texan left the police station and headed to the black Tahoe, where Fernandez counted her blessings.

"You better now?"

"Yeah, I guess," Lisa said and shrugged. Then both shared a laugh because Lisa was obviously lying.

"Take me home. I need a drink," the Texan mumbled, and Lisa drove off.

8

The first day of September was just an ordinary day in Chicago. The weather became windy. It looked like the trees were dancing because of the strong wind. The forecast reminded Chicagoans that the summer was coming to an end and the autumn was about to take its course. It wasn't cold yet, but people had to wear light jackets. The weather in Chicago didn't bother Tom Packer. He was mounting lights on the wall of a place that would become a Greek restaurant. The restaurant was supposed to open its doors at the end of the month, and Tom had to work extra hours to beat the deadline. This Greek restaurant was located in Deerfield, which might be considered one of the finest suburbs in northern Illinois. The interior was phenomenal. There were a few electric fireplaces that shone with glittering stones. The bar had cutting edge equipment and was fashioned in the shape of a Greek island. A few digital art projectors hidden in each corner would flash holograms at the bar. It was expensive equipment because it needed computer specialists to adjust a specific software that could produce particular images. The purpose of the hologram was to pop up among people who would visit the restaurant. That was a new gimmick that only a few restaurants could afford. Tom had to work overtime. Often, he didn't return home until midnight. His wife, Jennifer, lived in emotional shock. She could barely sleep at night. Mrs. Packer continued her visits with a psychiatrist, but she still felt sad. Any mother would be sad if her child was missing, and Jennifer was no exception. Usually, she locked herself in the master bathroom and cried there for hours. Her prayers were focused on bringing her daughter back home. Jennifer had imagined the joyous reunion with her baby girl a zillion times. She saw herself telling her story on live TV such as Dr. Phil.

Mrs. Packer didn't know what was right and what the wrong thing to do was. She asked her parents for advice, but they couldn't give her any because they had never been in a similar situation. Jennifer was devastated. She was lost. Often she looked at herself in the mirror feeling awful and not pretty. That was why she no longer wanted to be intimate with her husband. Tom was annoyed. Altercations between him and Jennifer had increased over the past few months. At times, the bond in their relationship became tenuous. Tom and Jennifer had multiple heated discussions over unimportant subjects, such as who was using the other's toothpaste or who should turn off the lights when no one was in a particular room. Brendan was forced to lock himself in his room to avoid the noise of his parent's bickering.

The computer genius disliked when his parents had falling-outs. Brendan was a quiet young man; he didn't talk much. He only spoke when he needed something. The cybersecurity guy spent most of his time at his laptop, and when he needed to go out, he didn't bother letting his parents know where he was going or when he intended to be back home. Tom and Jennifer had countless discussions about their son. They talked about his future and that it was time for him to leave their house and settle down with a nice girl. The problem was that Tom and Jennifer didn't talk straight to Brendan. They wanted to do it in a polite way, otherwise, Brendan would always take it the wrong way. The computer genius got easily offended when his parents talked about his future. It was because his parents shared a different outlook. The problems in the Packer family were coming out because of the stress over Ashley's disappearance. No one knew Ashley's whereabouts, or if she was even still alive.

***

Monday, the 5th of September, was a busy day in Chicago, especially for detectives McCarthur and Fernandez. The detectives were heading westbound on I-90 towards O'Hare Airport. Bob looked at his smartphone; it was around 2:00 p.m. He looked at the sky. The horizon was clear, and the sun shone upon the city of Chicago. For a moment, the Texan contemplated how exquisite this city was. At 2:30 p.m., the black Tahoe pulled to a stop on Northwest Hwy Street in Park Ridge. The detectives jumped out of the vehicle as quickly as if a bomb was about to explode. As he was emerging from the Tahoe, Bob waved at the unmarked police unit that was parked across the street. Matt and Damien waved back from their car. They knew they were to stay in their vehicle until Bob said otherwise. McCarthur and Fernandez walked to an ivory-colored apartment complex. They entered the residential facility and approached a white man with big glasses. His name was Jay Mayer. He was a Jewish entrepreneur who owned many properties, including this apartment complex. Mayer's face revealed a man who had been having a bad day. His nose was big, resembling a small cucumber. His brown eyes looked somehow angry. He was 5'8" with an overweight type of body. Jay was a wealthy man who wore clothes as if he was homeless. The Jewish entrepreneur looked to be in his late thirties, but he had the smile of a senior in high school.

"Hi, there! My name is Jay," the landlord announced and stretched his hand for a handshake. Bob and Lisa introduced themselves and immediately cut to the chase.

"How long did David Sparrow live in your building?" Lisa asked.

"About a year. He was a quiet tenant. Never heard any loud noises, and he always paid on time," Mayer replied and said, "Follow me, please!" The landlord trudged into the corridor and both detectives walked behind him. They stepped on a dirty carpet that only got cleaned once a year. Inside, the building looked antiquated. The old black sconces along the walls looked like lurking bats. The walls were painted half caramel, half gray. The building had a weird and nasty stench. The smell recalled a bathroom that hadn't been cleaned for months. Bob and Lisa exchanged glances as if they were asking, "*Where the fuck are we?*" Jay Mayer power-walked as if he was embarrassed by something. He went to a door that read "115." The Jewish landlord leaned close and whispered, "Gotta tell ya. I'm so glad that you caught this man before he killed someone else. Everybody in this building is scared to death." Hearing Mayer's words, both detectives nodded.

"Mr. Mayer," Bob said, "Have you heard any complaints about David Sparrow? Anything unusual?"

"Not really. Not that I'm aware of…" The Jewish landlord was uncertain, but he looked confident. A peculiar noise caught Mayer's attention. He leaned his left ear close to the door. His eyeballs shifted left and right in a state of confusion. He pulled out a bunch of keys and opened the door. Bob made a subtle sign, explaining that Mayer should stay in the corridor because he could contaminate vital evidence.

"We'll take over from here," Lisa said in a low and respectful voice. Jay lifted his hands up as if he was giving himself out to law enforcement officials. McCarthur and Fernandez proceeded into the apartment with caution. As they stepped inside, the two of them were shocked.

"What in Jesus' name is that?" Bob exclaimed, "What the heck is happening here?" Lisa was speechless. She couldn't find the appropriate words to describe what she was looking at.

***

Bob and Fernandez had never seen anything like this in their careers. They were in disbelief. The whole apartment was painted black. Around two hundred candles were lined up all over the apartment; each candle had a three-inch long wick. Some of these candles were on a coffee table that was at the center of the living room. On the ceiling, a sign of the satanic temple with a goat's head was painted red. The same satanic sign was painted on the east wall of the apartment. A bronze-colored statue resembling a satanic creature with a goat's head stood at the west wall of the apartment. The statue held a cue card that read: "THOSE WHO FOLLOW MY LEAD WILL PROSPER IN ETERNITY." Bob looked at the cue card and ignorantly blinked as if someone had just slapped him in the face. The windows in this apartment were covered with black drapes to prevent any light from breaking inside. On the south wall of the living room was a TV-stand filled with a books related to the Satanic Temple foundation, dubbed "TST."

An almost imperceptible, monotonous sound was coming from a pair of BOSE speakers. The noise coming from the speakers sounded like a weird "MMMM." It sounded as if someone was praying quietly without actually speaking. The Texan looked at a poster glued next to the TV-stand on the north wall of the apartment that read: FAIR JUSTICE. REASON. ADVOCACY. Both detectives were wordless. McCarthur had goosebumps. He tried to assimilate what was going on. Lisa Fernandez stepped into the bedroom. The UFC fighter looked around without touching anything. She kept distance from the furniture, avoiding any contact as if it might make her sick. The bedroom looked the same as the living room. Dozens of candles were set on the nightstand next to the bed. The walls were painted black, and a few posters of the Satanic Temple were glued to the wall. Inscriptions written on these posters were in what appeared to be Latin. Fernandez looked at a terrifying, framed picture of a black house. The house had satanic signs on the front door, and even a TST mailbox. That house stood as a symbol, portraying the community of The Satanic Temple. Detective Fernandez was frowning in disgust. She looked at the king-sized bed. Even the sheets and the pillows had TST's logos. The entire bedroom was embellished with souvenirs of The Satanic Temple. The air in the bedroom was foul, as if a human corpse had been rotting there for a month. Fernandez looked around, but she could barely see as she blinked in confusion. Detective McCarthur went to the bathroom. He looked at the black shower curtains with the logo of The Satanic Temple. The floor mat had the same satanic stamp. Even David's toothbrush was painted with a small image of The Satanic Temple. Bob stared at the toothbrush for a few seconds more.

"Okay, this guy is absolutely fucked up. I don't need a psychiatrist to tell me that," McCarthur was talking to himself.

"Chief!" Lisa exclaimed, "Come here!" Her voice sounded urgent, and that concerned the Texan. He speed walked to the bedroom.

"What is it?" he asked. Detective Fernandez pointed to the floor. A small bedpan next to the bed was filled with something that looked like blood.

"What the fuck is that?" Lisa asked while staring at her partner.

"I have no idea. But one thing is for sure."

"What?" Lisa asked.

"This man is a lunatic."

An hour later, David's apartment was overcrowded with a swarm of forensic experts. They were looking for fingerprints and anything else that could be useful. The investigators took pictures of every detail in David's apartment. Mayer, the landlord, was complaining and mumbling something about his property. He wanted to see what was going on, but his access was prohibited. Two police officers had to calm him down when he became belligerent. After four hours of thorough and detailed work, the forensic experts had found no fingerprints belonging to Kimberly, Josh, or Jack Hammer. There were no signs of Ashley either. Bob McCarthur and Lisa Fernandez were shocked.

"Where are we at now, chief? Fernandez asked while she was walking through the satanic apartment. Bob McCarthur stared at the bronze-colored satanic statue. It looked like he had ignored Lisa's question, but then he replied,

"When you left the interrogation room the other day, I asked David what he was doing on the day of Jack's murder. He said he was at his apartment. When I asked him if he had an alibi, Sparrow declared that his father could confirm his statement. But that's BS."

"What about Kimberly? Did you ask him what he was doing on the day of Kimberly's murder?"

"Yes, and his answer was the same. David said that he is a

homebody; he loves to stay in his apartment. He also claimed that he only leaves his apartment to buy groceries or in case of emergency. I don't know what the hell he meant by that," McCarthur declared in a low voice as if he was ashamed of what he was saying.

"Do you believe him?" Fernandez asked. Bob stared at her and flashed his crooked smile.

"Absolutely not. Sparrow is a whack job. What bothers me is that we still have no idea where Ashley is. Here is what I think. Look at all of those books on the shelf. David Sparrow is not a dumbass. Apparently he likes to read, which tells me he's a smart fuck," the Texan concluded.

It was 7:30 in the evening, and the forensic experts were still dusting for fingerprints. Chaos filled the entire building. Mayer had a headache; he had never been in a situation like this. The landlord felt embarrassed because his property overflowed with umpteen police officers, forensic experts, and other law enforcement representatives. Even though Jay Mayer instructed his renters to stay inside their apartments, some tenants were still peeking through their peepholes.

At half past eight, a Polish woman in her late fifties walked into the corridor. Her clothes were cheap; her jeans looked faded as if she washed them with bleach. Her breasts were so saggy that she might have stepped on them while she walked. Her name was Justyna Lavinsky. Justyna had a pear-shaped body. She was 5'6" tall with fat hips that bounced as she walked. Her hair was short and colored light pink. Miss Lavinsky had never been married. She didn't remember the last time she had sex with anyone. Justyna had emigrated from Poland thirty years ago. She had worked hard since she touched down in the USA. She cleaned offices in the downtown area for many years. Even though she had to take the bus on a daily basis, Justyna loved going to work. She had been saving money and financially supporting her niece. It was something that she felt proud of.

The Polish lady approached the satanic apartment. Her frowning face looked like she was saying, *"Don't bother me!"* Justyna's apartment was across from David's place. She looked at the police deputies and asked, "Excuse me, officers. What happened here?"

"Ma'am, I need you to step aside. At this moment, we cannot give you any information. But I can assure you that everything is under control," an officer replied. He was a short man in his fifties.

"That's fine, but you have to understand. I live across the hall. I don't want people making noise out here, bothering me. I've been living here for ten years, and I've seen people calling the cops too many times already. One guy who lived on the third floor killed himself a few years ago, and officers interrogated everybody. I mean, it was chaos. I cannot describe how..."

"Ma'am, I understand your frustration, and I promise you that everything will be fine," the short officer explained. Fernandez overheard the conversation between the deputy and the Polish lady and stepped over.

"Mitch! It's okay. I'll take it from here," Fernandez said to the deputy and continued, "Ma'am, my name is Lisa Fernandez. I'm a detective assigned to investigate this property. Do you mind if I ask you a few questions?" Justyna rolled her eyes as if she was saying, "*Here we go again! What does this woman want from me?*"

"Sure, but I don't have much time. I need to take care of my cats," Justyna said politely, but her facial expression looked as if she was offended. Miss Lavinsky hated when she had to talk to police officials.

"What is your name?" Detective Fernandez kindly asked.

"Justyna," Miss Lavinsky automatically replied as if Siri was talking.

"Okay, Justyna, what can you tell me about David? What kind of a person is he?" Lisa asked. The polish lady looked around nervously as if she wondered, "*Am I in trouble?*"

"I really don't know much about him. I see David once in a while, but that's about it. He doesn't talk much. Every time I see him, he always says hi. Hold on! Will I be in trouble?"

"Nah, ma'am, we just need to ask a few questions. That's all, okay?" Bob chimed in. He had heard the conversation between his partner and Miss Lavinsky. The Polish lady nodded politely, but she looked somewhat perturbed.

"Okay, have you ever heard loud or disturbing noises from David's apartment? Anything unusual?" the Texan asked.

"Not to my knowledge. Sometimes, his friend comes to visit him. But I can't really remember anything…unusual," Miss Lavinsky answered. Bob's eyebrows lifted in surprise; he didn't expect that kind of answer. Lisa's pupils enlarged because she too was surprised.

"Miss Lavinsky, can you describe David's friend," Bob asked. Justyna was holding her forehead as if she was in great pain. She then said, "I don't remember seeing his face, though. He was a white, overweight man. I would guess he was as tall as I am. I think he was wearing glasses, but I'm not sure. Excuse me. Can I go now? I'm tired from working all day, and now I have to clean my own apartment," Miss Lavinsky worded her frustration. She wasn't lying. She was a hard worker; she worked twelve hour shifts. Her legs and back ached painfully.

"Of course. Thank you for your cooperation. Have a peaceful night," Lisa declared and the Polish lady nodded. Miss Lavinsky went into her apartment and closed the door as quickly as she could. Then came the sound of a lock turning.

Around 10:00 p.m., the detectives walked to the black Tahoe.

"The CIA," McCarthur said, "reports that the YouTube video showing Ashley as a hostage was taken in Bulgaria."

"Is that even possible?"

"I don't know, dear. The CIA knows better. I doubt that they are wrong, but you never know..." The Texan slipped into another deep contemplation. His thoughts shifted onto another concern.

"What do you think, chief?" Fernandez asked as she entered the vehicle. Hearing her words, Bob flashed his crooked smile.

"What?" Fernandez snapped. Her voice sounded agitated, but she said it in a friendly way.

"I knew you'd ask me this question," the Texan said, "To be honest with ya, I'm confused a little."

"What do you mean?" Lisa asked while checking her eyes in the mirror.

"I don't know what is true and what is not. The Polish

woman talks about him as if he is an ordinary guy. Then, why would David want to kill Josh? There is another question that scratches my mind: where is Ashley, and did the murder of Kimberly and Jack Hammer have anything to do with David? Also, what was his motive?

"He is a weirdo!" Fernandez said.

"I get that. Hear me out, though. The guy where I buy booze is a weirdo too, but that doesn't make him a killer," McCarthur made his point. He wasn't wrong, but that didn't make him correct either. There was a pause. Silence filled the Tahoe.

"Do you really think that David knows where Ashley is?"

"Yes, I do believe he is hiding her somewhere, but he must have someone who helped him," the Texan answered.

"The stranger who the Polish lady described!" the UFC fighter exclaimed.

"Yeah, but we don't know what he looks like, other than that he is white and obese," the Texan spoke slowly. His words came out with frustration. Lisa sighed. She took a deep breath as if she was about to confess a shocking statement about her life. Both of them were tired. They had been working from 9:00 a.m. till 10:00 p.m.

"It's late. Let's get out of here," Robert said while staring at a random tree. He longed to go into his apartment and down a glass of cheap vodka. Half an hour later, the black Tahoe stopped on the side street where Bob lived.

"See you later, chief," Lisa said. Bob blinked faintly and flashed his crooked smile.

"Lisa. Drive safe. I'll talk to you later," the Texan said,

tapping politely on the Tahoe's roof. Lisa showed her charming dimples and sped away. She was soon out of sight. Not long after Fernandez drove off, Bob went into his apartment. It was pitch black in his condo. The Texan flipped the light switch, and the apartment shone brightly. The place looked messy, as usual. Bob didn't care how his apartment looked; a Hispanic lady cleaned for him once a week. McCarthur never invited guests to his condo. *No one comes here! Why should I clean?* his inner voice whispered while walking into his place. The Texan ran his hand through his curly hair. He peeled off his light North Face jacket and tossed it onto the sofa. He then went to the kitchen and opened the fridge. The only thing he wanted was to sip a glass of vodka. The Texan quickly poured and drained a few glasses. His head became a little dizzy. Under the influence of alcohol, Bob thought about his son, Jeremy. The detective felt guilty that his son didn't want to talk to him except at those times when Jeremy wanted something from him. Bob thought that he had failed at being a good father. He missed his son. *It is always ugly when the relationship between father and son turns sour,* he thought. The Texan knew he could be a better person and a good father. But Jeremy wouldn't give him a second chance to prove it. Robert had had multiple heated conversations with his wife, Teresa. Back in 2009, Jeremy was only five years old and often became the subject of his parents' altercations. Back then, McCarthur was in his mid-thirties, and his anger came out often. Because Bob tended to raise his voice to his family, Jeremy was terrified of him. The Texan was sad when he thought about his family. The flashbacks of his family were making him simultaneously sad and happy. The detective went to the kitchen and poured another glass. How many had he had already? He couldn't remember, and it didn't matter. His burning throat didn't stop him from draining another glass. At midnight, Bob sprawled on his couch and passed out. He had nightmares that night.

***

On Thursday, September 15th, the police department of Chicago was crammed with reporters from the local media. They were there for speech by Police Commissioner Lavance Makuba. He had to give an official statement about the investigation now that their main suspect, David Sparrow, had been charged with first-degree murder. The police department in Downtown Chicago was huge. The mayor of Chicago had passed a project plan for renovating the police facilities, and the city council had agreed to subsidize the plan. For the past six months, the police department had been under construction. The building interior was fitted with cutting edge technology and fancy lights. Also, the walls, on which many new Chicago signs were hanging, had been painted in black and blue.

Police Commissioner Lavance Makuba walked through the corridor to the room where the press was gathered. He wore an expensive black suit. His short-tapered afro hair looked fancy. Makuba slowly headed to the speaker's podium where he would make his statement. McCarthur and Fernandez were followed behind the Police Commissioner. Lisa looked outstanding. She was dressed in black trousers and a blue shirt that was tucked into her pants. Her black blazer coat was designed by an Italian brand, which wasn't that popular. Her ponytail wagged left and right as she walked. The Texan wore his light North Face jacket. His pants were also black, and his shirt white. Makuba casually walked to the lectern, surveying the crowded pack of reporters. The moment he stepped to the stand, the reporters started firing questions.

"Commissioner, can you tell us more about the missing Ashley Packer?" a young lady asked.

"At this moment, we are not sure where she is. But we are doing everything possible to find her. That is our primary goal. We're collecting information and working hard to determine Ashley's whereabouts."

"Commissioner, what are the charges against the suspect, David Sparrow?" another reporter asked. He was a man in his early thirties who wore big glasses. He was a handsome man, resembling the fictional character Clark Kent.

"Well, we found David's fingerprints on the gun that was used to kill Josh Rodriguez. It is clear that Mr. Sparrow is the perpetrator. His trial is scheduled for next week. Mr. Sparrow will be facing murder charges," Makuba explained. His voice sounded stern because this was a serious matter.

"What about the other two murders…uh… Kimberly and Jack Hammer? Have you found any connection between the victims and Sparrow?" another reporter asked.

"At this point, we have not determined if there is any connection between this person and the other two victims. I think the trial will come to a clear conclusion. I am hopeful that Mr. Sparrow will clear his soul. At this point, that's all I can say. Thank you!" Makuba said. The Police Commissioner turned around and walked back to where he had come from. The reporters kept asking questions, but the Commissioner was done with his statement.

***

Monday, October 3rd, was a busy morning in the city of Chicago. The Cook County Courthouse was filled with lawyers who wore expensive suits. The Courthouse wasn't that big, but it looked sumptuous, as if it was a museum. On that day David Sparrow would be standing trial in the courthouse. He was facing charges the minute the cops nabbed him back in September.

The bailiffs opened the courtroom's door, and people stepped inside. The spectator area was slowly filled by Chicagoans eager to witness the proceedings. Tom and Jennifer were two of the people who took their seats, as did Kimberly's and Josh's parents. Brendan couldn't make it. He had a fever, and it would not be wise for him to attend. Others could catch what he had. Twenty minutes later, David Sparrow was escorted by two deputies and seated not far from the judge's bench. David surveyed the courtroom. The court was immaculate. The bench where the judge would be sitting was made of wood material that glittered. The lights on the ceiling shone brightly. Some reporters from the local media were adjusting their cameras. The entire proceedings would be broadcast live on TV. David's parents walked into the courtroom. Even though they were separated, David's parents came together because they were worried about their son. His father had floppy gray hair. He wore an expensive corporate suit. He stepped to his son and whispered something to him. Listening to his father, Sparrow's eyes widened in a state of shock.

"All rise! The Circuit Court of Cook County is now in session. The Honorable Judge Karen Corndale presiding," the bailiff announced in an imperious voice, and everyone in the room rose to their feet.

In a second, a lady in a black robe stepped to the bench. She waved her hand, indicating that the people in the courtroom could return to their seats. Judge Karen Corndale was notorious in the city of Chicago. She had Irish ancestry of which she was proud. Judge Corndale looked to be in her mid-forties. Her beautiful blond hair was spectacular. She had a pretty face, but her blue eyes shot daggers. On this day, the judge wasn't in a good mood, and that wasn't a good sign for David. Corndale had a reputation as a stern but fair judge. She was a bit overweight, but her chin looked like she was taking care of herself. Judge Corndale put on her glasses and started reading the information about the case and the charges against the defendant.

David Sparrow sat fearlessly and listened to Judge Corndale. A man dressed in a manure-colored suit approached the defendant. The man was bald, with a horseshoe hairline. He was grossly overweight.

His name was Dean McMeyer, an attorney hired by David's father to defend the accused Sparrow. Dean whispered something to David. McMeyer wasn't just saying a few sentences, he was speaking lengthy. Sparrow just nodded. He gave the impression that he understood what his attorney was whispering, but the truth was that he had no idea what McMeyer said.

The trial took longer than everyone expected. The prosecutor showed all the evidence proving David Sparrow to be the main suspect facing the charge of murder first degree. On the other hand, Dean showed his courtroom skills by proclaiming that no one had in fact actually seen David Sparrow shoot Josh Rodriguez. Dean McMeyer was half Jewish and half Irish. He had grown up in the northern suburbs of Illinois. He had built a name as one of the best criminal defenders in the state. But Dean didn't come cheap. There's no such thing as a cheap lawyer, but McMeyer's fee was double what an ordinary criminal attorney would charge.

Everyone in the courtroom listened to the verbal virtuosity of each of the lawyers, except for one guy who was picking his nose. His name was Ben Dickens. Ben was seated in the spectator area. He was twenty-four years old and was one of David's closest friends. Ben had a slender type of body as if he was a rap dancer. Ben and David had grown up in the same neighborhood. Dickens had long hair, just like David. Ben took the stand Under oath, Dickens testified that his buddy had never been involved in a crime. He also proclaimed that David was a nice guy and a good friend. After a short fifteen-minute recess, the trial resumed.

David Sparrow was called to the stand. The audience watched the defendant taking the witness box; he wore a white shirt and black sweatpants. David looked a bit like a homeless person, but that didn't bother him. His mind fretted about what could happen in the next few minutes. His long greasy hair looked like he hadn't taken a shower for a week. The TV cameras were turned on and were pointing at the defendant. The prosecutor stepped closer to the bench. He was a man in his late thirties who had been considered one of the most successful people in Chicago. His name was Mark Dempsey. He was 5'11" tall with a seemingly fine body. He wasn't muscular, but he wasn't chubby either. Dempsey had been working in the city of Chicago for fourteen years. He became well-known as a prosecutor a few years ago after locking up a celebrity for child molestation. Mark had given multiple interviews on local TV shows because he was a brilliant lawyer who took his job seriously.

Back in the courtroom, Dempsey looked at David and asked, "Mr. Sparrow, do you know this person?" Dempsey showed a picture of Ashley Packer on the screen projector that was on the south side of the courtroom. David made an expression as if he had never seen Ashley before.

"Never seen her, sir," Sparrow confessed firmly. He seemed to be absolutely sure about his statement. Mark Dempsey took a deep breath.

"Okay then, you have never met her before," Mark repeated and asked, "Mr. Sparrow, did you know Josh Rodriguez?"

"Yes."

"So, let me get this straight. You have known Josh, but you have never met his fiancé. Is that true?"

"Yes, sir," David continued with his short answers. That was what Dean McMeyer had whispered to him earlier. Mark

Dempsey made a confused expression, like a man unable to understand something simple. He took another deep breath.

"Mr. Sparrow, how is it you knew Josh Rodriguez, but you have never met his fiancé, Ashley Packer? Josh had never introduced his fiancé to you?" Dempsey asked.

"Objection, your honor. Hearsay! Calls for speculation! I would strongly suggest my client not to answer this question," Dean McMeyer exclaimed.

"I'll sustain the objection," Judge Corndale cried out. Mark Dempsey took a deep breath, emitting a polite smile.

"Okay then. Mr. Sparrow, did Josh ever mention Ashley at any time?"

"Objection, your honor! Hearsay," McMeyer said disturbingly. Dempsey leaned closer to the mic and asked, "Your honor, may we approach the bench?" Judge Corndale gave a sign that she approved Dempsey's appeal, and both lawyers walked to the bench. The judge and the lawyers whispered something between each other for a few minutes. No one in the courtroom could understand or hear what the three of them were saying. It was interesting for the courtroom audience to observe the battle between the most popular criminal-defender in the state of Illinois against the most successful prosecutor in the city of Chicago. A few minutes later, both lawyers took their seats.

"Mr. Sparrow, how did you meet Josh Rodriguez?" Mark Dempsey proceeded. David looked at his attorney as if he was asking, "*Do I have to answer!*"

"Mr. Sparrow, did you hear my question?" Dempsey repeated. He was politely urging David to respond.

"Yes, sir. I met him at the gym where he worked. We talked about lifting weights and how to maintain a fit body. Josh showed great knowledge, and I said to myself, "*he seems to be a nice guy.*" And over the next few months, I started visiting the gym regularly," David lied. There was a pause.

"Mr. Sparrow, have you ever had any heated conversations with Josh Rodriguez?" Dempsey asked.

"Objection, your honor! Calls for speculation!" McMeyer exclaimed.

"Sustained!" Judge Corndale said sternly. Mark Dempsey took deep breaths repeatedly. It looked like he was enjoying the battle against the criminal defender.

"Mr. Sparrow, can you explain to the court what the Satanic Temple Foundation is and why your apartment has been decorated with materials related to this organization?" Dempsey asked.

"Objection, your honor! It has been proven that this foundation has nothing to do with any criminal activity. I would strongly suggest my client not to answer this question," Dean explained.

"Sustained!" Judge Corndale said.

"Mr. Sparrow, is that your gun?" Dempsey asked, and Sparrow saw a Glock 17 shown on the screen.

"Yes, sir! I do have a permit to carry a concealed weapon," Sparrow confessed, and Dempsey took a deep breath again. Breathing heavily in and out while working in courtrooms was one of Mark's patterns.

"Master Deputy Sheriff, Mason! May I please have you show the gun to Mr. Sparrow?" Dempsey implored, and an

African-American deputy stepped to the stand holding a gun that was sealed in a ziplock bag and showed it to the defendant.

"Yes, sir! That's my gun," Sparrow confirmed.

"Why would you carry a gun?" Dempsey asked.

"Objection, your honor! Calls for speculation!" McMeyer exclaimed. He was getting on Dempsey's nerves.

"I'll sustain! We are not here to discuss why people are having guns," Judge Corndale declared. Dempsey nodded and smiled.

"Mr. Sparrow, what were you doing in Josh's apartment a few seconds before he was killed?" Mark asked.

"Objection, your honor! Hearsay! Calls for speculation! There is no evidence of where my client was at the time of the murder!" McMeyer interrupted Dempsey. The criminal defender was using perfect timing to fire his objections.

"Your honor, I have testimonies of both police officers concerning the shooting," Dempsey protested.

"Sustained!" Judge Corndale said. Dempsey inhaled and exhaled annoyingly.

"Mr. Sparrow, why did you shoot at the police officer when he approached you," Mark asked. He was on a mission to prove how good he was.

"He screamed at me, and I got scared. That was why I pulled out my gun and shot into the ground. I wasn't pointing my gun at the police officer. I didn't intend to kill or injure the man," David answered. That was what McMeyer had advised him to say. Dempsey stared at the paperwork in front of him and said, "Let's take a look at exhibit 124. May we have the defendant's exhibit on the screen?" On the screen popped up a few cartridge cases photographed on the floor at Josh's apartment. Everyone in the courtroom was staring at the picture.

"Mr. Sparrow," Dempsey went on, "Are these cartridge cases from your gun?"

"Objection, your honor! Calls for speculation! It's not clear where these cartridge cases originated from! Furthermore, there is no evidence that my client had used his gun in Josh's apartment," Dean McMeyer didn't miss a chance to interrupt the prosecutor.

"I'll sustain," Judge Corndale said. Even the judge didn't like this ruling. But McMeyer had a good point, and she had to agree with his objection.

"Okay, but Josh Rodriguez didn't have a gun. Furthermore, it has been proven that the cartridge cases on the floor were from a Glock 17, the same gun David has. Also, we've checked and his magazine had some cartridges missing. And I would advise Mr. Sparrow to answer my question," Dempsey spoke with witticism.

"Objection, your honor! Hearsay! Calls for speculation. Your honor, may we approach the bench?" McMeyer asked politely, and Judge Corndale nodded agreeably. Both lawyers stepped closer to the judge. In a split second, the three of them started whispering among one another. The battle between the lawyers was tight. A minute later, the lawyers returned to their seats. Mark Dempsey wasn't finished. The prosecutor wouldn't quit until he put David behind the bars.

"Mr. Sparrow," Dempsey went on, "Can you tell me whose

blood was in the bedpan under your bed?" David made a confused facial expression, pretending that he didn't hear the prosecutor.

"Uh… I'm not sure if I understand the question," Sparrow mumbled. His voice was so low that Dempsey could barely hear him.

"Okay then. Let's take a look at exhibit 144. May I have state's exhibit 144 on the screen?" Dempsey appealed. In a second, on the screen appeared the image of the bedpan that Fernandez had found next to David's bed.

"Mr. Sparrow, is this bedpan yours?" the prosecutor asked.

"Ah! This one! Yes, sir! It's mine," David confessed. The defendant pretended that he was surprised by the question.

"Okay. Mr. Sparrow, whose blood was in this bedpan? Yours?" Dempsey asked.

"Objection, your honor. Calls for speculation! I would strongly suggest my client not to answer this question!" McMeyer was speaking like a robot.

"Overruled! Mr. Sparrow, you may answer the question," Judge Corndale said. David looked at Judge Corndale as if he was begging her to reconsider her decision. He then stared at the prosecutor and said, "It's from a chicken." David's voice sounded uncertain because he hadn't wanted to answer the question. The entire courtroom burst into laughter at this.

"A chicken!" Dempsey repeated, "Can you please tell us more about what a chicken's blood was doing in your bedpan?" The prosecutor had a good point. Everyone in the room awaited David's answer.

"Objection, your honor! Calls for speculation! Your honor,

may we approach the bench?" McMeyer appealed. Judge Corndale beckoned both lawyers to her bench. This time the conversation between Judge Cordale and both lawyers took a little over five minutes. After they finished the conversation, Judge Corndale adjourned the trial abruptly, scheduling it to resume in three weeks. In a few minutes, the people left the courtroom like rats scurrying out of a filthy dumpster. David Sparrow was taken to Harrison Street, downtown Chicago, where criminal defendants were held during a trial. McMeyer pulled all the strings he could to get bail for his client, but Judge Corndale was adamantly against it.

Bob McCarthur and Lisa Fernandez had been present in the spectator area surveying David's behavior during the trail. They had hoped that the defendant would reveal some useful information about Ashley Parker's whereabouts. However, their hopes faded after looking at the apathetic face of David Sparrow. Both detectives had compassion for the pain Tom and Jennifer were going through over their missing child. As the detectives walked out of the courtroom, Fernandez asked, "What do you think, chief?" Bob flashed his crooked smile. His small blue eyes were glittering like a man who just gotten laid by a hot chick.

"We got him!" the Texan replied, and Fernandez showed her beautiful dimples.

9

Thursday, the 29th of October, was a rainy day in Chicago. The sky was overcast and murky. It looked like the sun's rays would not show throughout the day. However, the bad weather didn't conceal the beautiful colors of the skyscrapers in the Windy City. It was the morning hours, and Chicago looked busy as usual. The gridlock in downtown was hectic. People honked their car horns in frustration. A few cab drivers cut the other drivers, which caused additional aggravation. Construction workers had closed some lanes, making the traffic even worse.

Kishan Shubham was driving his Honda Odyssey through the streets in Downtown Chicago that morning. He was a Lyft driver who had been working with the Lyft platform for more than five years. This job was his only income, and he was happy with it. Kishan had emigrated from India. He brought his beautiful wife, and together they'd had two wonderful children. Kishan was an amiable and honest man. He worked twelve hours a day, and he took care of his family. He had never had any problems with the police. On that day, Kishan had a rideshare request to pick up a passenger on East Illinois street. The fare promised to be lucrative, and the Indian man drove faster to get to the address as soon as possible. Shubham was speeding on Illinois street and switching lanes madly. A few minutes later he stopped his car and pressed the hazard lights. He looked around and checked the side mirrors to make sure that a PEO (parking enforcement officer) wasn't around. He hated when PEOs were strolling around because he might get a ticket for illegal parking. The Indian driver had already been waiting for a couple of minutes, and he became a little anxious. He looked at his belly, reminding himself that he had to lose some weight. He also was a hairy man. His bushy eyebrows looked a little scary, resembling *The Animal,* the fictional character from *The Muppets.* Kishan looked nervously at the Lyft app. He was to pick a guy named Alex. In the moment before Shubham switched to his phone app to contact the passenger, suddenly, BOOM! Something fell on the roof of his Honda. Kishan looked scared; his eyes widened.

"*What the heck was that?*" Kishan asked himself. The Indian driver heard screams outside. The alarm of his vehicle blasted loudly. Kishan opened the door and jumped off his Honda. What he saw made him speechless.

CHAOS IN CHICAGO

***

Fernandez sped through the city of Chicago. The sirens in her vehicle wailed, and the female detective was passing through red lights. Robert McCarthur sat on the passenger side. He looked through the window, but it seemed he wasn't watching anything. He was silent, but his mind was speaking. The Texan looked at his smartphone. The clock on the screen showed 9:30 a.m. Detective Fernandez took a hard right on La Salle Street, and after 500 feet, she made a left turn on Illinois Street. Jaywalking Chicagoans stepped into the street, but the Tahoe's sirens were loud enough to stop them. A few minutes later, the Tahoe stopped on Illinois Street, where other police vehicles, an ambulance, and a few firetrucks were parked. The block between East Illinois Street and McClurg Court was closed. Two police cars were parked horizontally, blocking the street. The officers were directing traffic away from the scene. Bob and Fernandez had to walk a few feet more because there were so many official vehicles and crowds of people in front of the building.

The detectives saw a blue Honda Odyssey, the roof of which was horribly smashed.

There was a female body on top of the Honda. The detectives stepped closer to the vehicle. She was dressed in black jeans and a blue turtleneck top. She had no shoes. She was beautiful.

"Oh my God! Can you believe it?" Fernandez asked. The way she expressed herself sounded more like she was praying. It wasn't a bad idea to pray at that moment. But both detectives were too busy for prayers, especially Bob. His mind was preoccupied with too many questions. He looked confused and disappointed. His scowling face looked as if he had an unpleasant case of diarrhea. The Texan was shaking his head in frustration because he recognized the body, and the same applied to his partner.

"We need to send the body for autopsy," McCarthur said in a low voice. The corpse was covered in blood. The crime scene looked ugly. Blood droplets fell from the victim's head like water steadily dripping from the faucet of a sink. The victim's eyes remained open as if she were not really dead. Police officers were asking the residents of the building to stay inside. Kishan, the Lyft driver, was complaining to a police officer. He grumbled about what had happened to his car. A helicopter owned by a local news outlet was hovering around the building, trying to get a better angle on the scene. The tabloids wouldn't miss the chance to cover this sad incident. Reporters gathered to get information about the victim. Some reporters asked the police officers for their comments, but the officers refused to give any information.

McCarthur beckoned the paramedics to come over. Four medical responders took the body down from the roof and placed it on a medical gurney. They put the woman in the ambulance and drove off. The dead person was Monica Shingles. It looked like she had jumped off the building and just happened to fall on Kishan's Honda. The chaos in Chicago grew bigger.

***

The next day the Chicago Morgue happened to be over-crowded. People were coming in and out from different rooms. Detective Bob McCarthur and Lisa Fernandez walked through one of the corridors, heading to the autopsy room. As they went through the double swing doors, Bob coughed badly. He felt dizzy and almost collapsed on the floor.

"What the hell! Are you okay, chief?" Lisa asked, staring at her partner.

"Yeah! It's from the tobacco," Robert replied.

"What! I thought you quit smoking," Lisa expressed her disapproval. She cared about her partner. McCarthur was like a brother to her.

"Do you need to see a doctor?" Lisa went on. Bob shook his head no. He placed his hand on her shoulder and said,

"I'll be all right, dear." The Texan sounded certain in his words, but Lisa wasn't completely convinced. The detectives went into the room where Marcus Johnson examined Monica's body.

"Hey, Marcus! How you doing, buddy!" Bob exclaimed joyfully.

"I'm all right. What about yourself?" Marcus responded in a low voice as if he was at the movies and was trying to be considerate of others in the audience.

"Can't complain. Living my best life!" the Texan answered. He sounded a bit snarky but in a positive way. Marcus nodded and greeted Lisa. He asked her questions about the UFC fighters who fought a week ago. Marcus loved to watch UFC, which was why he enjoyed chatting with Lisa. The female detective also loved talking about her passion. She was staring at Marcus with great interest. The coroner's hair was outstanding, as it always was.

"So what can you tell us about the deceased?" McCarthur asked. He couldn't wait to hear Marcus' opinion.

"I found a large amount of cocaine and MDMA in her blood. Monica was high on drugs when she fell from the building. There is something else… Monica took citalopram which means she was being treated for depression," the coroner stated. Both detectives were speechless. They hadn't expected that answer.

"Hold on! Let me get this straight! You're telling me she OD'd before she jumped from the building?" Lisa asked, and Marcus nodded.

"Wait a minute! At this point, we are not certain how she fell from the building," the Texan pointed out.

"Maybe someone threw her body out of a window," Marcus suggested.

"Huh?" Lisa said?

"What?" Bob snapped, "Was she dead before she fell from the building?"

"I can't confirm that, but my answer would be yes. I believe that Monica was already dead before she fell onto the vehicle," the African-American coroner stated. Both detectives looked at him in disbelief. Marcus' words confused them even more.

"That means we are not sure if it was a murder or a suicide. Or merely the improper disposal of a body," Fernandez said, and the two men nodded.

"I'll speak with my colleagues and get back to you later," Marcus said while looking at Bob.

"Okay, Marcus. I'll talk to you later," Bob said. The detectives walked out of the Chicago Morgue as fast as they could. They had a lot of work to do.

First thing the next morning, they drove to Royal Point, where Monica had lived, and interrogated every employee. The Chicago detectives chatted with Eric, the building manager. They needed to check the cameras from two days before, when Monica was found dead. The cameras covered the lobby, the front desk, and every exit from the building. But the problem was that there were not cameras on every floor, which meant that Bob McCarthur and Lisa Fernandez had nothing. The detectives searched Monica's apartment, but they didn't find anything. Besides the lack of evidence, there was another problem — Monica's parents, especially her father, demanded more information. He was a former governor of the state of Illinois and a prominent entrepreneur in the Chicago area. He was a big name in the city and demanded to know everything about his child, just like any other father would. Parents will do anything for the sake of their kids, and Monica's father was no exception.

More questions arose; why would Monica commit suicide? Or was she pushed from the building by someone else? And why did Miss Shingles take drugs? She was successful in her job and had built a remarkable career. According to her friends, Monica didn't have any enemies. Who could possibly want to push her from the building? Her boyfriend was in Miami on a business trip. There was no way he could have killed his girlfriend. Perhaps he had hired someone to do the job because he didn't want to be implicated in the crime.

Was Monica immersed in a sea of depression? Or maybe she was addicted to prescription drugs? These and many more questions remained unanswered. But Detective McCarthur was determined to find the truth— not only because that was his job, but also because the victims were kids, whom he could have been the father of.

At 4:00 p.m. the next day, Bob and Lisa were in their office downtown. The office space was chaotic; printers and fax machines were covered with hundreds of pages regarding the murders. More dead bodies meant more paperwork. There was also a tiny kitchen with a sink and long countertop bar on which sat a microwave and coffee machine. Also, a big modern fridge was placed by the left side of the sink. A large screen projector stand was left on the north side of the office. On the south side of the office were two brown leather couches positioned across from the screen. A long computer desk was installed at the corner of the southwest side. On the computer desk were two laptops at which Bob and Lisa worked. Detective Fernandez wore black khakis and a white shirt. The back of her shirt read: MY KIDS ARE THE POWER THAT GIVES ME THE STRENGTH TO FIGHT AGAINST CRIMINALS. Her athletic figure reminded McCarthur that he needed to work out at the gym. But he didn't have time for training: he was too busy at work.

As both detectives were reading the reports from Monica's case, Fernandez asked, "Does David Sparrow have anything to do with Monica? What do you think, chief?"

"That's a good question," the Texan responded, "It's possible. He could have known who pushed her from the building.

But how can we prove it? David has an alibi; he was in custody when she died."

"What about Monica's boyfriend? Did he have a motive to kill his girlfriend? I mean, we spoke with him yesterday, and he swore that he was in Miami on the day of Monica's death, but I'm not convinced that he was telling the truth. What you think, chief?" Fernandez asked. She was speaking her thoughts aloud. It was something that she did a lot.

"Well, he has proof that he was in Miami. Besides, every employee at Royal Point testified that Monica's boyfriend was a really nice guy. So the answer to your question is *no*. I don't think that her boyfriend would have killed her. But there is something that bothers me," McCarthur proclaimed.

"What?" Fernandez asked. She looked confused.

"I think the person who has Ashley is the same guy who has pushed Monica out of the building," Bob also expressed his thoughts aloud. Then Fernandez snapped, "Chief, that's a helluva leap. But wait a minute. Didn't you say the YouTube video was made in Bulgaria? I mean, was she taken to Bulgaria?" Fernandez asked. She became confused by her own question, which was something normal because the whole idea was bizarre.

"This question remains a mystery. I'm still waiting for the CIA to verify the origin of that video," the Texan replied.

"Really? That's weird! I thought that the CIA was taking this case seriously," Fernandez snapped. She hated when someone was working slowly or procrastinating on something important.

"Well, I spoke with the Bulgarian government and told

them about Ashley. I also sent them Ashley's files and a photo of her. 'We will be on the lookout.' That's what they responded to me," McCarthur said. He ran his hand through his hair and stretched out his arms. Both detectives were exhausted from work. They were doing everything possible to solve the mystery of the murders and Ashley's whereabouts.

"I'm getting old!" Bob announced and started laughing at his sardonic remark.

"Who said that?" Fernandez asked, and both burst into laughter.

"Okay. Let's get outta here," the Texan announced and sneezed so hard that his body jolted.

"Are you okay?" the UFC fighter asked.

"Yeah. C'mon. Let's go!" The detectives left downtown quickly, but the streets were congested. The heavy traffic annoyed Fernandez. She was holding the steering wheel nervously. Then all of a sudden a noise resembling a gunshot sounded from outside, and the Tahoe started to swerve.

"What the heck was that?" Fernandez asked in frustration.

"I don't know. Pull over into the emergency lane," McCarthur directed, and Lisa switched lanes. She parked the car, and both detectives jumped out to survey the vehicle. The front tire on the right side of the car had delaminated, the tread separated from the tire case. It looked as bad as if the vehicle had passed over police spike strips.

"FUCK!" Fernandez bellowed in a state of utter aggravation. She put her hands on her hips and turned around, leaving the vehicle behind her.

"Take a deep breath, dear. I'll take care of it," the Texan said while he was peeling off his coat.

"You sure? I mean, can you do it? I can call for roadside assistance," Lisa offered. Robert made a facial expression saying, "*Are you kidding? I have changed thousands of tires over the years.*"

"I used to change the tires of my truck back in Texas. Don't worry. Just give me forty minutes, and I'll be done," Bob assured his partner. It took him a little more than that. Two hours later, he was still struggling with the spare tire.

"Done!" McCarthur announced, flashing his crooked smile. His body was covered in sweat. He had worked hard, and Fernandez couldn't deny it, but the timing was way off. The UFC fighter looked at her smartphone.

"Okay! It took you only two hours and twelve minutes," the female detective declared.

"The clock on your phone is not accurate," Robert said with a smirk on his face.

"Oh, yeah. I know that!" Lisa replied, and both laughed happily. The next second, both detectives jumped in the vehicle and Lisa drove off.

Fernandez parked the Tahoe on the street where McCarthur lived and said, "Take it easy, chief." Fernandez showed her beautiful dimples. The Texan was so tired that he avoided using any words. He could barely see because his eyes were closing.

"Oh, I almost forgot. One of my daughters, Maribel, will be celebrating her birthday this Saturday. Stop by for a drink. I'll have some juicy steaks. So, set a reminder. I won't take *no* for an answer. Okay, chief?"

"Gotha. I'm not that old. Not just yet. When is this party starting?" Bob asked. He was yawning sleepily.

"You can come any time after 2:00 p.m.," Lisa answered. She was yawning too, and that made her laugh.

"Okay. I'll be there!" McCarthur stated and jumped out of the Tahoe. Fernandez smiled and drove off quickly. Bob went into his crib and opened a bottle of vodka. He was thirsty.

***

Saturday, November 5th, was a chilly day. The Windy City repeatedly proved how it had earned that name. The overcast sky blocked the sun, limiting its chances of breaking through it. The wind was pushing the gray clouds, making them look like they were alive. Despite the morbid weather, Chicagoans walked the streets, went to restaurants or stores, and enjoyed the weekend. The weather in the city didn't discourage McCarthur either. Around 1:00 p.m., he hopped in the shower. He needed to leave soon. Lisa Fernandez had invited him to her daughter's birthday party, and he had to go. He might have declined his colleague's invitation, but that would have been rude and inappropriate. Besides, McCarthur loved Lisa's kids. Also, he wanted to get out of his apartment because it was a complete mess; clothes were thrown everywhere, and the kitchen was covered with dirty dishes and silverware. Bunches of paperwork were strewn about the condo as if someone had been searching for an important document. After the shower, the Texan dried his curly hair and combed it a little. Robert's natural blond hair was starting to turn white. Getting older didn't make him happy, but he had to accept it because it was inevitable.

"What time is it?" Bob asked himself aloud and looked at his smartphone. It was close to 1:30 p.m. The Texan hated when he was running late. He put on his spiffy black khakis and his gray long-sleeve shirt. He then went to his closet and took one of his favorite *Guess* coats. Bob requested an Uber. He didn't have a car because he disliked driving in Chicago. McCarthur thought that Chicagoans drove too aggressively and that made him nuts. The Uber driver came unexpectedly fast. Bob left his apartment quickly, holding the birthday present, a beautifully illustrated children's book, and locked the door.

The Texan jumped into the Uber's vehicle, which was a white Tesla, and greeted the driver. The homicide detective couldn't comprehend how an Uber driver could afford to drive a Tesla. He tried to speak with the driver, but the guy refused to talk, as if the Texan had somehow insulted him. The ride took about thirty minutes. The Tesla parked on the driveway of a luxury house in Niles. Bob hopped out of the vehicle and looked around. This was his first time visiting Lisa's home. Lisa and her husband had bought the house a year ago. Fernandez got approved for a loan from the bank, and she happily put in a down payment to purchase the new home. A high fence surrounded the Fernandez's property. The front yard was as big as a half-basketball court. On the southwest corner in the back, a small pool was installed, and at the center of the yard was the kids' trampoline. Bob went inside and looked at the house. It was a beautifully designed home. He went to the living room, where the kids were chatting loudly and playing games.

"There you are! Chief, I thought you wouldn't come!" Fernandez said and hugged her colleague.

"Are you kidding? I won't miss the chance!" the Texan said and flashed his crooked smile.

"You bet! Let me show you the house. Come with me," Lisa enthusiastically exclaimed, and Bob followed her. A bling-bling kitchen was to the right of the front door. The living room had brand-new, white furniture and a massive TV attached to the wall. A full bathroom was on the left side of the house; it was furnished with pricy gray-white tiles with a luxurious shower and tub combo. The second floor had a master bedroom with a huge walk-in closet and a master bathroom where Lisa and her husband enjoyed their intimacy. The other three rooms were occupied by their kids. The walls in the hallway on the second floor were decorated with framed pictures of Lisa's family.

"So, what do you think, chief? This house isn't a bad investment, right?" the female detective asked. She waited for Bob's answer because she valued his opinion. McCarthur lifted his eyebrows. He hadn't expected that question, but he was elated that Fernandez sought his advice.

"The house is amazing! It is a good fit for your family. Your decision to buy this house is commendable," the Texan replied.

"Do you really think so? I mean, I don't know if we can handle this because…" Fernandez couldn't finish her sentence, she was nervous about the mortgage. Bob gave her a friendly hug.

"Listen, you're a good, hardworking woman. Everything is gonna be fine. Don't stress too much. Let's go downstairs. I need a drink," McCarthur declared, and Fernandez smiled as if to say, "*Thank you!*" As they made their way down the staircase, Robert looked around the living room. He saw how the kids were still playing loudly, and he instantly became crestfallen. Memories of his son playing as a kid arose in his mind. Bob took a deep breath. His inner voice said, *I need a drink!*

A few hours later, the Texan was feeling a little dizzy because he was mixing bourbon with brandy. He glued his ass to the chair by the alcove and looked out the window. He watched, but he wasn't seeing anything. His mind was filled with many thoughts about his messed up life. The Texan needed fresh air and went outside to the yard. He stared up at the sky. It was dark already. Bob gawked at one particular spot as if he was mesmerized by an eye-catching woman.

"Are you having fun?" Fernandez asked from behind. She surprised him because he hadn't seen her.

"Oh, yeah! Are you kidding me? Thanks for the invitation. I needed to hang out somewhere. I haven't been out since the Fourth of July," McCarthur answered.

"Stop shitting me! What is it? We've been working together for more than five years. I know you. I can read your face like I'm reading a book," Fernandez declared. Bob revealed his crooked smile.

"Okay, okay! You got me. I'm thinking about the missing girl, Ashley. Something, deep inside of me, is telling me that she is still alive. Also, I don't think she is in Bulgaria. As a matter of fact, I believe she is here, in Chicago," Bob declared in a low voice.

"Do you really think she could be here? But where?" Fernandez questioned. The female detective looked confused. For a moment, both detectives remained silent.

"David Sparrow knows where Ashley is," Robert asserted.

"I bet. But he won't talk. He's adamant. We need to interrogate him again. When was his next court date?"

"Holy cow! It's this Monday! We have to be there at 9:30 in the morning," the Texan declared.

"Yeah…" Fernandez whispered. In a blur, a noise came in. PAP-PAP-PAP. Terrifying gunshots startled the detectives. They hit the ground. All of a sudden, Lisa's house turned into a screaming nuthouse.

"ARE YOU OKAY!" Bob shouted, and Lisa nodded. Bob tried to grab his gun. He then realized that he wasn't wearing his sidearm.

PAP-PAP-PAP. More gunshots blasted somewhere close by. Fernandez waved at the others in the house to stay down and crawled to the fence. The wall surrounding her house was built of bricks and was 10 feet high. Fernandez couldn't see who was shooting at her house. A raspy sound of screeching the tires came from the street. Then Lisa ran to the front of the house and screamed, "Mother Fuckers!" Her blood was up. She was more than just mad. There was no sign of the car or the shooters. In a second, the Texan joined her. He was out of breath.

"Are you okay?" McCarthur asked.

"Yeah! I'm fine. Can you believe it?"

"That was a message."

"Huh? What do you mean, chief?" Fernandez asked. She stared at her partner and tried to understand what was going on.

"They didn't shoot into the house. I could tell by the sound of the gunshots. Whoever it was, he shot into the air. Someone is trying to tell us something!"

"Yeah. I see what you're sayin'. But who could it be?" Fernandez kept asking questions because she was confused.

"The same people who took Ashley," Bob declared, and Lisa nodded like a little girl agreeing with an adult.

Seconds after the shooting, Fernandez called the cops. Even though she was a detective, she needed to contact the local police and report the terrifying incident. The Niles cops came with a few patrol cars and lit up the street with blue lights. The neighbors across the street were observing Lisa's house with great interest.

Once she had calmed down a bit, Lisa got angry that someone had ruined her daughter's birthday party. She didn't have any security cameras installed around the house, and that pissed her off even more. Niles was a wealthy and quiet community; it had never occurred to her that a security system might be necessary. As a parent, she wanted her kids to grow up in a safe neighborhood, and Niles, Illinois, was one of her best choices. Or so she had thought.

The Niles police left Fernandez's property around 9:00 p.m. But Lisa would speak with them again first thing in the morning.

Robert McCarthur called an Uber and took off for his

apartment. He was in shock, just as Lisa was. Ironically, unlike his earlier ride, this time Bob was quiet and the Uber driver was talking too much, which made the detective tune out. As Robert was listening in irritation to the driver, he thought, *Oh, man! How can I get this guy to shut his mouth?*

The ride took about twenty minutes. As soon as the police detective hopped out of the rideshare vehicle, he was relieved that the driver was gone. But that didn't make him feel comfortable. His mind was preoccupied with a bunch of thoughts about the shooting earlier. He couldn't comprehend why or who would dare to shoot up Lisa's house. *Gosh, I need a drink,* Bob's inner voice cried out. He opened the fridge and took a bottle of vodka. Every time the Texan swallowed the alcohol, his face frowned as if he was holding a fart. *VODKA-BOOZER. VODKA-LOOSER*, the voice in his head whispered. The bottle was almost full when he grabbed it from the fridge. Two hours later, the same bottle was empty. The alcohol helped him forget about his messed up life and the problems he was facing at work. But the booze wasn't a solution, and the Texan knew it. However, he was still using it as a sleeping aid.

VODKA-BOOZER. VODKA-LOOSER, the same voice had proclaimed. McCarthur couldn't remember where he had heard those words. That wasn't important. Nothing was important when it came to the point of drinking alcohol. An hour later, Bob lay on the couch and drifted off to sleep.

10

It was Monday, the 7th of November. The Chicago court-house was busy as usual. A bunch of attorneys, wearing pricy suits, were walking in and out. Some of the people were heading to the courtroom with a sign that read "*110.*"

David Sparrow was back in the same courtroom where his trial had concluded three weeks ago. Sparrow was nervous because his future was now in the jurors' hands. His hair was messy, but that was the last thing he worried about. On this day, the jury would reveal their decision, and the judge would announce the verdict. The clock in the courtroom showed 9:25 in the morning. The courtroom started to fill with people. Ashley's parents, Tom and Jennifer, were in the crowd of people eager to hear the verdict. Brendan couldn't make it because he was working. David's parents were also there, waiting for the judge. They were restless because their only child faced a murky future. David's father would do anything possible to save his kid from prison, but his power was limited.

Bob McCarthur and Lisa Fernandez were also in the spectator's area. The detectives were whispering something to each other. Bob's face was pale as if he was about to faint. He had had a hard time waking up that morning. Nevertheless, his black duffel coat looked flashy, and his dark blue khakis were outstanding. Even Fernandez commented on his clothes. She was also dressed in expensive attire. She looked like a businesswoman who headed a large corporation.

"All rise!" the bailiff exclaimed. It seemed that he liked saying those words because they had an imperious effect. Judge Karen Corndale walked into the courtroom wearing her traditional black robe. The judge waved at the people, and they took their seats, but one man remained standing. That was Dean McMeyer, the attorney for the defense. He walked to the jury and declared why David should be exonerated. McMeyer spoke profoundly. His words spellbound the jury. The criminal defense lawyer tried to convince the people on the panel that David didn't kill Josh Rodriguez. He pointed out that no evidence showed David being the man who gunned down Josh Rodriguez. Also, he speculated that David didn't shoot at the police officer; he shot at the sidewalk because he got scared. He explained that the blood from the bedpan was from a chicken that David had bought as a pet. The chicken started shitting all over his apartment, and he had to euthanize it; it was Sparrow's mistake. However, according to the law in Cook County, killing a chicken didn't equate to killing a human. McMeyer's argument made a lot of sense. Dean concluded, saying that everyone has been in an awkward situation at times, and David was no exception. The criminal defense lawyer wrapped up his monologue by flashing a charming smile at the jury and took his seat.

The prosecutor, Mark Dempsey, didn't waste a second. He told the jury that no one else could have killed Josh Rodriguez, and all the evidence proved that David was the man who pulled the trigger. He emphasized that Josh was killed with bullets that had been fired from Sparrow's sidearm. Dempsey used his words wisely, and that was undeniable. He pointed out that society must take precautions and chastise people who commit brutal homicide, otherwise more people would be found dead. Mark concluded that it was society's duty to punish those who made such transgressions. He finished with the words,

"Sending someone to jail isn't our purpose but rather to mete out justice according to our laws. This murder was committed by David Sparrow and he must be made to pay for his crime. Thank you for your time."

Dempsey's words made people in the courtroom nod in approval of his point. Judge Corndale dismissed the court for a fifteen-minute break. After the break, everyone returned to their seats. David Sparrow was shaking. He was scared of what would happen next.

The judge spoke, "Ladies and gentlemen of the jury have you reached a verdict?" The jury foreman responded "Yes, your honor." He then handed a folded piece of paper to the bailiff, who brought to the judge. Corndale opened the paper, read it, and refolded it. "What is your verdict?" "We find the defendant guilty!" The courtroom erupted in gasps, cheers, and sobs.

The judge sentenced David Sparrow to twenty-five years. McMeyer promised David that he would appeal the sentence. After adjourning the court, Judge Corndale left the courtroom immediately, as if she had an urgent call to use the restroom. People in the court were discussing the sentence aloud. David Sparrow was immediately taken away. Later the same day, he was transported by paddy wagon to Cook County Jail, where he would be processed prior to his transfer to Stateville.

People rushed from the courtroom as if a bomb threat had been announced.

Tom Packer and his wife, Jennifer, were disappointed because they still didn't have any information about Ashley. They had hoped that David would reveal where he had hidden her. It was unclear to them how the police would find their daughter. Tom and Jennifer chatted with Bob and Fernandez. McCarthur promised to do everything he could to return Ashley. His words sounded confident because he was determined to resolve the mystery of the missing girl. Tom nodded agreeably, but Jennifer didn't believe in his words. She was losing hope. Her child had been missing since July. She could barely hold her anger. Mrs. Packer kept telling herself to remain strong, but she was losing her faith. The likelihood that she would never see her daughter again filled her with despair. Her body almost shook from trepidation. Her eyes filled again with tears. The conversation with the homicide detectives was making her restless. She couldn't stay in front of the courthouse any longer. Mrs. Packer nudged Tom and gave him a tacit sign saying that she wanted to go home. At first, Tom scratched his bald head in a state of uncertainty, but the angry eyes of his wife convinced him of what he had to do. Bob and Lisa watched as Ashley's parents took an Uber and left the courthouse.

"What do you think, chief?" Fernandez asked. She looked at Bob with her dilated pupils like a puppy staring at her master. McCarthur flashed his crooked smile. He admired how Fernandez concentrated on work.

"I think we have to roll the dice and interrogate David, again. He's got nothing to lose now, and I'm sure he'll spill the beans," the Texan said. He looked sure of himself, but in her heart Fernandez didn't agree with him.

"Are you hungry?"

"Yeah. I mean kind of," the UFC fighter responded.

"This whole lawsuit process made me hungry. C'mon! Let's get something to eat. I'll take care of the bill."

"You're buying me lunch!" Fernandez joyfully exclaimed as if she was a kid at Christmastime.

"Yeah. This isn't the first time I've bought lunch," Robert protested. Fernandez looked at him and showed her charming dimples.

"I'm not so sure about that," the female detective giggled, and Bob laughed out loud. In a matter of seconds, both detectives jumped in the Tahoe, and Lisa drove off.

***

The moment when David stepped into Cook County Jail, his only thought was of escape. The prison was old and its computers, surveillance cameras, etc., were outdated. McMeyer pulled some strings and got him into a cell without a cellmate. The criminal defense lawyer did his client a favor, but Sparrow took it for granted. David hated everything related to Cook County Prison. The guards were unfriendly, screaming and cursing at him. David had to stay locked in his cell for twenty-three hours. The only time he was let out was to eat and shower. David Sparrow avoided taking a shower. The fear of what could happen there tormented him. The food was cold and disgusting; even a dog would get sick eating it. The inmates looked at him with unfriendly eyes.

At first, David tried to speak with some of his ethnic group, but everyone shunned him, so he decided to mind his own business. He kept his mouth shut because he didn't know anything about being in prison. Sparrow hated his cell. There were roaches, rats, and bed bugs. He slept on a thin, uncomfortable mattress. David heard stories that people in this jail were dying every week. David's first night at Cook County Prison had been a nightmare. He couldn't sleep. He was afraid that the rats and the bugs would bite him. Sparrow became depressed to the utmost degree. He wanted to commit suicide, but he didn't know how.

The Cook County Prison was always cold, and that wasn't helpful to any inmate. David Sparrow didn't mind cold weather, but the cold in jail was a totally different story. He was 100 percent sure that he would get sick in a week and hoped that would kill him. But he was wrong. His immune system fought back and beat all the viruses. David had had no idea what it was like to be locked in the pen. He would do anything possible to get out of Cook County Jail. But it was too late for redemption. Locked up in his cell, David started losing his common sense. Although, he remained strong and continued fighting the consequences. He thought about nothing but leaving the horrifying jail, but his options were limited. He wanted to speak with McMeyer and beg him for a transfer to a different facility. What David didn't know was that the lawyers had their hands tied when it came to helping someone who had already been incarcerated.

During his first week in jail, David got into a fight in the chow hall. A Latino man dissed him about the food, and David couldn't take anymore. He jabbed the Latino. Then, the Hispanic guy jumped him and beat the shit out of him. His left eye was swollen, and blood ran from his nose. Not too long after his first physical fight in prison, David got into another one. On occasion, David encountered burly inmates who walloped his ass in seconds. The physical confrontations in jail put him in through rough ordeal. His nose was consistently bleeding, and he had lost a few of his front teeth. Almost every night, David burst into tears. He moaned like an injured animal. He would cry in his cell for hours. If he slept at all, his nights were filled with nightmares.

On one particular night, David was resting in his cell. He was curled up in the fetal position. Sparrow had no idea what time it was, but that didn't matter because time had stopped for him. He closed his eyes and fell asleep. In a little while, a noise of someone hitting the cell bars awoke him.

"Who's there?" Sparrow asked immediately. No one answered, but the same annoying sound was repeated. It was getting even louder.

"Who's there? I said. What do you want?" Sparrow spoke fearlessly, though he was scared to death. He knew that someone stood by his cell, and it wasn't a guard. There was no answer, and the noise continued.

"What the fuck do you want from me? If you come closer, I swear to God. I'll break your neck," David warned. He wasn't joking. He really meant it.

"HA-HA-HA!" a male laugh broke the silence. David couldn't see who was laughing because it was pitch black in his cell.

"David, you talk too much. I heard that you ratted to the police," the unknown man said. His voice sounded as if the devil himself spoke. David was in disbelief and on the edge of bursting into a tantrum. He hadn't expected someone would come to his cell and ask him questions about the police.

"I didn't say shit! I'm not a snitch," David snapped.

"I heard different, David," the man responded. His voice was eerie. David became speechless. He waited a second because he was in shock.

"Wait a minute! I didn't talk to the cops! I did what the Hacker instructed me to do. I went to Josh's house and talked to Josh while the Hacker shot him from the back door. Then I left the house. I didn't know that there were cops outside. I did my job. Tell the Hacker that I want my part of the deal, okay?" David's voice was loud and fearless, but he was scared like a chicken running from a farmer with a knife.

"What? The Hacker! What are you talking about, David?" the man asked.

"Oh, so now you pretend that I'm talking nonsense. Is that right? Let me tell you something! Fuck you, and fuck the Hacker. I want my money. You hear me?" David said. The words coming out of his mouth were spoken incredibly fast as if he was a talented rapper.

"There is an old saying: snitches get stitches. Ever heard that phrase, David?" The voice asked.

"I told you, man. I didn't say shit. You've got to believe me, man! I'm telling you the truth!" David was near to screaming. Fear crawled up his legs and over his body like slithering snakes.

In the next second, the creaking noise of an opening cell door echoed in the cell block. Someone entered his cell. David's eyes widened.

"No! Please, no! Noooo…"

***

Thursday, the 10th of November, was a cloudy day. Dangerous sleet rained across the city of Chicago. The weather informed Chicagoans that Christmas was approaching. The streets became busier. People were running errands, doing some early shopping, or going to the airport. The traffic got snarled, and drivers grew angry. None of that seemed to bother Detective McCarthur. He looked at the clock on his smartphone. It was 9:30 in the morning. *Where is she? She was supposed to be here half an hour ago!* his inner voice whispered. Bob grabbed his phone and was just about to dial Fernandez when the Tahoe pulled into his street. The Texan walked to the vehicle wearing his crooked smile.

"Hey, I thought you were going to pick up me at…"

"Don't say it… just… ugh! I had a little bit of a rough morning!" Fernandez snapped, interrupting her colleague. She had had a heated conversation with her husband. He burned his hand on the stove and blamed Lisa for his own mistake. The Texan nodded and declared, "Let's go to Starbucks. I need some tea. What do you think?" Fernandez nodded agreeably and drove to the nearest Starbucks. The detectives strolled into the coffee shop. Fernandez had a Chai Tea Latte, and McCarthur slurped an Earl Gray Tea. They sat facing the parking lot and discussed what they had to do that day.

"We need to visit our friend in jail," Bob spoke in a low voice as if he was a spy revealing top-secret information.

"Ugh! You mean David Sparrow," Fernandez asked, and her partner nodded.

"This kid knows more than he says. I'm sure he'll talk now. Hold on!" Robert said. His phone was vibrating. He looked at the screen and picked up the call.

"Yea. What! FUCK! Augh…dammit! Are you sure? Okay… I'm on my way," Bob mumbled and hung up.

"Who was it? What happened?" Fernandez asked. She could tell that something serious had transpired. McCarthur looked at his partner with a disappointed face and said, "Let's go. We need to leave."

"Where? Chief, what the heck are you talking about?" Lisa asked, and Bob bit his lip nervously.

CHAOS IN CHICAGO

"We need to get to Cook County Jail as soon as possible."

***

Cook County Jail was filled with a swarm of police officers and state troopers. It was chaos because the prison had been extremely busy that morning. Sirens and alarms were blasting out loud. Guards were running in different directions. Inmates had been taken to the dayroom area and put on the ground in handcuffs. The prisoners screamed and protested in confusion.

Thirty minutes later, a few forensic experts came to take pictures of the dead body. David had been stabbed multiple times. His stomach looked like Swiss cheese. Also, a sock had been shoved in his mouth. He lay on the floor as if sleeping. His eyeballs remained open, but his pupils weren't visible. The picture looked like a bad scene from a horror movie produced by Stephen King.

The Texan and the UFC fighter got there thirty minutes later. They walked hastily through the police officers and the guards and approached David's cell. The area was tiny, smaller than the size of a walk-in closet. McCarthur breathed heavily. He ran his hand through his hair. He hadn't expected to find David's dead body at Cook County Jail. The Texan was absolutely sure that David would talk and spill the beans about Ashley and the other murders. Fernandez observed her colleague with trepidation. She was disappointed but not in the same way Bob was. Every time Lisa had to deal with the dead body of a young person, her heart felt squeezed by

181

pain and sympathy. Whether that person was a convict or not, the female detective thought that people didn't deserve to be killed under any circumstances.

Both detectives knew that they would be working extra hours. When there was a murder, it meant that the homicide detectives had to work harder.

At noon David's body was sent to the morgue for an autopsy. The paramedics moved the cadaver as swiftly as if it were a living victim of a knife attack. The detainees, now back in their cells, looked quietly at David's body. Most of them were pissed about the handcuff lockdown.

Bob McCarthur and Lisa Fernandez started an urgent internal investigation. They checked security cameras and interrogated inmates. The prisoners had no idea who would have killed David Sparrow. The detectives learned nothing and became frustrated. There were no fingerprints and no weapons in David's cell. No one could tell who had opened David's cell, or how. The story of this accident didn't remain unknown for long. David's murder went viral in the tabloids, on YouTube, and social media. All local news channels acknowledged the tragedy that had happened in Cook County Prison, and that became problematic for the homicide detectives, because people would start asking more questions.

The next day, Bob and Lisa went to the Chicago Morgue. They needed to get more information about David's murder. The coroner, Marcus Johnson, reported that he couldn't find anything useful. Johnson confirmed that David died instantaneously, but he had no answers about who had killed him. The detectives left the Chicago Morgue disappointed. As they were walking to the Tahoe, Lisa asked, "What are we going to do, chief? We don't have anything?" McCarthur was wordless. His mind was looking for answers. In a little while, he said, "It could be anyone. An inmate confrontation. Maybe someone working in the facility, or one of the guards. Who knows?"

Fernandez agreed with her partner. The detectives could only guess at who could be the killer. They had no evidence except a dead body. There were too many questions that remained a complete mystery. Also, they still didn't have any idea where Ashley could be. Had she been illegally transported to another country to be used as a slave? The question of where Ashley could have been taken was still the top issue on which both detectives worked. McCarthur and Lisa needed to work harder and go back over every single detail in search of an answer.

11

"Noooo!" Ashley screamed hysterically. She was running through the trees in the dark forest. It was pitch black around her, but that didn't discourage the teacher from running. Someone was behind her. She couldn't see who was chasing her because she was scared to death.

"Nooo! Leave me alone! Help! Please!" Ashley yelled.

"You can hide, but you can't run! HA-HA-HA!" an unknown voice cried out. Ashley looked over her shoulder to see who was speaking. No one was behind her. Then she turned back and saw an ugly zombie right in her face. The zombie had no teeth and no eyes. The monster looked like a man in his forties, but dressed in a corporate suit like a banker or a lawyer. The creature grunted and snarled like an angry dog. The monster had skin partly torn off of its face. Maggots were crawling from its mouth. The creature looked like a cripple because it wobbled from side to side. But somehow, the zombie seemed larger than a 200-pound man.

"Nooo! Please, noooo! Aaaah!" Ashley kept screaming.

***

Ashley awoke after a bad nightmare. The terror she felt was indescribable. The teacher looked around. She was trapped in some cage-like structure in an unknown basement. She was locked in the cage like an animal in the zoo. The cage was built with thick bars that didn't have much space between them; it looked like the teacher was in a prison cell. The entire basement looked creepy, resembling a haunted house with ghosts. Also, ominous noises were coming from a furnace, which additionally petrified her. The basement seemed to be in an ordinary house, but it was too dark to know because the lights were turned off. Even though it was dark, she could partly survey the basement; there was a washing machine that looked like it had never been used before. On one side of the basement, there were a bunch of construction tools and materials such as plywood, drywall, barrels, and many other things. Also, there were shovels, spades, rakes, and a mattock left by the staircase. Ashley had goosebumps; the basement terrified her. The teacher was scared to death of that creepy place. It was so scary, she felt as if at any second ugly zombies could crawl out from somewhere and attack her. To the left was a room with a single door that had always been locked.

Ashley didn't have any major injuries. The knee she had fallen seemed not to be serious, and the pain was tolerable. She walked around the cell. It wasn't spacious, but she could move around. There was a toilet in the cage, which was convenient for her. It was surrounded by sliding drapes so she could have her privacy. She went to the toilet and pulled the drapes. After flushing, she rose to her feet and looked into the little mirror, which was hanging on the wall next to the toilet. The mirror was cracked as if someone had punched it. Despite the broken mirror, Ashley continually stared in her reflection in it. Her golden hair looked disheveled and dirty.

The teacher couldn't remember the last time she had combed her beautiful hair. She recalled receiving compliments from friends about it, but that was before she'd been kidnapped. The moment she found herself locked in the cell, her hair looked unclean and filthy. She wore a tracksuit and a gray blouse that looked billowy on her. The Creep gave her these clothes a week ago (she called, The Creep, the person who kidnaped her). Ashley turned around, making sure there was no one in the basement, and took off her clothes. She looked at her naked body in the small mirror. Her butt was smaller than she remembered it being. Ashley felt she must have lost around 15 pounds in the past few months. She looked a tad like a street-walking crackhead. Ashley couldn't tell what her weight was, but she could imagine she was no longer at 110 pounds. The Creep fed her with salads bought from Aldi, which was fine with her. Ashley grabbed her rounded breasts; they looked smaller because she had lost weight. The teacher turned again to examine her entire body.

Although she looked fine and healthy, Ashley was dirty. She felt like a homeless person who hadn't showered for months. The teacher put her filthy clothes back on and left the toilet.

She slept on an old mattress that had dirty sheets. It was gross, but she had to deal with it. Ashley thought about her parents and her brother, Brendan. She missed them a lot. The English teacher also thought of Josh, Kimberly, and one of her best friends, Jack Hammer. She had no idea that all of them had been murdered. Ashley knew nothing of what had happened in the world since she had been imprisoned in the spooky basement. Ashley remembered the moment when she found herself trapped in the cell for the first time—she screamed and cried for hours. But later on, she figured that the screaming wouldn't help her. Even though she tried to be brave, Ashley cried whenever she curled up on the mattress.

What it seemed to be an hour later, the heating system kicked on, which implied that it was cold outside. Ashley had no idea which day it was or even which month it was. The English teacher sat on the mattress. Her inner voice told her that she needed to escape from the animal cage. *But how can I get out of here? The door is always locked. I don't have anything that I could use to open it! What should I do? If I try to seduce The Creep, would he show mercy and let me go? Nah! That's impossible*, the voice in her head said. The teacher had already determined that the Creep was a man, based on his behavior and manner of speaking. *There is no way a woman could talk like that and behave so oddly*, she concluded. The turmoil she felt frustrated her even more. But she didn't get discouraged. Actually, her predicament gave her the will to fight for her freedom. She then surveyed the spooky basement yet again, trying to find something useful. It wasn't easy because it was always dark, except when the Creep was there. The teacher stared at a few small windows out of reach. She would need a step ladder in order to get to the windows, but there was the fundamental problem; she didn't have any access to the windows because she was locked in the cage. At least the windows gave her an indication of whether it was a day or night.

Ashely curled up in the mattress and tried to sleep, yet she couldn't. Her mind was preoccupied with the fear of what could happen next. She thought she might need more physical strength. That was why she had started doing pushups and sit-ups on the floor. She couldn't do pull-ups, which was a bummer. After a couple of weeks and constant training, she could see how her body was becoming more muscular. She looked like a professional boxer who just became a world champion.

The next day, Ashley awoke from another nightmare. The kidnaped girl wanted to shriek from terror, but was smart enough to remain silent. She looked at the small window across the room and saw that it was still night. She rose to her feet and went to use the little restroom. She pulled the drapes and sat on the toilet. Not long after she flushed it, Ashley splashed her eyes at the sink, which stood under the small mirror. Even though it was dark, she could easily see herself in the mirror. She then realized that something behind her was moving. *What was that?* her inner voice asked. The teacher turned around and surveyed the spooky basement. It looked like nothing was there, but she remained focused. Her eyes shifted in different directions. She couldn't see anything, but she could *feel* something unpleasant, like the presence of an alien.

"Maybe I'm losing it!" she spoke out loud. The teacher stepped out from the tiny toilet, and her eyes widened. She couldn't believe what she was witnessing. Her eyes were utterly shocked, and her eyelids rapidly blinked.

"Oh my God! Aaaah! What the heck is that?" she almost screamed. The teacher was so scared that the hair on her unshaven legs bristled. She saw a baby mouse scurrying through her legs. Ashley freaked out. She jumped on the mattress and peeled off her tracksuit to use it as a weapon. She screamed in a panic. The baby mouse took off in a different direction; the little rodent was scared to death of her, but Ashley couldn't have known that. She wasn't an expert on animals, mice included. *Where did it go?* her inner voice exclaimed. Ashley looked around, but there was no sign of the baby mouse. The teacher surveyed the spooky basement. Her teeth were grinding from anger. The one thing she really hated was mice. Ashley vividly remembered how her father killed a mouse when she was five years old. Since then, she had been terrified of rodents.

Ashley's eyes filled with tears. She couldn't bear it in the spooky basement anymore. The teacher went to the small restroom and stared at the broken mirror. She thought about getting a piece of the glass and cutting one of her veins, but she couldn't hurt herself, not like that. The beautiful hostage returned to the mattress and curled up. She tried to sleep, but her eyelids couldn't stay closed longer than few minutes because she was afraid that the baby mouse could come back. A couple of hours later, bright sunlight broke through the window and lit up the basement. It was morning. Ashley knew that the Creep would be back soon. The teacher wasn't wrong. Not long after sunup brought the light as if an angel were approaching, the sound of the creaking hardwood floor overhead broke the silence. The noises caught Ashley's attention, and she looked up. The footsteps from upstairs were moving from room to room as if someone was in a big rush. Creaks from opening doors disturbed her. Ashley looked at the staircase, which was right across from the cage, and her eyes flashed with great anticipation. She waited for the Creep. The teacher went to the restroom and pulled the sliding drapes. She unzipped the top of her tracksuit just enough to expose her impressive cleavage. She looked at the broken mirror and tried to fix her messed-up hair. The teacher had a plan. She had to look more presentable because it was time for breakfast.

A few minutes later, the door at the top of the stairs opened. The eerie sound of footsteps slowly descending the stairs quickened Ashley's heartbeat. She stared at the approaching figure. The man was dressed in the same black robe as he wore in the popular YouTube video where Ashley was involved. Also, he was wearing the same hacker mask with the ominous face. A weird-looking device was hooked on his belt. He used this to distort his voice. That was the person who Ashley called — *The Creep.*

"Morning!" Ashley greeted, using her pleasantly faked

voice. The man wearing the hacker mask approached the cage, opened a small slot in the door, and threw a sealed plastic bowl of lettuce, some chopped chicken, and a white dressing that looked more like sperm.

"Thanks! Where's my water?" Ashley asked, and the Creep tossed in a bottle of water. Ashley briskly grabbed the bottle of water and took a few gulps.

"When am I gonna hear your real voice? It's been…what… three months since you brought me here, and you haven't said much. Why? Are you scared of me?" the teacher asked in a low voice. She walked with an attitude to the bars. She made a pose as if she was a fashion model doing a shoot. The Creep took a few steps back. For some unknown reason, the villain kept his distance from the hostage.

"I'm not scared of you. Why would I be? You're my asset," the Creep replied. Ashley frowned. She didn't expect that kind of answer.

"So, you're the guy who thinks he is the master of the universe, huh? Tell me something, smarthead. Why are you keeping me here? Why don't you just kill me?"

"This is part of the plan," the Creep responded. Ashley rolled her eyes in frustration. She didn't like the conversation, but she needed information.

"That's part of your plan, huh? And what is your genius plan? To rape me and demand a ransom for my life? Is that what it's all about, smarthead?" Ashley kept using her voice in a sulky way which sounded annoying. She did it on purpose. The teacher wanted to entice the Creep and get him to talk more. Her idea wasn't bad.

Dimitry Salchev

"I can't tell you, sorry," the man behind the mask spoke with his fake voice. Ashley wanted to crack up. She had been kept in the cage for over three months, and the man who had kidnapped her was starting to sound like a virgin nerd. The whole idea amused her.

"You're so pathetic! Who are you anyway? A computer specialist who needs attention? What's your purpose? What's all this bullshit about?" Ashley kept asking question after question. She had been studying the man behind the mask, and it seemed he was innocuous.

"So, you want to know who I am. I don't have to give you any explanations. But you know what… I'll tell you anyway because soon you'll be deleted from human society," the Creep proclaimed.

"Go ahead, smarthead. I'm desperate to hear your story." Ashley declared. The man behind the mask had never heard the word "smarthead", but it was clear to him what it meant.

"Well, I'm the Hacker. The guy who does what is called— ransomware. What does that mean? Hear me out; I consider myself a *black-hat* type of hacker. What is a black-hat hacker? The Black hat hackers are those people who aren't bound by any ethics. So what do I do? I write codes and send them out to large American companies that are vulnerable to hacker attacks. I'm looking for operating systems that haven't been scrutinized before. I found some information by searching and understanding how sites are built up, or put together and how things work. Then I can change that process and take control of it. So ransomware is a computer attack that has been used for many years. Also, ransomware is like malware that gets on a particular system, encrypts all of the data, and then holds it as a hostage, demanding assets under a preferred currency. Once I take the money, I write some codes to decrypt the data and give it back to the company that has been hacked. Over the years, the ransomware techniques drastically increased because it turned out to be very remunerative for hackers, just like me. And I'm not talking about thousands of dollars; I'm talking about millions of U.S. dollars. Many governmental institutions seek help in better understanding the notion from equipped sources. These sources could only be the hackers," the Creep paused. He saw Ashley's bulging eyes and asked, "Do you get what I'm saying?" Ashley smiled from ear to ear. It looked like she was enjoying the conversation. She looked down at her feet and then back at the Creep.

"You may be surprised, but I do get what you are saying. My brother understands computers better than I speak English. I bet you and my brother could talk for hours. Wait a minute," Ashley paused and continued, "So that's why you kidnapped me— to get in touch with my brother?" The teacher asked an essential question. Then she waited for an answer.

"Listen, I have to go. I'll talk with you later," the man in the hacker mask declared and headed to the stairs.

"Wait! You didn't answer my question. Hey, come back here. I wasn't finished," Ashley protested, but it was too late. The Hacker climbed the stairs and turned off the light.

***

Ashley ran through the trees. She was in a remote area far from the city.

"I'm coming!" the Creep with the computerized voice screamed. Ashley stopped for a second and turned around to survey the man who just had spoken. She saw the man with the hacker mask approaching and holding a knife.

"Nooo!" Ashley shouted in terror and started running. She ran into a dense forest. It was dark, and the teacher had a hard time seeing which direction she could take.

"I'm coming," the Creep called. Ashley started running as fast as she could. For a moment, she thought that she had escaped from him because it was quiet around her. She stopped and took a deep breath. *Where is he? Did he quit chasin' me?* her inner voice whispered. Ashley surveyed the perimeter. There was no sign from the Creep.

"I'm coming. You can run, but you can't hide, bitch," the Creep yelled and sneaked out from a tree that was just a few feet away from her.

"Noo!" She exclaimed and started running again. The Creep seemed slow, but somehow he moved faster than her. It seemed as though the hacker was inside a computer game and using some codes to cheat by teleporting himself near her.

Ashley kept running, sprinting as if she was competing in the Olympic Games. *Faster! Run faster!* her inner voice commanded. Ashley wore the same tracksuit she had been wearing for weeks. Somehow her hair was tied in a bun. The teacher couldn't understand how that could be because she didn't have any hair ties. But there was no time to answer the question because she was running for her life.

"Help, help!" She screamed out loudly. The teacher hoped that someone would hear her voice and come to save her. As she ran through the forest, the trees seemed to move as if they were alive. After a few seconds of running, Ashley stopped.

"What the heck is that?" She hollered in great panic. Ashley couldn't run any further because a huge, gray-colored wall built from solid concrete was in front of her. There was no way she could climb over that obstacle. The wall was about eight feet high, and it looked long. Ashley tried to find her way out, but it seemed like there was no exit. *Oh my God! What am I going to do now?* her inner voice pleaded. Then she had an idea; she looked around and grabbed a tree limb. She needed a weapon. She had to fight for her life; there were no other choices. Her heart was racing because she was terrified. Her hands were shaking from the ominous feeling that something unpleasant was about to happen.

Ashley held the weapon, but she looked uncertain of what she was doing. She had never been in a fight before; she never had to because she was a benevolent and lovely person who always found a way to avoid physical violence. But at that moment, she had no choice.

"I'm here, bitch! HA-HA-HA. There is no way out," the Creep's voice echoed from somewhere, but she couldn't see him. The teacher looked around. *Where is he? Oh my God! How am I going to get out of this?* the voice in her head asked.

"Aaah!" Ashley screamed. Terror was written all over her face, as if she was living in the pages of a horror novel.

"There is no escape! HA-HA-HA," the Creep cackled. He loomed from somewhere and was just about ten feet from her. He wore the same black robe. His mask fit well on him; it looked like that was his actual face.

"I have a surprise for you!" the Creep announced with his computerized voice. Ashley had no idea what the villain had just said. Then, in just a few seconds, the Creep's body started shaking convulsively. Blood poured from his neck. The hacker turned away as if ashamed of what he was doing. His body transformed into something that Ashley had never been seen before. All of a sudden, the Creep's body started to tear apart. More blood streamed out of his body as if he'd been blown up by dynamite. Something much bigger came out of what was left of the Creep's body. It was a terrifying monster, seven feet tall, and covered in fur and had muscles bigger than Levan Saginashvili's. The creature then turned to Ashley and showed its face.

"Aaaah! Oh my God! What is this?" the teacher asked herself in utter shock. Even though she asked, Ashley knew what it was. It was a big-ass werewolf. The monster's eyes were furious, like an angry tiger, ready to attack at any second. The werewolf's muzzle was huge. It had long fangs and a nose from which dripped a nasty liquid such as Ashley had never seen before. Saliva drooled from its jaws as if the monster were preparing to eviscerate its prey. The werewolf growled like a rabid dog.

"Oh my God! Noo! Don't do anything! Please, don't hurt me! I didn't do anything wrong. Please!" Ashley begged, but it seemed the werewolf didn't understand English. The monster looked so big and scary that it seemed no human could survive him. Its gray fur was brisling as if it was angry at Ashley.

The creature stood on its hind feet like a human, but it was hunched over like an animal. The werewolf was repeatedly growling and walking toward her. *Oh my God! It's coming at me! What am I going to do?* her inner voice whispered in her head. The werewolf stepped slowly, but it seemed that it could move faster than lightning. As it approached, the werewolf opened its arms wide and continuously growled.

"No! Please, no! Nooo!" Ashley screamed hysterically.

***

Ashley woke up. There was no werewolf and no trees. The teacher was on the mattress in the spooky basement. *Oh my God! I must be dreaming!* Her inner voice declared. She was covered in sweat, as if she had just finished engaging wild intercourse. The hostage went to use the small restroom. After flushing the toilet, she splashed her face in the sink and looked at herself in the mirror.

Gee! I don't really feel pretty. My hair is such a mess! My eyes look like the eyes of a vampire. I need to get out of this house, but how? Think, Ashley. Think! the voice in her head said. The teacher contemplated the options she had. She thought about starting a fire that would activate the fire and smoke detector systems. This would bring the local fire department. The idea wasn't bad, but she had no way of starting a fire. Then another thought came into her head. The window on the left side of the cage was around 10 feet from her. The sunlight came through the window and fell on Ashley's ankles. The teacher had a brilliant idea. She rushed to the mirror and with her long nails tried to remove a small piece of the cracked glass. At first, she struggled vainly, but then she managed to detach a tiny piece of glass.

The size of that piece was around two inches, but it was big enough. Ashley kneeled on the floor and held the mirror up to the sunlight. She was signaling out the window using the heliograph method. Her hope was simple— to keep signaling until someone saw it. Ashley kneeled with the piece of mirror in her hand for about two hours, but no one seemed to recognize the subtle sign. The teacher knew that if she was patient, someone would eventually respond.

Ahh! My knee hurts! I'm going to have to take a short break, her inner voice spoke. The desperate hostage kept signaling until the sun sank behind the horizon. She put in a lot of effort, but there were no results. Let down by the unsuccessful endeavor, the teacher hopped onto the mattress and closed her moist eyes. She was tired and hungry. The Creep hadn't shown up throughout the day. But fifteen minutes later, steps made creaking noises from the floor above. *Speaking of the Devil, here he comes!* Ashley thought. In a little while, the Creep walked down the stairs. It seemed he was in a rush because his legs moved quickly. The villain approached the cage and left a sealed bowl of salad and a few Cheetos puffs for dessert. He also left a bottle of water.

"Here's some food," he said. His computerized voice resembled that of *Darth Vader*, the character from *Star Wars*. Hearing his creepy-sounding words, Ashley refused to answer. She was still curled up on the mattress. She was so scared of the Creep, the villain from her nightmares, that she didn't want to move from there. The flashback images from her nightmares disturbed her.

"Why don't you just kill me," the teacher mumbled in a low voice. The Creep froze when he heard Ashley's statement. He was silent. Ashley felt tormented and simultaneously disappointed. The teacher needed answers because she was confused.

"Why can't you answer my question? I think I deserve to know. You keep me here as a hostage, like an animal cooped up in a cage, and treat me like a piece of shit without any explanation. At least you can be decent and answer the simple question," the hostage demanded a response. She felt that she was entitled to have answers.

"It depends," the Creep answered. Ashley was flustered. She sat up on the mattress and surveyed the man responsible for her turmoil.

"Depends on what!"

"Depends on how obedient you are going to be. That's all I can say," the malicious man responded disdainfully. Ashley suddenly realized that the Creep was teasing her on purpose. Her facial expression rapidly changed. The teacher squinted and announced, "We know each other, don't we? You seem kind of familiar to me." All of a sudden, silence hovered over the basement. The Creep froze like a statue. He seemed shocked by her announcement.

"No, I have never seen you before," the Creep answered.

"Haven't you? Hmm... Are you sure? That's why you cover yourself with this black tablecloth and wear this stupid mask. You want to stay anonymous because you're scared I'll recognize you. Am I right? Oh, yes. I think this is exactly why you're playing your foolish games. Am I right?" Suddenly, the fear she always felt towards the Creep disappeared. The teacher was confident that she was onto something.

"Even if we do know each other, that doesn't mean I won't kill you," the Creep spoke. His computerized voice sounded insulted for some reason, and Ashley knew it.

"So we do know each other. You've just confirmed it," she declared.

"I didn't say that. Those are your words," with that said, the Creep turned around and walked to the stairs. He looked composed, but his rage was about to burst out.

"Hey, where are you going? Did you get the book I asked for?" Ashley had to yell because the man with the black robe and hacker mask was just about to take the stairs. The Creep turned around and asked, "What book?"

"*Blood Covenant* by Michael Franzese. You know the man who publicly quit the mob and lived," Ashley declared. The teacher was intrigued by this book. A colleague from school had recommended it, and she wanted to read it.

"Hold on!" the Creep said and climbed the stairs. Ashley had no clue what he was about to do. Less than five minutes later, the Creep returned and snuggled a hardcover book between the bars.

"Here!" the ominous voice of the Creep blurted out. Ashley grabbed the book and opened it.

"But that's not what I was asking for…this is a book about teaching computer terminologies," Ashely's words came with disappointment. Seemingly offended, the Creep blurted out.

"This is not a library. So shut your mouth!" His voice wasn't loud, but it clearly said what he meant. Ashley had pushed some buttons and made the man upset about something trifling. The Creep left the house almost immediately. Ashley opened the book and started reading. After an hour, she grew tired. She couldn't keep her eyes open and put the book down. The teacher snuggled under the sheets of the mattress and closed her eyes. *Who is this guy? Why do I have the feeling that I know him? Think Ashley! Think! Who is the man behind this Hacker Mask? And why does he keep me here as a hostage? Does he want to kill me?* The teacher sank into deep thoughts. Her thoughts transformed into questions, but she couldn't come up with a straight answer. Who could be the man behind the mask? That was the question that many asked themselves.

12

Bob McCarthur looked nervously at his smartphone. The clock on the screen showed 5:40 p.m. The detective was at the upper level at O'Hare. He had just flown back from Dallas, Texas. He had spent two nights with Jeremy his son on Thanksgiving. Jeremy would never come to Chi-Town, so McCarthur had to take the plane. The detective couldn't stay longer in Texas. He had to be in Chicago by Friday, the day after the holiday. *Where is he, dammit?* his inner voice whispered. The detective was waiting for an Uber driver at Terminal 2, Door E. He anxiously looked at the Uber app to track the driver's location. The driver's icon on the app was going in weird directions as if it was circling around the airport. The detective called the Uber driver to acknowledge his location. The driver spoke a few words in a foreign language and hung up the phone. Then the app notified McCarthur that the driver had canceled the ride.

"Ah! Dammit!" McCarthur mumbled under his breath. He thought about calling Lisa Fernandez, but then he recalled that she was on vacation in Wisconsin with her family. McCarthur had no choice; he requested another Uber driver. The second driver came unexpectedly fast. This driver operated a white Toyota Sienna model 2020. The car was big and spacious, but that didn't matter because McCarthur had only one carry-on bag. The Uber driver looked posh, dressed in a black fedora as if he was ready to attend a Christmas party organized by a big corporation. Bob was amazed at how the Uber driver was dressed. He was an Asian-American man in his early forties. He was also easygoing with a friendly demeanor. Bob had an engaging conversation with the Uber driver throughout the ride. Half an hour later, the white Sienna parked on Lincoln Street where Bob lived. The detective took his luggage and waved goodbye to the Uber driver. His legs swiftly climbed the stairs to his condo. He unlocked the door, and his jaw gaped. His condo looked immaculate. Everything inside was glistening. The furniture gleamed as if were brand new. Every single room was pristine. Maria, the housekeeper, had cleaned the apartment while Bob McCarthur was in Dallas. The Hispanic lady had done a phenomenal job, and the Texan resolved to acknowledge her effort by giving her a bonus. The clean apartment didn't stay that way for long. The detective searched around, throwing clothes and items everywhere. He then went to the living room and sat on the couch. He opened his laptop and started punching the keyboard. His fingers moved crazily fast. Weird noises were buzzing from the printer that Bob was using. After an hour of intense work, Bob went to the printer and collected the pages from the printing machine. The printer worked so hard that it looked like it would break at any minute. The Texan hung a corkboard on the wall in his living room. On the board, he pinned the printed images of every victim in the cold case, including Ashley's photo. Also, there were many other printed pages with detailed information about every dead person. Bob stared at the board and contemplated for a second. He ran his hand through his curly blond hair and breathed heavily. *There must be some connection between Jack Hammer, Kimberly Shimmers, Josh Rodriguez, Monica Shingles, David Sparrow, and of course, Ashley Packer*, the voice in his head said. Then the Texan raised his curved eyebrows. His eyes were blinking rapidly. His facial expression changed to a surprised man who had just met Jesus.

"The murderer knew all the victims!" McCarthur said out loud. *But who could be that person? Who could know all of the murdered people?* The detective looked around as if he was searching for something. His gut feeling was telling him something essential. Then the burly Texan sat on the couch and started punching the keyboard of his laptop. The printer started spitting out more printed pages. It looked like the printer was vomiting because the printed pages were coming out of the machine madly. The detective took all the pages and started thumbing through each one. Bob moved so fast that sweat started dripping from his forehead. He was so focused on the paperwork that he lost all track of time. The sun disappeared from the horizon as if it would never shine again. Bob flicked the light switch and continued reading the printed pages. At 9:00 p.m., the detective took his eyes off the pages. He was exhausted from reading for several hours straight without once using the restroom. The Texan yawned as he had not slept for days. His red eyes could barely stay open. He stood up and walked around the condo. His belly was making weird noises because he hadn't eaten for the past couple of hours. Bob took his smartphone and opened the DoorDash app. He ordered food from an Indian restaurant that had good reviews on Google. The delivery took longer than he expected. McCarthur didn't know that most of the restaurants were extremely busy on Fridays, and deliveries usually took longer. Around 10:00 p.m., someone knocked on the door of his apartment.

"I'm coming!" the Texan shouted and looked for his wallet. He then opened the door, and a twenty-year-old boy smiled at him while handling a brown paper bag. The boy was of Mexican descent. His body was so scrawny that he looked like a heroin addict who didn't eat any food because he was saving his money to buy drugs. McCarthur took the brown paper bag and stretched his arm, handing over a $5 gratuity.

"That's your tip," the detective declared.

"Gracias, señor," the boy spoke quietly and bowed to Bob as if he was his royal master. McCarthur flashed his crooked smile and closed the door. The detective was starving so badly that he ignored anything else and focused on the Indian food. He took the items from the brown paper bag and surveyed what was inside. The bag was filled with butter chicken, lemon rice, Kachumber salad, baked potato wedges, Cucumber raita, and Naan. *Where are the utensils? They never put them in, dammit,* the voice in his head spoke. The food was a little too much for a single person, but Bob was a big man, and he was hungry. The Indian cuisine was delicious, and the detective was happy with his choice. He devoured everything in just a few minutes. After he had finished, he cleaned the coffee table on which he had eaten his dinner and went back to reading the files. The Texan kept reading for a few hours more. At half past midnight, he stopped the research process and took a deep breath. It was ominously quiet in his room. The big Texan went to the bathroom and brushed his teeth. He was so tired that taking a shower seemed too much for the night. *Tomorrow, I'll do some work! I need more answers. Yes! I know exactly who can help me,* his inner voice whispered. McCarthur was thinking about work, but he should have been relaxing because Thanksgiving weekend was supposed to be his vacation. However, the Texan was determent to resolve the case that he and his partner had been working on for months. His gut feeling kept pushing him to work even when he was off duty. The Texan knew that he was one step closer to unraveling the mystery. At around 2:00 a.m., Bob crashed on his couch. He laid there as motionless as if someone had just put a bullet in his head.

***

The following day Saturday, November 26th, Bob aroused from his nap and jumped up from his couch. He felt beat up because the couch wasn't comfortable to sleep on it. He moved slowly, like a man struggling with ninety percent heart blockage. McCarthur went to the bathroom and sat on the toilet. He looked like a chicken that was about to lay an egg. His number two's were so big and long that Bob got scared at what he saw in the toilet. *Gross!* his inner voice rattled off. Bob flushed the toilet and looked in the mirror. His eyes bulged as if he had awoken from a five-day coma. *Why am I sleeping on the couch when I have a bed? Ah, whatever. Who cares? I need to get ready. C'mon, old man! Hurry up,* the voice in his head commanded him as if Police Commissioner was talking. Despite his slow movements, McCarthur got dressed incredibly fast. He looked dapper; he wore a black Guess duffle coat, a gray shirt with black and red stripes, and some ordinary silver khakis. His curly blond hair looked neat in spite of the fact that he hadn't been to a barbershop since October. McCarthur requested an Uber. The driver showed up in a few minutes. Bob hopped into the Uber vehicle, which was a blue Toyota Camry, and the driver asked, "Hello, sir. Your name is Robert, right?" Bob just nodded without saying a word. His mind was too busy to chat with the Uber driver. The ride took about twenty-five minutes. The blue Camry stopped at Northwest highway, and the detective jumped out. He walked a few feet and approached the building where David Sparrow had lived. The clock on his smartphone showed 10:30 a.m. It was time for some real detective work. Bob was just about to call the landlord to get the access code for the building, when a Hispanic family on their way out let him in. He walked into the corridor and knocked on the door of the Polish lady who lived across from David's apartment.

"Who is it?" Justyna Lavinsky asked in her Polish accent.

"Detective Robert McCarthur, ma'am. I need to ask you a few questions. I just need some information. That's all. Is it a good time for you to have a quick chat? It won't take long."

"How did you know that I would be here? Are you spying on me?" the Polish woman asked. She was suspicious because no one ever came to visit her. She didn't have time for friends because of her work schedule.

"No, ma'am. I remember the last time we spoke you mentioned that you are off on Saturdays, so I was hoping it would be fine if I just stopped by. May I come in?" Bob asked politely. He knew that people could be terrified if someone knocked on their doors unexpectedly, but he didn't have a choice.

"Give me a second!" the Polish lady shouted. She walked into her bedroom and changed her clothes. Then she checked her face in the mirror. She wanted to make sure that her European face looked pretty. The detective waited in the corridor for a little longer than five minutes. *What the heck is she doing out there?* He was wondering. Patience wasn't his strong suit. A few mutes later, the door opened, and Justyna popped up. She smiled at Bob with her yellowish teeth. The Polish lady looked spiffy as if she was going on a date. She wore an expensive pink, long-sleeved shirt and black pants that looked fine on her. The detective surveyed the Polish lady and smiled back at her.

"I apologize for interrupting you. Usually, I don't show up like this without calling," the detective said.

"That's fine. Please, come in. Pay no attention to the apartment. It's a mess. I'll have to clean it today," Lavinsky declared. McCarthur looked around. The apartment looked neat and squeaky clean as if a team of four people had just finished cleaning.

"Are you kidding? You should look at my apartment. It's like a spoiled pop star is living there," the Texan replied. He had a remarkable dry sense of humor.

Justyna laughed out loud. Her laugh sounded harsh and awkward, but that didn't bother the detective. "You gotta take off your shoes. I'll give you slippers," the Polish lady proclaimed, and Bob obediently did what he was told. "Here! Put these on and come with me," Lavinsky said sulkily, but she didn't have any bad intentions. It was just the way she talked.

"Meow, meow!" Two cats briskly approached the detective. The cats meowed as if they were begging for food.

"This is Nancy, and the white one over there is Bamby. They are two lovely girls, and I love them so much. Girls, say "hi" to the man." Justyna talked to her cats as if they might respond in English. McCarthur waved at the cats. He felt like an idiot, but he was just being polite.

"Sit here! Would you like coffee or tea? I think I have apple juice too," Lavinsky offered. At first, her attitude seemed grumpy, but that was part of her Polish hospitality. In fact, Justyna was a lovely lady. She was an outgoing person, despite her deadpan face that looked like she would start bitching about something petty.

"I'm good, thank you," the detective refused kindly. The Polish lady frowned at him. She didn't understand his answer.

"So, you want something, or you don't?"

"No, thanks," the big man said and continued, "Can you describe the guy who visited David Sparrow? Do you know what I'm sayin'," Bob spoke colloquially, hoping it would put Lavinksy more at ease.

"Aaa, yeah. I know what you mean. The boy was young... in his early twenties. He was fat. I mean not fat, but... what is right word..."

"Overweight?" McCarthur suggested.

"Yes! I would say so. He was around 6'1" tall. His hair was blond and like... what is the right word. Hold on. I'll show you what his hair looked like," Justyna said. She took her smartphone and started typing something. Nancy and Bamby kept meowing as if they were saying something vital.

"Shush! Quiet, girls. Mama is busy now. Here! His hair looked like this," the Polish lady said and showed the screen to McCarthur. She almost shoved her phone at his face.

"Oh, I see. Okay!" he cried out. His eyes sparkled. The Texan bit his lip and showed his traditional crooked smile. He looked surprised and simultaneously disappointed. The Polish lady sensed that something important had just happened and asked, "Is everything okay?"

"Oh, yes! Absolutely," the detective responded politely. Lavinsky grinned, but she felt awkward. "Would you like to try my cake? It's made from a Polish recipe. It's really good," the lady offered.

"No, thanks. Do you know what time it is?" Bob asked. He could look at his smartphone, but something preoccupied his mind.

"It's almost 11 a.m.," the Polish lady replied. Then McCarthur started coughing badly. He sounded like he might choke.

"Hey! Are you okay?" Justyna asked. The Texan needed a second to respond because he was breathless. He was holding his stomach because he struggled with a lot of pain.

"Yeah. I'm fine."

Are you sure? You don't look okay." The Polish lady showed sympathy because she liked McCarthur. The detective took a deep breath. After a few seconds, he proclaimed.

"Ma'am, thank you for your time. I gotta go. I'm late for a meeting," Bob lied. He did it on purpose because the Polish lady would start asking more questions, and he had no time for answers; it was time for actions. The detective rose on his feet and went to the front door. Bamby and Nancy were meowing as if they were saying *bye,* but actually, they were hungry. Justyna Lavinsky opened the door, and the Texan immediately slid out. He walked fast through the corridor. McCarthur left the building as fast as if he was being chased by a dozen hoodrats. He took out his smartphone and made a call.

13

At 10:30 a.m., while McCarthur was still talking with Justyna Lavinsky, Tom Packer was working in his garage. The garage was a complete mess. The electrician had promised Jennifer to clean it up and organize things. The pile in the garage was the subject of their heated discussions for months, and Tom had finally made the time to clean it. Jennifer was doubtful. She preferred to check on him in person. "Tom, how long will it take you to clean the entire garage?" she asked, standing at the threshold of the door. Tom stopped his endeavors and turned around. He was sweating because he was working hard.

"I'm not sure, honey. It may take some time. I have to sweep the floor and organize the shelves. Why are you asking?"

Tom countered. He was scratching his bald head— a trait that Jennifer found annoying.

"I also need you to hang the Christmas lights. It's 45 degrees outside. Soon it will start getting colder," Mrs. Packer declared. Her phone rang, and it disturbed her.

"Hold on! I gotta take the phone call," Jennifer said. Tom watched how his wife disappeared into the house. *Who is she talking with? Well, I better get back to work before she gets mad.* Mr. Packer started sweeping the floor. He was so focused that he didn't notice the silhouette behind him. Something was slowly approaching. The electrician stared at the floor as if he was searching for something important. Then a baseball bat hit the back of his head, and the electrician immediately collapsed on the ground. Blood covered his head. Tom was unconscious. He was still alive, but he looked like a dead man. The person who attacked Mr. Packer moved with incredible speed and the same time was as silent as a cat. The assailant lifted Tom onto an old chair and tied his hands and legs. He then wrapped duct tape around Tom's mouth. The electrician sat on the chair like a rat captured by the mafia. Tom's head lay tilted on one of his shoulders and he remained motionless.

Jennifer finished the phone call and started wiping the countertop in the kitchen. She was a clean freak. Everything in her house had to look immaculate. She used an expensive spray to keep the countertop in order. Just like her husband, Jennifer was focused on cleaning. The dishwasher was making loud noises because it was working at full speed. Jennifer didn't realize that someone was approaching from behind. The noisy dishwasher gave the assailant a perfect chance to make his move. Then, BANG! Jennifer was floored in a second. Unlike Tom, she remained conscious, but she could barely move. Vertigo shook her head as if she had drunk a whole bottle of vodka.

"Aaaah!" Jennifer moaned in tears. She was hit with the same baseball bat that knocked out her husband.

"Don't kill me! Please, don't kill me!" Jennifer begged. She couldn't see her assailant because her face was pressing against the tiles. Mrs. Packer was hurt badly. She could feel how the blood was flowing from her head. Her hands were trembling from the terror she felt.

"Please, don't kill me! Take whatever you want just don't kill me!" Jennifer talked hysterically. There was no answer as if she was talking to herself. Silent, the assailant grabbed both of her hands and tied them behind her back. He then tied her legs together.

"Please, don't kill me! Please, don't kill me! Jennifer screamed in a panic.

"Shut up, bitch!" the voice of the assaulter grumbled. Jennifer's eyes widened. She knew that voice, although she was so scared that she couldn't say a word. The man who attacked Jennifer lifted her and carried her to the bathroom on the first floor. The man briskly moved around as if he was doing drills in the military. Jennifer was tossed into the bathtub like a fish. She looked at the assaulter and couldn't believe her eyes.

"Brendan! What the fuck! Are you insane? Untie me for Christ's sake! I'm your mother. What the hell are you doing?" Brendan was surprised. Even though he wore a balaclava, his mother still recognized him.

"Shut up, bitch! Mother, huh? What kind of mother are you? Berating me since I've known my name!

"Brendan, what are talking about? I love you! You're my son! Untie me! What do you want from me?" Jennifer kept spilling words hysterically.

"Shut up! I said! I don't need your excuses!" Brendan commanded. His eyes were the eyes of an insane killer.

"Brendan! Listen to me carefully. Don't do anything stupid. Your father will be very pissed," Mrs. Packer said. She was wiggling in the bathtub like a catfish. Brendan smiled hellishly.

"Don't worry about him. He is as silent as a corpse," the computer genius said.

"What are you talking about? Did you kill your father?"

"Shut up, bitch!" Brendan said and turned on the water. The bathtub was filling with cold water.

"No! It's cold. Brendan! Don't do it, please! We can work this out! Think for a second! I'm your mom! Brendan!" Jennifer was screaming, and that annoyed her son.

"Shut up! I said!" the cybersecurity guy piped up. He was furious.

"Brendan! Hear me out! The detective will be here soon. He called me earlier and asked to come over. He had something important to tell me but he didn't give any…details…" Jennifer stopped before finishing her sentence. She then realized that she had made a foolish mistake by revealing this information. Brendan's face changed. He looked happy.

"Thank you, mom! I love you."

"Brendan! No! Brendan…" Jennifer couldn't talk anymore. Her son put duct tape on her mouth because she was talking too much. The cold water almost covered her body. Then Brendan stopped the water, kissed his mother on her forehead, and left the bathroom, locking the door as he closed it. The insane assailant looked around. He needed something important.

***

Bob McCarthur was in an Uber vehicle. The driver was a Ukrainian guy who acted sullen, as if he had been insulted. His driving skills were impressive and he deserved a tip. The Uber driver headed south from Park Ridge to Norridge, where Tom and Jennifer lived. McCarthur looked at the clock on his smartphone. It was around 11:15 a.m. He also checked Google Maps; the GPS on his phone showed 10 minutes ETA. Bob was pondering how to tell Mrs. Packer what he had just found out. He had called Jennifer and asked if he could stop by her house and chat with her. The detective thought it would be inappropriate to reveal the reason why he needed to talk with Ashley's mother over the phone, so he wanted to speak with her in person. Mrs. Packer had agreed to talk with the detective, but Bob was uncertain of what he was doing. He had never had to do something like this before. How could he tell Jennifer that her son could be implicated in a crime that was connected to her daughter? This theory sounded ridiculous. The Texan was carefully choosing his words for the speech that he was about to give. As a parent, he felt foolish coming to the Packer's house to throw accusations about their son. McCarthur just wanted to tell Jennifer the facts. However, any parent would be pissed if a cop knocked on their door and started accusing their child of a brutal crime. Bob didn't want to sound like an asshole. That was why he chose his words carefully and hoped that he would sound more like a thorough professional who had some serious reasons to think that Brendan might be involved in a murder. *I know that the Polish lady is telling the truth. But that wouldn't be enough,* he thought.

"Here, boss!" the Ukrainian driver said respectfully. Bob handed him a five-dollar tip and jumped out of the vehicle. The sun's rays shone on the luxurious house where Tom and Jennifer lived. Bob looked around, making sure that no one was watching him. The Texan was nervous. Each step he took made him feel more awkward. The detective deliberately surveyed the house. *Am I doing the right thing? Or maybe I'm not. I guess there's only one way to find out,* his inner voice spoke.

"Aaaah, dammit!" the Texan cried out. Shortness of breath bothered him. As he walked up to the house, he felt dizzy. Although, the pain he had didn't deter him. *Come on! You old fart! Move your fat ass!* his inner voice encouraged him.

McCarthur walked to the main door and rang the bell. The white front door seemed new as if Tom had just put it in. The bell was one of those Nest hubs that had a camera on it. For a moment, Bob thought about his house in Dallas. It was a lovely house, and he took care of it for the sheer joy. After a few seconds of daydreaming, Bob rejected the memories from the past and focused on work. He rang the bell again because no one was answering. And again, no one was responding. *That's weird! I spoke with Jennifer just thirty minutes ago! She said that is okay to swing by. Why is no one opening the door?* McCarthur was confused. *Maybe the bell is not working,* he thought and started knocking on the door. The detective had no idea what had already happened after he finished the phone call with Jennifer. He took his smartphone and dialed her. The following second, he could feel the barrel of a gun digging into his spine.

"Get inside. The door is open!" a man quietly said from behind. The detective did what the voice told him. His gut feeling already knew whose voice it was. *What now?* McCarthur's inner voice asked.

***

"Brendan, let's talk about it!" Bob offered while turning the doorknob. There was no response, and McCarthur set foot inside the house. The young man kept the pistol jammed into Bob's back. Brendan swung the door shut without looking away from the detective. He pointed the silenced gun at the detective's head.

"Brendan! Where are your parents?" McCarthur asked. That was a dumb question because he could connect the dots and figure out what had happened.

"Brendan…"

"Shut your mouth, bitch!" the hacker hectored sulkily. He then patted the detective down and found a 9 millimeter. He took it and stepped a few feet from the detective to keep a safe distance.

"Brendan, we don't need to go that far. You know what exactly I am talking about."

"Put your hands up so I can see them," Brendan commanded. He pulled off the balaclava and put it into his pocket. He then took Bob's smartphone and smashed it on the floor. The boy looked angry and bitter, like a man who had lost all of his money in a poker game.

"Everything is all set. Let's roll," the hacker said

"Huh? Where are we going?"

"We are goin' for a ride."

"A ride? Where?" The Texan was flummoxed.

"You'll see. I think you have to meet a friend since you're already snooping around with your big nose. Let's go. I don't have the entire day to waste," the cybersecurity guy commanded.

"Brendan, think for a second. You're not gonna get away with this. The police are not far from here. They will shoot you without hesitation," Bob bluffed. He tried to put doubt into Brendan's head, but his attempt failed.

"Shut up! You think my MS-DOS is not functioning?" Brendan piped up.

"MS...what?"

"I don't have time to explain. Here's the modus operandi: we are going outside slowly. You'll casually take the driver's seat, and I'll sit behind you. Don't move too fast, and don't forget that the gun is pointed constantly at you. You'll keep it low profile. Got it?" the hacker finished his monologue.

"Yeah, I see what you're saying," the Texan replied. He could jump and take the gun from Brendan's hands, but his gut feeling was telling him that the hacker would make a mistake. In a minute, both went outside by the garage.

"The Ford Fusion?" Bob questioned, and Brendan nodded. The hacker wore a hoody with a blue jacket. He hid the gun in his sleeve; it was a very ingenious trick. He did it on purpose because no one was supposed to see him.

"Wait a minute! Am I driving?" McCarthur asked.

"Of course! Who do you think is driving? Jimmy Hoffa! Let's go. Jump in the car," the hacker gave orders, and McCarthur followed his instructions. Both men got into the blue Ford Fusion, and McCarthur fired up the engine.

"Take East River Road and then make a left on Lawrence Avenue," the hacker commanded. He was right behind the driver's seat because he knew that from there, Bob wouldn't be able to disarm him.

"Brendan, listen to me. The cops will be behind us in a minute. Let's talk. That's all I'm asking for."

"Is that so? Now you're doing me favors? You think that you're making me feel good with your words? Cut the crap. I'm not stupid. If that were true, the cops would have been here already. You weren't sure that I might be the one you were looking for. You just came to speak with my mother. You think I don't know that, huh? You dumb fuck! Mr. Policeman." Brendan sounded like a sarcastic douchebag. Robert remained speechless.

The kid is clever. He is a frigging genius. What am I going to do? I must find out what his plan is, the detective thought.

"How did you find out about me? Who told you?" Brendan asked.

"My informer told me that you'd been hanging out with David Sparrow. The rest wasn't that hard to figure.

"Who is your informer?"

"I can't tell you that. A-aa... Are we going straight?" Bob asked for directions.

"Make a left on River Road and then another left on Irving Park," Brendan said. McCarthur didn't know the area because he worked mostly in Chicago.

The blue Ford Fusion approached a cul-de-sac and parked on the driveway of an old house. The building looked rundown as if it was a drug den. The windows were covered with plywood. The front porch was rotting. The entire house looked dark as if Dracula lived there. The haunted house looked like nothing was functioning, but in fact most of the appliances worked perfectly fine. Both men jumped out of the car.

"Come on! The door is open!" Brendan snapped urging the detective to walk faster. Bob set foot on the stoop. As he was walking on the porch, he had the feeling that at any second his foot might sink into it. With each step, the floorboards creaked. Bob opened the front door and surveyed the first floor. The living room was well-furnished and had a TV set. There was a bunch of suitcases on the couch.

"Are you flying somewhere?" the detective asked.

"Shut up, bitch! Here, this door," the hacker pointed out a door to the left. Bob had a bazillion questions, but he decided to keep his mouth shut, at least for the moment. The detective opened the door and felt for a light switch. It was remarkable that the lights were working in this rickety house.

Ashley was curled up on her mattress. Hearing unusual

noises, she sat up and watched as two men were walking down the stairs. *Gee! What's going on! Who are these people? Wait what? Brendan! Is that Brendan? Oh my God, Brendan just busted the Creep! Yay! Hold on! Wait a second! No! That cannot be true! The unknown man couldn't be the Creep. He's too big,"* the teacher thought.

"Brendan, what's going on? Who is this man?" she asked. Her brother didn't seem to pay attention to her question. He unlocked her cage.

"Get inside!" Brendan said to McCarthur, and the detective stepped into the cage where Ashley had been locked for the past few months.

"Who are you?" Ashley asked Bob. "Brendan! What are you doing? Put that gun down. Brendan!" Ashley kept shouting to her brother without understanding the situation. She was confused. She would never have expected to see her brother walk into the basement with a gun in his hand. Her eyes were wide with puzzlement.

"Brendan!" Ashley yelled at her brother.

"Shut up, bitch!" Brendan yelled back at her. His voice was sulky, like a man in a bad mood. Brendan's behavior made Ashley speechless. She couldn't comprehend why her brother was here, speaking to her like this.

"I'll leave you two birds to chirp. I gotta go upstairs," Brendan said, and locked the cage. He then speed walked up the stairs.

"Who are you?" Ashley repeated her question and stepped back because she was scared of Bob. He looked big, and that intimidated the teacher.

"Ashley, you may not believe it, but I am the detective who has been searching for you since July. My name is Robert McCarthur, but you can call me just Bob," the detective declared. Ashley shook her head no. She thought he was lying.

"You're right. I don't believe you. And what's up with my brother? Why is he acting like that?" Ashley asked. She was disappointed and simultaneously confused. The teacher had never seen her brother acting so aggressively.

"Ashley, I know you're shocked, and that's absolutely normal. I'd love to show you my badge, but your brother took it from me. I hate to say it, but I think your brother is a murderer.

"Noo! It cannot be. My brother is not the Creep. Brendan wouldn't kill an ant. No way. You gotta come up with something else. I'm not buying it. No," the teacher cried out.

"Who's the Creep?" the detective asked.

"That's the guy who wears the black robe and this stupid mask!"

"I see. I think your brother is the guy you call— the Creep."

"No! No way! Brendan cannot be the Creep!" Ashley said.

"Okay. How did you end up here?" McCarthur asked. That was the question he had been asking himself a bazillion times already.

"Well, on the fourth of July, I spoke with my mom around noon. I had to stop by Mariano's, and then I took an Uber to a friend's place."

"What was his name?"

"Jack Hammer. Why, do you know him?" the teacher asked, and Bob nodded.

"Anyway, so Jack needed my opinion on his first book.

He was working on a story about zombies. I graduated with an English major, and I love writing, so I promised Jack I'd stop by and check his draft. Jack is one of my best friends. I've known him since grade school, he is the only guy who has never wanted sex from me. Anyway, at 8:30 p.m. I left Jack's apartment and called an Uber because I was supposed to be at my parents' house to celebrate the holiday. I had been waiting for the Uber for about 10 minutes. I wondered why it took so long, but then I remembered it was the 4th of July. So I waited a little more, and finally a black Toyota Camry with one of those Uber light signs approached. I jumped in the car, but the driver was a little weird."

"What do you mean by *weird*?" the detective asked.

"Well, his voice sounded as if he was faking it. Anyway, I asked him if he had the correct address, and he confirmed it. I remember that the driver covered his face on purpose. He wore a mask for COVID-19, sunglasses, and had a hoody. There was no way I could identify him," Ashley said and stopped for a second.

"Then what happened," McCarthur asked. He was deeply focused on Ashley's story.

"Well, the ride took a little longer than usual. I wasn't paying attention because I was watching Dave Chappelle on Netflix on my smartphone. Then suddenly the car stopped. I was like, *why are we stopping*? I asked the driver the same question, and he said that he needed to check the tire. He jumped out of the vehicle and opened the trunk. I looked around and realized that we were on Lawrence Avenue between East River Road and River Road. Right by Robinson Woods, between

Schiller Park and Norridge. I asked myself, *why is the car west of Lawrence?* My parents' house was on the east side. It didn't make any sense because we came from the east side. So I looked back to check on the driver. There was a small gap by the opened trunk, and I could see what he was doing. Then I saw that he had a gun. I got panicked and immediately jumped out of the car and started running towards the trees. It was already getting dark. I shouted for help, but people were shooting fireworks, so it was impossible anyone to hear me. I was so terrified. I didn't know what to do," Ashley stopped her monologue and started crying.

"Okay, but why you didn't call 911?"

"Well, as I was running, I realized my phone wasn't on me. I must have left it in the car. I was terrified. I was trying to escape, but the man was chasing me. I remember that I stumbled and fell to the ground. I hit my knee badly. Then as I was trying to get to my feet, someone hit me in the back of the head with some object. Next thing I knew, I found myself here in this cage. I'm so ignorant," Ashley said and started weeping. Bob opened his arms and hugged her as if he was her father.

"It's okay, dear. You didn't do anything wrong. You were attacked by a psycho," he consoled the teacher. Ashley snuggled in Bob's arms and hugged him back.

"Ashley, do you remember the last person with whom you spoke before the kidnapping?"

Ashley's eyes widened as if she saw the devil. She realized the essential fact that could explain the confusing situation. She looked straight into Bob's eyes and said, "Brendan! I texted him before jumping into the fake Uber. He knew where I was. I told him that I would swing by my friend Jack and that at around 8:00 p.m., I would be heading to Norridge. Oh my God! BRENDAN IS THE CREEP!" Ashley blurted out. She was stunned by her brother's deeds.

"It's okay, honey. It's okay," the Texan kept reiterating the expression—*It's okay*. Although he had no idea how they would find their way out of this predicament.

"How are we gonna get out of here?" The teacher asked the question that Bob had been asking himself.

"I am not sure, but don't worry; I'll come up with something," the Texan replied. He sounded positive, but she was doubtful. The door opened, and footsteps interrupted their conversation. Brendan was holding a 9 millimeter pistol.

"Brendan, what is wrong with you? Why are you doing this?" Ashley asked. She couldn't be quiet. She had too many questions.

"I'll tell you that later. First of all, I need to kryptonite this cop," Brendan replied. He was pointing the gun at McCarthur. Bob looked a little surprised. He was caught off guard, but he had a plan.

"Brendan, before killing me, why don't you tell your sister what you did to Jack Hammer and the rest?" the Texan suggested. It was the perfect time to ask this essential question.

"Yeah, Brendan! What did you do to my friend Jack? Tell me! I think I deserve to know," Ashley questioned. Her words came quickly because she was pissed. Brendan looked straight into his sister's eyes and smiled hellishly. He looked fierce.

"I guess I can tell you the story before I blow this place

out. Ashley, remember when you texted me that you were coming to our house?" Brendan questioned.

"Yes, I told you I was takin' an Uber, and I would be there in half an hour," Ashley replied without hesitation.

"Guess what! I was the guy who drove you that night. I was the Uber driver. And the funny thing was that it was easy to rent an Uber car for the night.

"You little dipshit! Why did you do that? Ashley asked.

"Hear me out! I hate when people interrupt me. So I had to stop the car on Lawrence. I needed to get my gun from the trunk, but then you ran out off into the trees. The moment I was about to shoot, you fell on the ground. That gave me some time to get closer. However, you got back on your feet and started running again. You didn't go far because you stumbled and hit your knee. As I got closer, you screamed hysterically, so I had to hit you with my baseball bat to knock you out. You were unconscious, and that made it easy for me to bring you here. The streets were abandoned because everyone was celebrating the 4th. Anyway, it wasn't difficult to carry you in up here, to this basement. Let me emphasize. I own this this dump. Why? Buying property was an essential part of my plan. I did my research, and I bought it last March. The price was reasonable, and I took the chance…"

"Then what did you do?" Ashley interrupted Brendan, and he shot back "Don't interrupt me, bitch! Augh! I hate that, and you know it! Anyway, where was I? Ah, yeah! So after I put you here, I had to return to our parent's house. Mom and Dad started asking where you were. They called the cops, and two officers stopped by our home to speak with us. The timing was fine. No one suspected me of anything. However, I had to get rid of your friend, Jack Hammer because he was the last person who saw you, and he knew me. So, I texted him and told him that I needed to speak with him. He agreed, and I came to his apartment. I bought a bottle of whiskey, and we shared a drink. Jack asked me why I was wearing gloves, and I told him that I had burned my hands on the stove. Fucking idiot. He believed it. Anyway, I put poison in his drink and gave it to him. A few minutes later, Jack told me that he didn't feel good, and I put him on his bed. I told him that I had called the ambulance. I lied, and he believed it. I took his phone and left his apartment. I assume he was dead after an hour or so. Then your roommate, Kimberly Shimmers, started to bother me on Instagram. I had no choice. One night, I went to speak with her. I told her that I needed to discuss something important with her, and she let me into her apartment. We talked a bit, and then I stabbed her a few times. Then, I wrote a suicide note to make it look like an accident. Then I stole her smartphone and took off," Brendan finished his speech.

"What! You bastard! Brendan, you are a sick maniac!" Ashley screamed. She was mortified, screaming and crying emotionally. She hadn't known about her roommate's death or about Jack Hammer's murder. The teacher moaned like a puppy that had just been hit by a car.

"Did you use gloves?" McCarthur asked.

"Of course! What do you think? That I'll leave you my fingerprints, huh? You dumb fuck. Do you think I am stupid, huh? Whatever. Then I had to make it a little more interesting because the police could suspect me. I had to wear this hacker mask and the black robe. I brought a pricy camera, shot a video with my sister, and posted it on YouTube. I wrote some codes and made it look like the video was uploaded from Bulgaria. It was a good way to confuse the cops. And, of course, my lover, Josh was about to make a big mistake," Brendan declared. He stopped for a second.

"What? What are you talking about? What do you mean by saying— *your lover*?" Ashley grilled. The teacher was still in tears, but after she heard the name of her fiancé, she became furious.

"Yes, that's right, Sis. Josh and I had a secret relationship. We started seeing each other in January 2022. We wanted to live together, but first, I had to get rid of you."

"Oh, my God! You've got to be kidding me! Josh is not gay! We were supposed to get married, remember? Brendan, why you're lying to me? Please, tell me the truth!" Ashley begged her brother. She was on the verge of having a panic attack. She wanted to scream out loud because the pain in her heart was intolerable.

"Josh was bisexual, not gay. I'm gay. I like men, got it! Ashley, I'm telling you the truth. Josh and I were supposed to move to Greece and live there, but he fucked it up. He said that the police were bothering him and blah-blah-blah. I got sick and tired of him. At first, I loved him, but then he became obnoxious and annoying. Josh knew where you were, and he was about to rat to the police, and I had no other choice. I had to get rid of him."

"Nah! It cannot be true! Are you kidding me! Are you

for real? Josh loved me! He was buying me gifts and took care of me when I needed him. Brendan, you're a fucking psycho. How could you do this to me? What have I done to treat me like this? And since when are you gay?" Ashley kept asking questions. Her voice rose hysterically, and she was about to scream.

"Since elementary school I've known that I was different. I liked boys, but I couldn't reveal that to anyone, not even to you, Sis. Mom and Dad have never cared about me. They don't want to know how I feel. That's why I hate them.

"Brendan, this is not true, and you know it..." Ashley countered.

"Shut up, bitch! I'll put a bullet in your head! Shut the fuck up, okay? Back to my story. Where was I...? Ah, yes! So I contacted a man named David Sparrow. I needed an alibi, and he wanted money. David agreed to make it look like he killed Josh. I promised him 10 million dollars in cash, and he gave me a green light. My plan worked like a charm. On one particular day, I visited Josh at his house. I told him I needed to see him, and he said yes. I called David Sparrow and told him to meet me at Josh's apartment. I paid a visit to my dear friend, Josh. Sparrow came a few minutes later. Josh asked me who David was because he had never met him. I told him that David wanted to start training, and Josh got happy about having another customer. Whatever! As Josh and David discussed personal training, I pulled my gun and terminated Josh. David had the same kind of gun. His gun was used as bait for the cops. After I shot Josh, I had to sneak out the back door. David was instructed to lock that door from the inside to make it look like no one had used it, and then he left from the front door. That was the plan, and everything worked just the way I wanted. But David Sparrow was an idiot. He thought that he would get away with it, but he was wrong. I knew the cops were watching Josh's place. I hoped that they would spot David, and I was right. The cops saw David leaving Josh's apartment, and he fucked it up. He got scared, and I guess he shot at the cop if I'm correct. Is that right, Mr. Policeman?" Brendan grilled the detective.

"Yeah, that was written on the police report. But how did you kill David? He was in prison," McCarthur asked. The confusion about the murders started to clear out in his head.

"I couldn't do it by myself. I called some friends, and they did the job. The guards helped me too. It wasn't a problem because a lot of the guards will take bribes. It wasn't cheap, but I took care of that," Brendan explained.

"Who was the man you hired to kill David?" McCarthur asked.

"I can't tell you that, Mr. Policeman!" Brendan replied.

"So you were the one shooting up my partner's house in Niles?" the Texan asked. Brendan frowned at McCarthur and said, "Maybe...I know where she lives, you too." The hacker replied with a smirk in his face.

"Yeah. That's what I thought. What about Monica?" Bob asked.

"Who's Monica?" Ashley asked, grimacing.

"Yea, Mr. Policeman. Who's Monica?" Brendan repeated. His voice was snarky, and that was making the Texan nervous.

"You don't know about her?" the detective asked. Ashley

shook her head no. *That's weird! So Monica had lied! She never met Ashley! But why would she lie about her?* the Texan thought. He was confused because Monica had given him a false statement, but it was too late for answers. She was gone—her funeral had been a week ago. McCarthur sighed. He then said, "Monica was Kimberly's friend. One particular night, Kimberly and Monica had a drink in your apartment. Josh came there, and the three of them had a little fun together."

"Huh? What do you mean had a little fun together?" Ashley asked. She was baffled and could barely stay still.

"You know like... They had a..."

"A what? Say it!" the teacher demanded an answer.

"Yes, Mr. Policeman? What happened that night?" Brendan asked in a playful voice.

"Okay! Apparently, Josh, Kimberly, and Monica had a threesome. They must have been having a lot of fun because Josh knocked Kimberly up. She was carrying a baby before your brother killed her. That was what I was told at the Chicago Morgue," McCarthur finished his speech. Silence hovered in the basement. Brendan didn't know that Kimberly was pregnant, but that didn't mean anything to him. But as for Ashley, she was thrown in a loop. She didn't know what to say. Her jaw was left hanging. She then sat on the mattress and held her head. She was in great pain. The headache was making her dizzy. She had too much information just in a few seconds to consider. The teacher didn't know how to react. Tears filled her eyes.

"Brendan!" the teacher said, "What about Mom and Dad?" Brendan didn't answer. He was ignoring Ashley because his eyes were staring at his smartphone. Ashley was mortified and repulsed. Although, she wanted to remain strong for the sake of her own life.

"Brendan, did you hurt Mom and Dad?" Ashley repeated her question. This time, her voice was imperative. Brendan looked at his sister and said, "Dad is tied in a chair in the garage, and mom is in the bathtub. I took the batteries out of the carbon monoxide detectors and opened the furnace gas valve. In a few hours, the entire house will be filled with carbon monoxide."

"Why would you do that? Why have I been kept here like a hostage? What is all this about anyway?"

"Remember when Mom and Dad left me at Disneyland, huh? Do you have any idea how miserable and embarrassed I felt?" Brendan asked. His eyes were furious as a pitbull preparing to eviscerate another dog.

"Ashley, what is your brother talking about?" Bob chimed in. His body strained against the bars, because he longed get out and pull Brendan's face off of his skull.

"Yeah, Ashley! Why don't you tell Mr. Policeman what happened at Disneyland," the hacker said and stepped closer to the cage. The teacher shifted her eyes and explained, "Back in 2005, Mom, Dad, Brendan, and I went to Disneyland. The weather was hot and humid, and the park was packed with people. Anyway! As we were leaving the park, we thought Brendan was behind us. There was a boy who looked just like my brother, and we all thought that the boy was Brendan. As soon as we reached the exit gate, Dad asked, 'Where is Brendan?' We looked everywhere for him, and after an hour, one of the guards found him on the east side of the park, by the exit. That was all. My parents didn't leave Brendan on purpose," Ashley concluded.

"Bullshit! That's bogus, and you know that perfectly well. It wasn't what actually happened. I was scared to death, running with tears and screaming for Mom and Dad. They forgot me because they didn't give a fuck about me! Doesn't your software collect this information?" Brendan asked. His computer language seemed to be weird at times.

"Brendan, is this all about the day in Disneyland?" Ashley asked. She couldn't comprehend why her brother could have held this grudge for so long.

"Noo. Absolutely not. Mom and Dad have always loved you more; you are their priceless darling. Our parents have always been proud of you, Sis. In the meantime, they have always been ashamed of me for whatever reason. It makes me sick. Every time I hear Mom or Dad praising you I feel like shit. Mom and Dad have never told me 'I love you' or 'I'm proud of you.' Never!" Brendan was belligerent. His anger could have been sensed from miles away.

"Brendan, let's talk like grownups. I think there is a misconception between you and your parents," McCarthur suggested.

"Oh, yeah. Is that what you're thinking, Mr. Policeman? Who the heck do you think you are? What the fuck do you know about my family and me, huh? Do you know who I am? I have stolen millions of dollars from banks and large corporations with poor cyber security. I have so much money that I can make myself disappear without a trace. You got that?" the hacker shouted aggressively. He pointed the 9 millimeter at

McCarthur's face and said, "You better get on your knees and start prayin' because I am about to blow your head off! How about that, Mr. Policeman?" While the computer genius was talking, the detective caught a silhouette that moved behind Brendan's back. Bob recognized the person who was slipping up slowly. The hacker kept his eyes on McCarthur, which was his mistake. Ashley also saw the person approaching Brendan's back.

"Don't move a muscle!" a voice behind Brendan whispered as the barrel of a Glock G17 touched the back of his skull. The hacker raised his eyebrows. He was surprised by the person behind him and panicked. His mind ran through several options on how he should proceed.

"Lisa!" McCarthur exclaimed and lifted his hands high as if he was a boxer who'd finally knocked out his opponent.

"I got this, chief!" Lisa said. She didn't take her eyes off Brendan. The situation became a nail bitter. Ashley looked confused. She whispered to the Texan, "Who is she?"

"I'll tell you later," Bob said, giving Ashley a subtle sign to hold it steady.

"Brendan Packer, you're under arrest! The house is surrounded by dozens of police officers. There is no way out! Drop the gum, and put your hands up!" Lisa Fernandez said solemnly. She was just a foot away from Brendan and had the drop on him. But it looked like the hacker didn't want to give himself up.

"Brendan, do you understand what I said? Don't make this any harder than already is. The game is over," the female detective announced. Lisa's words annoyed him, and he got bent out of shape.

"It's over when I say so!" Brendan screamed. He turned around and went for Fernandez' neck. That was a wrong move because he underestimated the power of the beautiful detective. Fernandez stepped aside, quickly ducked under Brendan's arm, and dug a punch into his ribs.

"Aah!" Brendan moaned. The pain in his ribs seemed to paralyze him for a second. Fernandez moved with incredible speed. She armlocked Brendan and floored him in a second. Lisa bent one of Brendan's hands, and he had no choice but to drop his weapon.

"Aaaah! The computer genius screamed. The pain was making him weak. Brendan realized that he had messed with the wrong woman. Because of her training, she had a cat-woman-like agility. Her martial arts skills were impressive.

Fernandez handcuffed Brendan and asked, "Where is the key for the cage?"

"Upstairs!" Brendan lied. He wanted to buy some time and confuse the female detective. To some degree his plan worked because Fernandez shifted her eyes in confusion. But she said, "Don't play games with me, Brendan. I'm not in a mood." She was pissed because Brendan had attacked her. She took assaults on her personally. While Fernandez patted Brendan down, McCarthur explained to Ashley how good his partner was.

"Where is the key? This is your last chance! Talk, you little scumbag," Fernandez asked, demanding a quick response.

"Brendan, gave up! It's over. You know that," Ashley urged her brother, but he ignored her appeal.

"How did you find me?" Brendan asked the female detective. Fernandez was filled with disgust. She had been listening from the shadows and overheard the story of how Brendan killed most of the victims, and she was sickened.

"Well, McCarthur sent me a text. He said that he wanted to talk with your parents. Something in my head was telling me that I should come too. When I approached your parents' house, I saw how you and Bob were getting into the blue Ford. Bob sat behind the wheel and drove off. Bob doesn't like driving. So I realized that something was happening. I decided to follow you before calling for backup. The ride took about 10 minutes, and that was fine with me. I saw where Bob parked the blue Ford, and I parked my vehicle the next block to prevent suspicion. Then I walked to this house and called for backup," Lisa finished her monologue. The Texan frowned.

"Lisa, why didn't you wait for the backup?" McCarthur asked, but he already knew the answer.

"You know me, chief! I couldn't miss the show!" Lisa said, and Bob flashed his crooked smile. He comprehended what his partner meant. He was worried about Lisa because she had risked her own life by entering the house without backup. But the problem remained— Lisa needed the key to open the cage.

"Brendan, where is the key for the cage? I'm not playing games. Where is the key?" Lisa kept repeating the same question over and over again. Brendan didn't respond to her questions, and that made Lisa angry. She grabbed Brendan's ear and twisted it painfully. The hacker loudly moaned as if he had been stabbed with a knife.

"Upstairs! I left the key upstairs!" Brendan screamed. His face was pushed into the floor. Detective Fernandez lifted Brendan. The hacker tried to attack Lisa by ramming his head into her stomach. That was another wrong move because Lisa did a karate trick and threw him on the floor. He fell so badly that he broke a rib when he landed on the ground.

"Aaaaaah" he moaned like a dying animal.

"No more lies, Brendan. Tell me the truth! I'm not here to play any games. Don't push my buttons, okay?" Lisa was furious. She had been asking about the key for the past three minutes, and her patience was already gone.

"I told you! The key is upstairs! I'm not lying," the cybersecurity guy grumbled. He spoke with tears in his eyes. The pain he felt was unbearable. Lisa Fernandez sat on the sprawled body of Ashley's brother. Just a second before she rose to her feet something creaked from the stairs.

"Drop your weapon and step a few feet back!" a male voice ordered. The person pointed a .357 magnum at Lisa. He was standing on the stairs, his face was in the dark and could not be recognized.

"Who are you?" Lisa asked the man in the dark. She dropped her weapon and stepped aside, just like the man had ordered. The guy came closer and showed his face. Everyone in the basement stared at the unknown man. McCarthur squinted. He couldn't see clearly at that range. He then identified the man who was pointing a revolver at Lisa.

"Jeremy! Is that you?" Bob asked. He couldn't believe his eyes. He was far more disappointed than surprised.

"Do you know him?" Ashley asked.

"Yes! That's my son! Jeremy, what the fuck are you doing here? Why are you in Chicago?" The Texan demanded answers. His facial expression exposed his growing anger.

"Who? Huh?" Fernandez scolded. She kept her hands high, but her mind was going over options.

"Jeremy, put that gun down for Christ's sake," the detective with curly blond hair snapped.

"Shut up, old fuck! I'm sick and tired of your ignorance!" Jeremy yelled. He was a lanky guy, about 6'1". His slender body made him look like a volleyball player. Jeremy had a sleepy face and beautiful blond hair, just like his father. His brown eyes were sparkling. Jeremy was a young kid at age of eighteen, but he looked like he was in his early thirties. McCarthur's son stepped up close to Fernandez and said, "Turn around and keep your hands up! Are you okay, Brendan?" Jeremy looked at the hacker.

"Do I look like I am okay? I think this bitch just broke my rib," the hacker complained. The pain he felt had forced him to talk in gasps. Jeremy approached Fernandez and patted her body down; he took her smartphone and continued his search. He only used one of his hands because the other hand was holding the .357 magnum. The boy from Texas was touching Fernandez intimately. He used the chance he had and grabbed her breasts, then her ass. Fernandez became furious.

"Okay, now I want you to go over there!" Jeremy said and pointed to the north side of the cage. He then took a key and opened the door. Apparently, he had opened the cell more than once because he worked the lock quickly.

"Now, get inside and stay there," the boy from Texas ordered, and Lisa went into the cell. Fernandez looked at her partner as if she was saying, "*Don't worry! I got this.*" Lisa stepped inside, and Jeremy locked the door behind her. The female detective gave a hug to Ashley. She saw the turmoil that the teacher had in her eyes. The boy from Texas was smiling as if some dumpster slut had just finished doing a handjob on him.

"Jeremy, what are you doing? Do you really want to kill us? What is all this about? I'm your father. I think I deserve an explanation," McCarthur declared. He was stalling for time hoping that more cops were on their way. Jeremy was fuming. He eyeballed his father aggressively.

"Jeremy, we don't have much time! C'mon, get the key and uncuff me, you idiot!"

"Shhhh! Brendan!" Jeremy said. He disliked when someone was giving him orders.

"Jeremy, did you kill Monica Shingles and David Sparrow?" Bob asked his son. The boy from Texas didn't answer. His silence spoke out loud of what he had already done. McCarthur realized this. He was more than disappointed.

"The key! Jeremy, get the fucking key!" Brendan kept urging the boy from Texas. McCarthur's son wasn't the smartest kid. He forgot to get the key from Lisa who was already locked in the cage. The boy bellied up to the cell and pointed the pistol at Fernandez.

"Give me the fucking key! Now!" Jeremy threatened. Lisa pulled out a keychain from her police jacket.

"You want these!" she asked teasingly.

"Yes! C'mon, hand them over," the boy said. He stretched his arm into the cage to grab the small keychain. His fingers were jiggling impatiently.

"You want these, right?" Lisa kept teasing the boy from Texas.

"Yeah," the boy replied.

"Jeremy! Stop wasting time! Take the keychain from that bitch!" Brendan shouted. All of a sudden, the sound of sirens caught everyone's attention.

"You see, Jeremy! The backup is here! There is no way out. Put the gun down! You can't get out of here. Think about it!" McCarthur spoke to his son. He begged his kid to act like a reasonable man, otherwise things could get ugly.

"Give me the keychain!" Jeremey repeated. His body was glued to the cage. The tension in the basement was hovering like a ghost. Everyone in the room was impatient. The three hostages waited to be rescued. Brendan longed to free his hands. His buddy was his only chance. But Jeremy's mind was fogged by mixed thoughts.

"Give me the fucking keychain! I said. Or I'll shoot you!" Jeremy clamored! His calm eyes looked like he was about to fall asleep, but his mind was on the edge of pulling the trigger.

"Here!" Lisa yelled and threw the keys up in the air. The keychain flew through the bars and headed up to the ceiling. Jeremy was distracted; his eyes were tracking the trajectory of the keychain, and that was his mistake. Lisa Fernandez pulled out a small pepper spray and streamed it right into Jeremy's eyes.

"Aaah! My eyes!" the boy screamed. His eyes burned, and he howled with pain. Jeremy dropped the .357 magnum and covered his eyes with his hands. He couldn't keep his body in balance and collapsed on the ground. Lisa stretched her arm and tried to reach the revolver, but the gun was too far away.

"Jeremy! You stupid idiot!" Brendan screamed aggressively. He knew his chances of escaping from the house were now down to zero. His accomplice did a sloppy job while he was body-searching Fernandez and had missed the pepper spray. Bob was ashamed of what had happened. He didn't like what his partner had done to his son, but then he realized he would do the same thing in a similar situation.

"Can you reach the gun?" Bob asked his partner.

"I'm trying, chief! Fernandez exclaimed. The tips of her fingers were an inch from the gun. Then both detectives were frozen like statues. No words could describe what they saw. Brendan also witnessed what was happening. Jeremey missed it. His eyes were aching badly. Silence descended in the basement, except for Jeremey's moaning. No one could explain what then happened. Bob's jaw hung open because he had never seen anything like this, nor had Lisa or Brendan. Ashley's eyes were closed. She stretched out her arm, and with some unseen power, the keychain for the cage was slowly transported through the air from Jeremy's pants to her hand. It was like Ashley had some force to move metal objects with the power of her mind.

The teacher had the keychain in a few seconds. Her eyes

were still closed while she whispered, "Take them!" At first, no one reacted to her appeal, and she repeated, "Take them!" Fernandez stepped slowly and grabbed the keychain from the girl. As soon as Lisa took the keys, Ashley collapsed on the floor. Blood slowly dripped from her nostrils. Bob blinked in utter disbelief. He couldn't take his eyes off Ashley. In the meantime, his partner unlocked the door and quickly opened the cage. She grabbed the .357 magnum and her smartphone. Then, she made a phone call.

***

Fernandez contacted the approaching police and told them that the house was under control. She then sent a firetruck to Ashley's parents. The firefighters broke into the Packer's house and rescued Tom and Jennifer. Tom had severe dizziness, and his wife was repeatedly coughing. They were taken to the hospital.

***

Just in a few seconds, Brendan's house was invaded by a bunch of cops and deputies. The police arrested the hacker and his accomplice, Jeremy. Fernandez had to call the bomb squad because Brendan told her that the house had explosives with timers.

McCarthur carried Ashley because she was unable to use her legs. The detective handed the teacher to the paramedics, and they took her over. The house where Brendan kept the hostages was filled with over sixty people. A chopper from the media was hovering over the rundown house. Reporters were asking questions, but no one was willing to answer. Bob sat on the curb in the cul-de-sac. He tried to keep it together, but his eyes were filled with tears. He was incredulous. His son was implicated in not one but two murders. A second later, his partner joined him.

"Are you okay, chief?"

"Yeah," McCarthur said staring at his shoes. He wasn't okay.

"Look, I'm sorry what I did to your son... I didn't..." Lisa couldn't finish the sentence because she was ashamed. Bob waived his hand. He clearly meant to say, "*Please! Don't bother!*" The two detectives sat on the curb for quite some time.

At 9:30 p.m., Lisa parked the Tahoe on Lincoln Street, where Bob lived. He jumped out of the vehicle and said, "Thanks!"

"I'll call you tomorrow, chief," Fernandez said. Bob showed his thumbs up without saying anything. The Texan longed to be alone. He stepped into his apartment and looked around. His condo was a mess again, as always was, but that was the last thing he cared about. That night, the detective drank a large amount of vodka and passed out on the couch.

14

Ashley and her parents were taken to the same hospital, but all three of them were in different rooms. The teacher looked fine. Her vitals were showing good results. Her mom had mild flu. While she had been tied up in the bathtub, her skin had gotten macerated. Jennifer looked like a jellyfish and she needed special care. Other than that, she was fine. Tom's medical report was a little more serious. He had a concussion caused by the baseball bat that Brendan had used. The electrician also had an open wound on the back of his head. The doctors needed to do forty-eight stitches to close the cut. Tom had to spend two weeks in the hospital. The doctors told him that he was a lucky man because he had been just a few inches close to certain death.

***

Three days after Brendan was arrested, he had his trial in court. The judge sentenced the hacker to life. He was charged with the murder of Jack Hammer, Kimberly Shimmers, and Josh Rodriguez. It was clear that Brendan would not be released anytime soon.

***

Thursday, December 8th, was a cold day in the Windy City. The sky was filled with clouds and looked like it was about to start raining. The clock showed 1:00 p.m., and the streets of Chicago were filled with cars. Chicagoans were getting ready for Christmas. Some of them were rushing from store to store and buying gifts. Many people were looking for the perfect present but one man didn't need to buy any Christmas gifts. That was Detective Robert McCarthur. He was walking through the corridor of the police precinct in Downtown Chicago. Next to him strolled another white man. He was dressed spiffily; his trench coat looked expensive. His name was Joseph Kulamov. He was a Jewish guy who had come from Russia many years ago. He was 5' 9" with an overweight body because he loved to eat. Joseph was in his early forties, but he looked much older. His nose was big, but his blue eyes were beautiful. Kulamov was a respected lawyer in Chi-Town. McCarthur had called him for help, and he agreed. A few minutes later, the detective and the lawyer entered an interrogation room where Jeremy waited. He was handcuffed because he had been charged with the murders of Monica Shingles and David Sparrow.

"Jeremy, it's nice to meet ya. I'm Joseph Kulamov. I'll be your defense attorney," the Jewish man declared. McCarthur didn't say a word. He was still shocked to find his son involved in murders in Chicago.

"I'm fine... I guess... What's gonna happen to me? I mean. Am I going to jail?" the boy from Texas asked. The lawyer shifted his eyes in a way as if he was saying, "*I don't know how to tell you this.*"

"Jeremy, it depends on a lot of things. First of all, I need to know what exactly happened. Don't lie to me because I am your only chance, okay? Tell me the whole story. What are you doing in Chicago? How did you meet Brendan?" the Jewish lawyer said.

"Come on, son. Tell the whole story. I'm here with you," Bob encouraged his son. Jeremy looked at his father, then at Joseph, and said, "I've known Brendan for five years. We used to play a computer game on the same server. Brendan and I hit it off from the get-go. In 2019, Brendan flew to Dallas, and we went to a few bars, hanging out with some bad bitches and... you know," the boy stopped for a second. He thought of choosing his words carefully.

"Aha! Go on," Joseph said.

"Last year, Brendan came to Dallas. He said he wanted to talk to me in person. I agreed, and we met at a dive bar where a few people were stoned and almost snoozed by the boring music. Anyway. So Brendan had a plan to get rid of his family and make it look like an accident. He wanted to escape somewhere in Europe… I think he said Greece," the boy in the handcuffs said.

"Why would he want to obliterate his family?" Joseph asked.

"Brendan mentioned that he found a way to steal a lot of money from large corporations by doing some cyber-attacks, and he wanted to leave the country unnoticed. He said that his family had been treated him badly, and he was sick and tired of them," the boy explained.

"Aha. Including Ashley?"

"Yes. Brendan offered me a lot of money if I would help him, and I couldn't say no. I'm talking about more than ten million in cash," Jeremy confessed.

"Aha, and what was Brendan's plan?" the lawyer asked his next question. McCarthur just listened to the conversation. He sat next to his son and hoped the Jewish lawyer could work a miracle.

"Brendan didn't reveal his entire plan. He told me I had to be in Chicago when he needed me. The hacker was taking care of all expenses. I'm talking about hotels, flight tickets, and he even gave me money to spend on whatever I wanted, except for guns of course. I went to the mall and bought new clothes, food, games, and whatever I saw. The list was long," Jeremy confessed.

"Aha. When was the first time Brendan told you to come to Chicago for work?"

"I came here in March this year. Brendan had bought a house a few miles from his parents' house, and the hacker needed me there. I worked on his property, doing whatever he told me to. The hacker hired a Polish company to build the cage and install soundproof insulation around the entire house."

"Jeremy, you said you don't like to come here because it is too cold during the wintertime," his father interrupted him.

"McCarthur!" Joseph snapped. The lawyer gave him a sign saying, "*I'll take care from here!*"

"Jeremy, tell me about Monica Shingles," the lawyer conjured the boy to talk.

"So Brendan called me in August. He said I had to be back here by the first of October. I flew into Chicago and checked in at a hotel by O'Hare. The hacker gave me Monica's information. I knew where she lived, where she liked to go, where she shopped— everything. Monica snorted a lot of cocaine and took MDMAs. I had to get in touch with her and became her *provider* if you know what I mean," Jeremy stopped to see if his father and the lawyer got the hint. Both men made a sign to proceed.

"I met Monica in a bar that she liked. I came onto her, and I gave her a *tester* for free. She loved it. So I started supplying her with a bunch of cocaine that Brendan gave me. Two weeks later, the hacker called me and said that it was time for me to do the *hit*. On Wednesday, the 28th of October, I paid a visit to my new friend, Monica. She hosted a small party in her apartment, and I swung by. She needed me because I had the drugs. We spent all night long doing some coke and talking about every bullshit thing you could think of. We partied all night long till the morning hours of the next day. By sunrise, Monica and I were left alone in her apartment. She was out of control. Snorting coke every five minutes or so. Then I suggested we go upstairs and watch the sunrise. I don't think Monica understood what I was asking, but she agreed, and we both went to the roof. Monica was so high that I had to hold her because she could hardly walk. We went to the roof, and I just let her walk to the edge of the building. The chick fell on her own. I didn't have to push her. It was so easy," the boy finished his monologue. McCarthur and Kulamov were speechless. Both of them had so many questions that they didn't know where to start.

"Jeremy, since when you're doing drugs?" McCarthur asked. He was traumatized by what his son had done. As a father, he couldn't take it. His disappointment grew bigger.

"Honestly, I don't like it. I have tried it a few times, but it's just not my thing," his son replied. He looked like a boy who was telling the truth. Joseph rubbed his left ear.

"Let's leave the questions about drugs aside, Joseph said and continued, "Jeremy, tell me what happened next?"

"After Monica fell from the roof, I snuck out immediately and took an Uber to my hotel. An hour later, I was on a plane flying back to Dallas."

"Aha, and why did Brendan want to kill Monica Shingles? What did she have to do with him and his plan?"

"I'm not sure. Brendan hated Monica for whatever reason. He mentioned that this chick slept with Kimberly and Josh Rodriguez. The hacker was furious when he found out. I don't know why. He just told me that she had to be *erased*. That's what I remember," the boy from Texas replied.

"Aha, when did you come back to Chicago?"

"I came back on the sixth of November... Yeah... I think

that's the correct date. Brendan called me and said that he had a job for me. As usual, he didn't mention any details over the phone. The hacker hates sharing details in his phone calls. So I flew to Chicago and went to a Holiday Inn. The next day, I had to meet him at his house. Brendan talked about a guy named David Sparrow. He said that this guy fucked up really bad and that I had to take him down. The hacker explained the whole scenario. He contacted some people who worked as guards in the Cook County jail and gave me some work clothes. I had to be there at 10:00 p.m. At that time, the shifts were changing, and I had to sneak through the guards. A burly guy was helping me out. He took me through the fastest, and I guess, the easiest way to get to the C Block. The burly guy told me that I had no more than half an hour. I was told where David's cell was. I moved fast because the timing was crucial and essential. Brendan gave me a small shiv and told me it was easy to carry a small weapon in prison. Honestly, I didn't care about what weapon I would use. I just wanted to do the job and leave fast. So I went to David's cell and told him a few words."

"Aha! And what did you say to him?" Kulamov asked.

"I don't remember the exact words… it was something like… no. Actually, David started asking questions like, 'Who's there?' I told him that he talked too much, and he moaned like a little girl. He was asking about his money or something like that. I had no time to waste. I opened the cell with the key that the burly man had given me and I stabbed David a few times," Jeremy admitted. His father took a deep breath.

The shame forced him to cover his face using the palms of his hands.

"Aha! Then what happened?" Joseph grilled. His work was remarkable. Kulamov wanted to have every detail of Jeremy's story. That was his way of acquiring the information that he needed.

"I had to leave the cell as fast as possible. The burly guy was waiting for me by the stairs. I handed him the keys to the cell, and he walked me out of the prison. I flew back to Dallas the next day."

"This burly man, do you know his name?" the lawyer asked his next question.

"No, sir."

"Aha! Aside from being burly, what does he look like?" Joseph quizzed. Bob just listened to the conversation. He stayed quiet, as if he wasn't in the same room.

"Honestly, I can't tell. He wore a COVID-19 mask and a cap. Also, it was so dark that there was no way I could see his face. I wouldn't be able to recognize him," the boy with the handcuffs replied.

"Aha. You said that you returned to Dallas. When did you come back to Chicago?"

"I boarded on Thanksgiving, which was Thursday evening, November 24th. The day before we got caught…I guess. Brendan needed me to help him with something. The next day, on Friday, we worked on the house. The hacker called some guy. This guy had installed C4 with timers in the entire house."

"Aha, and this bomb man, what did he looked like?"

"Honestly, I've never met him. When I got to the house, the bomb man had already left," the boy admitted.

"Go on! Finish your story," the lawyer said kindly. He was surprised by the words that came out of Jeremy's mouth.

"We finished what we needed to do on Friday, and the hacker told me to go to my hotel room and rest because, the next day, we would have more work to do. On Saturday, I had to be at the house in the afternoon… around…2:00 or 3:00 p.m. I took an Uber to the house. I saw Brendan's blue car that was parked on the driveway, and I went into the house. As I was opening the front door, I overheard unknown voices that were coming from the basement. Brendan kept a .357 magnum in a safe box, and I decided I needed the gun. I grabbed it and went to the basement. That was it. My father knows the rest," Jeremy finished the story. He was telling the truth, but Joseph still felt iffy.

Jeremy's confession made McCarthur embarrassed. The detective wanted to pull out a gun and shoot himself, but as a father, he had to be strong. *What are the odds of having my son involved in one of the most brutal string of murders that has ever happened in Chicago?* Bob asked himself. He knew that the answer to this question would remain a mystery.

"So what now? What's gonna happen?" Jeremy asked. The boy from Texas didn't realize how difficult his situation was. He was just a kid, immature and inexperienced. He didn't grasp how messed up his life had become.

"I can't answer your questions, not right now. Excuse us. Your father and I have to talk for a second," Joseph said, and both men left the interrogation room.

"What do you think? What are his chances for a fair trial?" Bob asked impatiently.

"There is no such a thing as a fair trial when it comes to a murder, and Jeremy had killed two people. Even though he didn't technically push Monica, he was there, and he fled a crime scene. That would not look good to the judge. I think Jeremy needs to plead guilty, and maybe the judge could show some leniency. Either way, the kid is looking at up to 30–35 years in jail. That's the law in Illinois. I'm sorry, Bob. I'm really trying to help you out, but your boy is in a seriously bad situation," Joseph stated. He tried to sound reasonable, but McCarthur didn't buy any of his words.

"Okay, I'll talk to you later," the Texan said and returned to his son. The detective wanted to spend a little more time with his boy because he wouldn't see him again for a long time.

"What do you think, dad?" Jeremy asked his father. The Texan couldn't remember the last time he heard the word "Dad" spoken aloud from his son. Bob encouraged his boy. They talked a little more.

The following week, Jeremy had his day in the court. The kid confessed his guilt, and the judge gave him forty years. McCarthur promised his son he'd do whatever it took to get him out of prison sooner, but his chances were at zero.

***

The next day, Lisa and Bob went to Presence Resurrection Hospital in Park Ridge, where Ashley was a patient, to pay her a visit. Fernandez parked the black Tahoe, and the detectives strolled to the hospital. Ashley was seated in a medical room filled with fine furniture and a flat screen TV that hung on the wall.

"Hey, Ashley! It's good to see ya. How are you feeling?" Lisa said and handed her a bouquet of beautiful red roses. Fernandez figured that bringing flowers was a good idea. She wasn't wrong.

"Oh my God! I love roses! How do you know that?" Ashley exclaimed in surprise.

"I figured a strong woman like you deserves some treats," Lisa smiled with her charming dimples and hugged the patient. Detective McCarthur also hugged the teacher. The three of them had created a special bond after being locked together in the cage.

"My hair looks awful! I'm sorry. I…"

"Your hair is gorgeous, love. I wish I had your hair. Who's your hairdresser?" Lisa teased Ashley. She sat on the bed next to the teacher. The two young women were lost in girl-talk conversation while Bob remained silent. After a few minutes of casual chat, Fernandez changed the subject.

Ashley, what did you do that day… you know when we were in the cage. I'm not asking to start some sort of investigation. This question is off the record, and it'll stay between the three of us," the female detective pointed out.

"I don't know. I just closed my eyes and started praying. I have never done anything like that before. I don't even know what to call it — telekinesis?"

"It sounds like… I thought this only happened in the movies, but in real life, it's much more terrifying. Ashley, this may sound odd, but can you do it again? Can you try to move an object in this room?" McCarthur implored. He admired what Brendan's sister had done a few days ago and wanted to see it for a second time. Lisa didn't approve of Bob's appeal. She thought that Ashley had been through enough, and she had to rest. Regardless of her thoughts, the female detective said nothing.

"I can try… I guess."

"Dear, you don't have to," Fernandez chimed in. Ashley gave a sign, saying it was fine, and closed her eyes. Both detectives were staring at the teacher and waiting for a miracle to happen. But nothing happened. No items were moved or anything like that. Ashley opened her sparkling green eyes and declared, "I don't think it would work like that. I don't know."

"Dear, forget about it. Did you speak with anyone about the telekinesis?" Fernandez asked.

"No. How could I? It's so weird. People may have thought I am insane," Ashley explained, and both detectives nodded.

"We didn't say anything. No reports, nothing!" Lisa proclaimed. Robert looked at his partner as if he was asking, "*Are we going to do it?*" Lisa approved her partner's suggestion with no hesitation.

"Okay, let's take an oath that we won't tell anyone about this bizarre…thing. Sounds good?" McCarthur offered. Lisa and Ashley agreed. The three of them held their hands in a circle and promised to keep the telekinesis story secret and not share it with anyone.

"When will you be going home, love?" Lisa asked.

"Actually, I think tomorrow. That's what the doctors told

me," Ashley replied with her innocent green eyes. She was happy that her stint in the hospital would end soon.

"Okay, love. Heal faster. We'll talk with you later," Fernandez said, "Oh, one more thing!"

"Yes?" Ashley said surprised.

"You do look like the actress Beth Behrs," Lisa proclaimed, and Ashley burst into laughter. Then both detectives left the inpatient room.

Around 4:00 p.m., Mrs. Packer swung by the hospital to visit Ashley. Jennifer had been released the day after she was taken to the hospital. She was worried about her daughter. They preferred to avoid any discussion related to Brendan. They talked for a bit about nothing in particular. Then Jennifer kissed her daughter and told her how much she loved her. Mrs. Packer left Ashley's room and went to check on her husband. Tom Packer was doing fine. However, he was still advised to stay in the hospital for a few days more.

***

Later the same day, Ashley looked at the electronic clock which was next to her bed. The clock showed 10:00 p.m. The teacher couldn't fall asleep. Her restless mind wouldn't give up. She had tried a few times, but she failed. She turned the light on and looked around. Her room was quiet as if the entire hospital was empty. Ashley went to use the restroom. After she finished her business, she looked at herself in the mirror. The gorgeous teacher recalled staring at herself in the broken mirror while she was kept as a hostage in the spooky basement. She had spent a few months there, and the unpleasant memories piled up from that house wouldn't disappear with a snap of her fingers. Ashley washed her face and returned to the hospital bed. She climbed on and closed her eyes. Then she heard knocking at the door.

"Come on in!" Ashley said. She sat up on the bed and stared at the door. The knocking was repeated.

"Yes! Come on in," the patient repeated, wondering who that might be. The next instant, her face became pale. She looked at the door, and her eyes froze. The fear made her mouth agape.

"Aaaaaah!" Ashley screamed at the top of her lungs. She couldn't believe her eyes. The terrible werewolf of her dreams was standing at the door, growling and baring its fangs. The monster's gray fur bristled. The beast sneaked through the doorway and headed toward Ashley. The fury lycanthrope was hunchbacked, but it still looked big. The werewolf had a wolf-like muzzle that looked long and scary. The beast opened its jaw and showed its huge fangs. Saliva was drooling from its mouth. The monster's eyes were wild and furious as if it would attack at any second. The teacher jumped out of her bed and went to the window, maintaining a maximum distance from the monster. Goosebumps crawled over her body. The terror made her cry.

"Oh my God! Please don't! Please nooo! Aaaaaah!"

***

Ashley awoke from her nightmare. It was dark in the room.

She turned on the lights, and surveyed the place. There was no werewolf or anything like that. A brunette nurse had rushed to Ashley's room to check on her because she was screaming. Ashley was somewhat relieved that it was a nightmare, but she couldn't stop crying. At midnight, she finally nodded off. There were no more nightmares, not yet.

15

On Monday December 19th a big celebration was organized in a vast ballroom in Downtown Chicago. The guest list was long, filled with big kingpins and famous moguls. The event was organized in the names of Detectives Robert McCarthur and Lisa Fernandez. They were to be awarded with special recognition for conducting criminal investigations and successful homicide case prosecutions. The awards recognized acts of great courage and honor and were given by the mayor of Chicago. The detectives were holding their awards with pride and respect. Even though he was acknowledged by the mayor and the City of Chicago, Robert McCarthur felt that he had lost the most important award that any human could want, and that was his son, Jeremy.

CHAOS IN CHICAGO

***

Jeremy McCarthur and Brendan Packer were taken into the same prison but were kept in different cell blocks. Jeremy had no idea how terrifying the pen in Cook County was. He wished to leave that daunting place, but there was no turning back. He had to face the consequences of a criminal who committed two brutal murders.

Unlike his accomplice, Brendan seemed to have no problem being around other convicts. His brain worked remarkably well. He started building the name *The Hacker*, and it seemed like he was making a lot of friends. Brendan needed a strong backbone in the prison, and he was doing a good job. The hacker was looking for options and ways to be released on parole. An early release from prison seemed almost impossible, but the money in his bank account could possibly change the game.

***

On Thursday the 22nd of December a 911 call was received at the emergency switchboard in Chicago. Four police units and an ambulance rushed to Lincoln Street in Roscoe Village. It was noon when the police deputies barged into a residential apartment located in a newly remodeled townhouse. The officers nervously checked all the rooms. The condo was a mess. A Hispanic lady in her fifties was crying in the kitchen. Her hands were shaking from the shock she had experienced. The deputies tried to talk to her, but she refused. Instead, she pointed to the bedroom, and the officers went in there. The cops found Robert McCarthur dead, lying in his bed. His eyes were closed, but it seemed that somehow his soul was still there, watching the crime scene. Robert McCarthur had passed away from a heart attack. He was supposed to stop drinking because he had a severe heart blockage. His primary physician had repeatedly urged him to quit, but Bob ignored his suggestions. The Texan needed open heart surgery, but he refused to take any action, not after Jeremy's indictment. Bob had just received an award from the mayor, and a couple of days later he was in the Chicago Morgue. Robert McCarthur went to be with God a few days before Christmas. It was a tragedy that hit not only Chicago but the entire country. One of the most successful homicide detectives in the history of the U.S. was gone.

***

Ashley moved back to her family home because she was so traumatized by her recent ordeal. Her father, Tom, was discharged from the hospital. He took a month off from work because his head was still injured. Jenifer spent more time with her daughter. She had missed her little girl. Mrs. Packer thought she would never see her baby girl again, but she was wrong. The future served her a raw deal; her daughter had returned home, but her son would probably spend the rest of his life in prison.

On Friday the 23rd of December Ashley came home from a shopping tour. She had bought her parents gifts and even got something for her unhinged brother. As she was walking into her parents' house, Ashley realized she was alone. She looked at her new iPhone 13. The clock displayed 2:15 in the afternoon. The teacher was exhausted, she decided to take a short nap. She went upstairs to her room and closed the door. Then, she took a shower. After that, she climbed into her bed and closed her eyes.

"Hello, Ashley! HA-HA-HA!" a terrifying voice spoke out loudly. The voice sounded as if a man spoke with a sore throat. Ashley awoke from her nap. She wasn't sure if the voice was realistic or a product of her imagination. The teacher thought she was dreaming and once again closed her eyes.

"Wake up, Ashley!" the same voice spoke. This time she heard it clearly.

"Who are you?" she asked. The gorgeous young woman looked around. The room was empty, but it felt like someone was hiding there. There was no answer, but Ashley waited patiently. She could feel the ominous presence of something as if a ghost was hovering around. The eerie silence gave her goosebumps. The room was quiet, but it felt like someone was watching her. Ashley kept waiting, but there was no response. She closed her eyes for the third time.

"Don't be afraid, Ashley! I won't hurt ya. HA-HA-HA," the same sore voice cackled. Then Ashley jumped off the bed and looked around. She was petrified. Her legs were trembling from the terror she felt.

"Huh? What are you talking about? Who are you?" the gorgeous girl asked, but again there was no response. Ashley searched the room, yet no one was there. She was confused and scared.

The questions about her momentary telekinetic power and the disembodied voice that had spoken to her remained unanswered. Some things just cannot be explained.

The chaos in Chicago seemed never-ending.

Author's Note

According to the National Missing and Unidentified Persons (NamUS) database, which is funded by the U.S. Department of Justice, more than 600,000 people go missing annually. Approximately 4,400 unidentified bodies are recovered each year. Nationwide, there are roughly 6.5 missing persons for every 100,000 people.

Check the other of Dimitry's bestsellers on Amazon and everywhere books are sold.

Bridge of Pain: How My Life Become a Roller Coaster

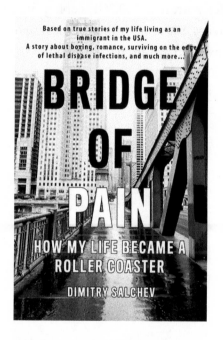

Dimitry's autobiography is based on ten years of his life, and it's primarily focused on the years between 2014 and 2019. Dimitry talks about how he prevailed over countless obstacles in those years. You will witness how his routine life turned into a nightmare. In this book, he portrays how many times he nearly died, and how he returned to life. He also emphasizes how wrong he had been and how important his faith in God was.

James Dobrev: The Cold Murder

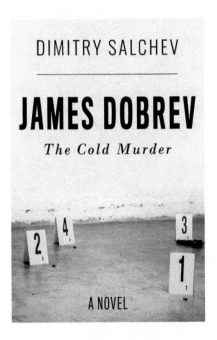

James Dobrev was a prosperous author. He lived all of his life in Chicago. One night, he stopped working on his novel for a trip to the closest liquor store. When he got to the store something unpleasant happened. Since then, James' life became a nightmare. He was accidently involved in a murder. The target was a Russian man who had been kidnapped from Moscow. The police detectives couldn't understand how the Russian man looked the same as he had sixty years earlier. The police sent James to Bulgaria for witness protection. His trip to Bulgaria was bizarre. James realized that some people were watching him. Just as things seemed to be going okay,

James received shocking news. His mother had disappeared. He had to fly back to Chicago. A few weeks later, one of the most brutal firefights in the history of Illinois occurred.

About the Author

Dimitry Salchev was born and raised in Plovdiv, Bulgaria. He immigrated to the US in 2014. In 2018, he was diagnosed with endocarditis. He was urged to have complicated surgery and had to fight for his life. He had four surgeries in two years. Twice, he had to relearn how to walk. Before his last surgery, he became a hundred percent paralyzed. He lost the ability to talk, see, and move any of his muscles. The doctors thought they were losing him. Nevertheless, Dimitry woke up after two weeks of induced coma. It took him some time to heal after his last surgery. In 2020 he met a beautiful girl. They decided to get married in 2021. Three months after the wedding, his marriage turned into a nightmare. The following year, he tried to work on his marriage with hope that it would be fine. His situation got worse, and he had to move out of his wife's apartment. He had nowhere to go. He was forced to live in his car somewhere in the Chicago area. However, that didn't discourage him. When he came to the US, the author could barely say a word in English, but in 2022, he wrote two books in the same year. During that time, he never quit his job. Dimitry would not stop writing books. God bless America.

CPSIA information can be obtained
at www.ICGtesting.com
Printed in the USA
JSHW081236120623
43031JS00003B/157